# OF VALOR & VICE

## A REVELRY'S TEMPEST NOVEL, VOLUME 1

# K.J. JACKSON

First Edition: May 2017
ISBN: 978-1-940149-23-3
http://www.kjjackson.com

# K.J. Jackson Books
## Historical Romance:
Stone Devil Duke, *A Hold Your Breath Novel*
Unmasking the Marquess, *A Hold Your Breath Novel*
My Captain, My Earl, *A Hold Your Breath Novel*
Worth of a Duke, *A Lords of Fate Novel*
Earl of Destiny, *A Lords of Fate Novel*
Marquess of Fortune, *A Lords of Fate Novel*
Vow, *A Lords of Action Novel*
Promise, *A Lords of Action Novel*
Oath, *A Lords of Action Novel*
*Of Valor & Vice, A Revelry's Tempest Novel*

## Paranormal Romance:
Flame Moon
Triple Infinity, *Flame Moon #2*
Flux Flame, *Flame Moon #3*

Be sure to sign up for news of my next releases at
www.KJJackson.com

# DEDICATION

– AS ALWAYS,
FOR MY FAVORITE KS

# { CHAPTER 1 }

The marriage, on all accounts, had been a disaster.

The web of black lace on her veil tickled the tip of her nose, and Lady Pipworth stared at the black box being lowered into the ground, determined not to sneeze. The ropes under the coffin creaked under the strain, several of the frayed cords snapping. Her right cheek lifted in a half cringe.

Her husband always had been generous in the belly.

She had come to the burial against the advisement of her late husband's cousin. Sitting in the confines of the drawing room, sobbing—as was usual and proper in this situation—was for a wife that would actually miss her husband.

Adalia would not.

Nor did she wish it to appear so. She would see her husband into the ground. Pay him that respect. And then attempt to wash the last two years from her mind.

Dirt thumped onto the black wood. One thud. Two. Three. Four. Until the dirt fell quietly into the hole, piling in covert silence upon itself.

The dirt began heaping above the gravesite and the small crowd around her started to shift, dispersing. Six more shovels dumped, and the black mound was complete. Adalia was the last to turn from the gravesite.

Due respect, whether he deserved it or not.

She walked slowly down the serpentine path of the graveyard, lifting her gloved fingertip to scratch her nose. As long as she kept the crowd in front of her, she could avoid the distant relatives of her late husband that had appeared at his death. They would have questions for her, and she had no answers.

She could already tell by the pursed lips, the looks of curiosity during the funeral, that they had discovered how thoroughly her husband had driven the Pipworth estate into the ground—never a creditor he could not charm, or a bauble for his mistress he could not resist. His second cousin, the new Marquess of Pipworth, had inherited a mess along with the title. But that was the extent of Adalia's knowledge on the matter.

She looked up to the trees dotting the hillside between the rows of neat granite headstones, slowing her gait as she avoided the pointed, backward glances of the relatives. They were rabid for a target to unleash their anger upon, and she preferred to escape the day without being torn apart.

The sudden steps next to her made her jump. A quick glance up at the tall man appearing at her right told her he was not a relative of her late husband. Or at least not one she had been introduced to.

"Forgive my presumption of speaking to you before introductions, Lady Pipworth, but this appears to be the one moment in time at which I will have easy, private access to you."

Adalia continued walking, her steps speeding up slightly as she looked up at his face, not quite believing the gall of the stranger. Fearing her cocked, scathing eyebrows were hidden too well behind her black veil to make an impression, she laced her words with as much haughtiness as she could muster. "Sir, you go beyond all measure with your uncouth presumptiveness."

"I am aware, Lady Pipworth. I would prefer this to not be my only access to you. But it is."

She stiffened. "Who, sir, do you think you are to approach me at this time?"

"Careful, Lady Pipworth." His look stayed forward, casual, as though they were old friends out for a stroll and a chat on a crisp spring day. "Your late husband's family is ardently studying you at the moment. Best to pretend we are acquaintances so they do not question our association."

Adalia glanced forward, scanning the group milling about the line of carriages. Unabashed glares were still focused her way. "My husband's family is the least of my concerns, sir. Now I ask you again, who are you?"

He nodded, clearing his throat. His height gave length to his stride, which he was clearly not accustomed to reining in. Especially to the snail's pace she had committed to. "Forgive me, Lady Pipworth. I should have started with my name and purpose. Your brother, Theodore, was my good friend. I am the Duke of—"

"You know Theodore?" Her feet stopped, her look whipping to him. "Have you heard word from him?"

"I do know him, but I have heard little word from him since he left for the Caribbean. Much as I imagine is the same for you."

His tone, incredibly arrogant, made her bristle. "You know nothing of my correspondence with my brother."

"That is true. But if, as I suspect, you have not heard from him in the past months, I am here to fulfill a vow made to him."

Adalia exhaled a slight sigh, the sudden hope for Theo's return that had flared in her chest extinguished before it could catch fire. She needed Theo back on English soil. Her two oldest brothers dead and buried, he was her last remaining brother, and she needed him. Desperately. "What was the vow?"

"To offer my assistance to you, should you need it. You have just lost your husband, so this appears as though it is the appropriate time to come forth and extend my help."

For an excruciatingly long, dumfounded moment, she stared at him through the black threads of her veil, her mouth slightly askew.

A blackbird squawked, landing on the weathered point of an obelisk gravestone behind his head. It spurred her from her stunned state.

"This is the appropriate time, sir?" Her arm flew up, pointing to the gravesite at the top of the hill as her voice went slightly shrill. "Did you not notice I was just walking away from my husband's grave—his very *fresh* grave? And you think to approach me here? You think this *appropriate*?"

His look flickered up the hill and back to her face. "I— well—"

"Well nothing, sir. I do not care who you are, or what my brother asked of you. This is my *husband's* funeral. And why would my brother ever ask a vow such as that of you?

I do not even know you, sir. I have never heard of you. So please take your assistance and move out of my sight."

"Adalia, come, you must ride in my carriage." The soft voice of Adalia's friend, Lady Vandestile, wrapped her protectively—calm against her storm. Violet moved to her side, her hand on Adalia's elbow, prompting her forward down the path.

It snapped Adalia out of the sprouts of a rant before it became an actual tirade, and she looked to her friend. "Yes, Violet. Let us take our leave."

She gave one curt nod to the man that had accosted her and then turned, starting down the path with Violet.

Her hand still on Adalia's elbow, Violet leaned in as they walked, her voice hushed. "I did not recognize that man. Who was that?"

Adalia shrugged. "He told me, I think, but I did not hear him."

"Why not? Your veil is not that thick." The edge of Violet's lip curled in a mischievous smile. Of course Violet could not keep a solemn façade, even at a funeral—particularly when she knew how Adalia truly regarded her late husband.

"He mentioned Theodore, and then I heard not another word he said."

"Theodore?" Violet pointed backward over her shoulder with her forefinger. "That man has heard from him?"

"No. That man was of no use. No use at all." Her fingers clasped over Violet's hand on her elbow. "I did not expect a vulture to descend so quickly upon me."

Violet snorted a stifled chuckle. "Exactly—wait at least a day, please." She squeezed Adalia's elbow, steering her

off the path and toward the Vandestile carriage. "You, my dear friend, have enough madness in your life dealing with Pipworth's family. They are a sorry lot. I do not envy you the task at hand."

Adalia's eyes went to the family members slowly entering the carriages. "Once they are convinced I know nothing, have no pots of coins stashed away, I will be useless to them. Just another drain on the estate to contend with."

"Lady Pipworth."

The sudden voice in her ears spiked hackles onto the back of her neck, and Adalia turned to see a small, wiry man approaching her. He tugged his ill-fitting black tailcoat against his chest, attempting to right it as he approached her.

There would be no avoiding him this time.

"Lady Pipworth, please, a moment of your time." Hired by her eldest brother long ago, the current solicitor of the Alton estate scurried in front of her and Violet, effectively blocking her path. She stopped.

"Can this not wait, Mr. Chesire? As you can see, I have other matters to attend to this day."

The man didn't budge. "I fear not, my lady. As you have refused to see me the last three times I have come for an audience with you, this is the moment I must seize."

Adalia knew she should be more generous with the man. She knew he had kept the Alton estate afloat for as long as he could. Valiantly so, even. But she didn't want to hear the news. She didn't want to hear what she had been avoiding for the past month.

His lips tight, Mr. Chesire glanced pointedly at Violet.

Violet looked to Adalia, her pretty blue eyes questioning. Violet knew all about meddling solicitors. "You will be fine? I can stay."

"You can excuse us, Violet."

"Cass and I will wait for you in my carriage." With a nod and a searing glance at Mr. Chesire, Violet stepped away.

Adalia looked to Mr. Chesire.

He wasted not a second. "I will come to the point, my lady, lest you escape me again. The coffers have been spent near to dry. There is not a thing left to leverage for more funds."

She stared at him through her dark veil, the lace sending a web of black strokes across his weathered face. The familiar feeling of her chest curling inward upon itself, growing thick, slowed her breath. After her husband's death, she'd had a reprieve from the constant fatigue caused by her heavy heart, but now it was back. She had only been granted two days of respite. "You are positive? There must be something we have not looked at."

"There is not, my lady. We have already let most of the staff go at Glenhaven House. Only three servants remain here in the London townhouse. And we do not have the funds to continue the tutor for the twins."

"No, we will not disrupt my nieces' education, Mr. Chesire. That is unacceptable. Whatever it takes, their education is the most important thing—that tutor is brilliant and it was very hard to convince him to take on the twins. That is the first place any income must go to."

"But, my lady, they are only girls and the creditors have been most insistent—"

Adalia took a quick step forward, lifting onto her toes to gain enough height to bear down upon him. "Do not ever—ever—speak those words again, Mr. Chesire."

"My words, my lady?"

"They are not 'just girls,' Mr. Chesire. They are my nieces. They are my brother's legacy, and they are intelligent and witty and proud little girls, and they will remain so. They come above everything. Do you hear me? Do not ever dare to dismiss them again—not in front of me, and most certainly not without my knowledge."

He wavered for a breath and then shuffled a step backward, his head bowed. "Of course, my lady. I apologize." He hazarded a glance up at her. "But the money—"

"I will get you the funds, Mr. Chesire. The girls will continue with their tutor and you will keep up all appearances until Theodore returns to assume the title." She glanced to her left to see the Pipworth carriages moving away from the cemetery. Her look went back to Mr. Chesire, pinning him. "And you will keep this private between the two of us, Mr. Chesire. If I hear so much as a whisper of slander on the Alton name, I will come down upon you with a vengeance unknown to man."

His face visibly paled. "Of course, my lady." He backed away from her, because of the threat, or because he suddenly believed he was dealing with a madwoman, she wasn't sure. "I await word from you on the funds, my lady."

She waved her black-gloved hand in his direction, dismissing him. He turned and hustled past Violet's carriage, hurrying down the street. She stared at his back until he disappeared around the far corner, attempting to calm the boil in her body that tried to steal all her breath.

What mad world had she stumbled into where random men thought approaching her at her husband's funeral was appropriate?

She shook her head and stepped into Violet's carriage.

Madness of addled men she could deal with. She'd done so for the past two years.

The madness of creating coin out of thin air—now that was to be an actual challenge.

~ ~ ~

Gripping the weathered chunk of galena in her right hand, her left palm mindlessly tapped the top edge of the rock—the very first ore pulled from the lead mine that had produced the wealth her family's estate had enjoyed for eleven generations. Adalia stared at the portrait of her parents on the wall adjacent to the door as she sat upon the edge of the desk in Caldwell's study.

*Correction.* Caldwell was dead. This was now Theodore's study, if he would ever see his way back to England to take over the title and the estate. Take over all of the burdens that were swallowing her whole.

Her mother and father stared down at her. Faces she had no memory of, except for this painting. Pride was always the thing that tantalized her about the portrait. Pride in both of their faces. What they had been looking at when the artist had captured them—what would have created that unabashed pride? The question she asked every time she looked at the portrait. Had it been her three brothers? All of them had been alive when the portrait was done, according to Caldwell.

She could easily picture her brothers when they were young, dancing behind the artist, demanding attention. The three of them had always demanded attention. Theo would have been the rascal, dragging his brothers into misbehaving, claiming the whole time with laughter about how much joy they were spreading. Alfred, always thinking, would have been engineering a way for the mischievousness to abound. And Caldwell would have been directing the mayhem, if not antagonizing it into a higher level with a wicked smile.

Three blond heads bobbing madcap about. Once, as they had been their whole lives.

Her chest tightened.

*Where the hell was Theodore?*

Her husband was dead. Two of her brothers in the ground. The third missing.

*No. Not missing.* He just had not replied to her last letter two months ago, which had reiterated Caldwell's death. Nor had Theo replied to the five letters before that reporting the very same thing.

She shook her head. *Not missing.*

But gone. And that meant she was the sole one to support the Alton estate with what little was left of her dowry—and her widow's third from the Pipworth estate that barely bought enough bread for the three servants here at the Alton townhouse.

She had moved back to her family's townhouse because of the twins—in truth, she had wanted to continue to live here to be near her nieces after Caldwell died nearly two years before. Five years old at the time of their father's death, the twins had found themselves motherless, fatherless. But they still had Adalia.

Yet after she married Lord Pipworth, he had not allowed the girls to come with Adalia and live at the Pipworth townhouse. Nor would he allow Adalia to leave and move back into the Alton home.

So Adalia had wasted no time in packing her belongings and moving back into her family's home the day her husband died, even though the Pipworth dower house was now hers to use. Her nieces needed her. And she needed them.

At least her husband's death had allowed her to right one wrong.

Adalia let the rock slip from her fingers, thudding softly onto the desk. Damn the mine. They had spent far too much time and resources attempting to find a new vein to source, and now they had nothing.

She needed money. Needed it desperately. She needed to keep her family's name, the legacy—her nieces' chances for proper matches one day—intact until Theodore returned. She was the only one left to do it.

At the sound of the ore thumping onto the desk, Hazard, Caldwell's wolfhound and fierce protector of the twins, sat up next to her and nudged her thigh with his nose. She scratched the wiry grey hairs behind his ears, calming his alarm.

Her gaze shifted to the glowing coals in the fireplace. The day had been warm, but now a definite chill had set into the air. Spring not yet quite free of the shackles of winter.

Even the coal for warmth would be hard to come by in a month's time.

Damn that she had no skills to make money with.

Marriage was out. She had been an utter failure at that. No heir. A husband that barely regarded her presence. No. She would not subject herself to that again.

Adalia's stare slipped to the sideboard next to the fireplace, her eyes riveted on the half-filled decanter of brandy. If she was to ever start imbibing the vile liquid, now would be the time. Her tongue curdling, she scraped it on the edge of her front teeth. The one time she had tried it with her brothers while in the throes of a particularly long night of playing whist had been enough.

Her look skittered along the sideboard to the ebony card box that held playing cards and counters. The brass inlaid cover was flipped open, displaying the two decks of worn playing cards and the brass gaming counters minted with the Alton crest. The twins must have been snooping into it, as it was usually closed, though everything appeared to be in place.

Walking to the sideboard, she stopped, flipping up the top card from the deck on the right. Queen of diamonds. The queen of diamonds always went on top. Always in charge. When she was younger, she always liked to imagine that the queen of diamonds represented her, because wasn't that what her brothers had always done for her—put her on top?

Except the reality of being in charge in no way aligned with what she had fantasized. Being in charge was exhausting.

Her thumb slipped down along the corners of the cards. Soft, smooth, the edges of the cards were tattered from wear. She had long since memorized every bend and scratch on each card—an advantage she had never confessed to her brothers. Though she was pretty sure Alfred knew she had—just as she suspected he had memorized them all as well. And Alfred had always insisted on not replacing the decks, no matter how Caldwell and Theodore grumbled upon the worn cards.

Devil take it, they had probably *all* memorized the cards.

Exhaling the memories that had landed like a brick in her chest, she shook her head, even as she could not tear her eyes away from the symbol of the past. She needed to concentrate, plan—not wallow.

Money. She needed money.

She could learn to scrub floors. Take in sewing. But she also knew how very little that would add to the coffers. Not nearly enough to keep the Alton estate sound. To keep the creditors at bay. Or even to feed the girls.

No. She needed a healthy source of income. One that didn't entail a husband. But how could she scheme it?

Her gaze locked on the worn brass counters in the card box. Truth told, she had no skills other than with the cards. She had always been able to turn her pin money into double in nights when the opportunity arose. That was what being raised by three brothers who loved to gamble got her.

The thought started small, a tiny, niggling idea that refused to shrink away, only growing bigger with each second that passed.

She *was* particularly canny with the cards.

She had a dower house at her disposal.

She did have a wide set of wealthy friends that loved to gamble.

What had her brothers always said? The house always wins.

Perhaps.

Her eyes captivated on the card box, her head tilted. Her brothers had raised her to possess one outstanding skill. To gamble.

And shouldn't one always bet on their one outstanding skill?

She could open a gaming house. She wouldn't be the first woman to do so.

*But no.*

She couldn't. It would mean scandal.

But…but if it was successful, it would also keep her family's estate solvent until Theodore returned home. And she would be as discreet as possible. It would save her family's good name, and save the possibility for the twins to marry well—or well enough.

Those two things she had to preserve at all costs.

Scandal for her, she could accept that. As Lord Pipworth's widow, it was primarily now his family's name that she would taint. Their dower house. Any modicum of guilt she should feel on that matter had shriveled when her husband jumped into the Thames to save his drowning mistress.

Scandalize the Pipworth name. Save the Alton estate.

Yes. She could live with that.

# { CHAPTER 2 }

JUNE, 1813

Toren Felshaw, fourteenth Duke of Dellon, took a long sip of port, studying the elegant ballroom from the slight cove offered by the back right corner of the room.

Could Theodore possibly have known his younger sister had this in her?

Alive with merriment in all nooks, the Pipworth dower house sparkled, with shouts of victory and robust clapping cutting into the air above the lively music of the string quartet. Everywhere Toren glanced, laughter flowed, along with the coins streaming from purses.

*The Revelry's Tempest.* The most exciting gaming house to capture the *ton's* fancy in years.

She had turned her dower house into a den of gaming. A successful den of gaming, by the looks of it. Wellington's latest victories on the peninsula had apparently bolstered confidence and loosened purse strings.

The tall, white wainscoting along the walls of the ballroom and the attached drawing room reflected the candlelight of the chandeliers, keeping the rooms bright into the darkest part of the night. Five hazard tables scattered throughout the ballroom were full, a crush of people three deep around each of them. Twelve smaller card tables held various pleasures—baccarat, whist, and piquet.

In the corner opposite him a crowd of men and women had gathered for caterpillar races. At the far end of the drawing room, bets were flying on blindfolded wives being able to identify their husbands by feeling foreheads.

No matter how one wanted to wager—the Revelry's Tempest, apparently, served it up on a bright, shiny platter.

He shook his head slightly.

He hadn't thought Lady Pipworth was capable of all this. The woman he had met at Lord Pipworth's funeral had been diminutive. Utterly quiet. Drowning in hastily bought black mourning crepe.

That was, she had been diminutive until she had opened her mouth. He should have known in that moment not to underestimate Theodore's little sister.

His height giving him an advantage, he looked over the tops of heads, scanning faces in the room until he spotted the proprietress. Or, at least the person he assumed was Lady Pipworth. She had been buried under so much black lace at the funeral he hadn't seen her face fully.

Lady Pipworth stood beside the large fireplace in the ballroom, her face strained as she listened to the man at her left. She nodded to the man, her lips searching for a contrived smile. The same height as Lady Pipworth, the man was portly, bald, and talking at a speed that sent spittle to gather at the corner of his mouth.

Admonishing Lady Pipworth, perhaps?

She shook her head in sudden disagreement, interrupting him as she pointed to several tables around the room, and her eyes turned sharply to the man. Whatever he had just told her, she did not care for.

At least the woman was contrary with others as well—
the same as she had been with Toren.

He stared at her in the glow of the ballroom's
candlelight. Her hair piled elegantly with one bandeau of
black securing a single black ostrich feather to her head, the
dark color of it set off the blond in her hair and highlighted
the strands of red that mixed haphazardly through her
upsweep. Unique coloring. And charming.

Her black silk gown, simple, but cut low across the
swell of her breasts, floated outward as she spun toward the
ballroom again, pointing at more tables as she spoke. It gave
Toren a full view of her face.

Pretty, and he hadn't expected her to be pretty.
Beautiful, even. Her bone structure was delicate, with finely
carved cheekbones. Full, heart-shaped lips, and wide green
eyes—so light that he had to study her irises for a long
moment to decipher the exact color—almost a green mixed
with gold, or at least it looked like that with the distance
between them.

Toren had expected her to look like Theodore. Why, he
wasn't sure. But that had always been how he had pictured
her. A female version of Theodore.

One of her guards, dressed head to toe in imposing
black, moved to her side, dwarfing her, and Toren noted
the slight limp in his step. Peculiar. All of the guards he had
seen that night had a limp in their steps. Not noticeable
unless one was studying them, but there nonetheless.

For as much as she had managed to put this place
together, she had made dismal choices in her guards. That
could very well cost her.

Lady Pipworth looked up at the guard, giving him her full attention. With a quick glance over her shoulder to the man she had been speaking to, she dismissed him with a slight wave of her hand.

The portly fellow glared at the guard, a foot taller than him, and then slunk away along the edge of the room.

It wasn't until he was well out of range that Lady Pipworth nodded to her guard. She smoothed the front of her gown and moved into the crowd, smile wide on her face as she greeted her patrons, laughing and clapping and squealing with the best of them.

A sigh settled into his chest.

Lady Pipworth was apparently made of sterner stuff than he had credited her for.

What madness had Theodore managed to thrust upon him?

~~~

"I do not know how you do it, Adalia." Lady Desmond closed the front door of Adalia's dower home turned gaming house.

Adalia turned from chatting with Logan, the head of her guards, and also an exceedingly tall, handsome, and fiercely strong man. The little old ladies—and the young ones as well—loved her guards, which was exactly why she had chosen them so carefully. Not only was it impossible not to feel safe with Logan's crew hovering about, they were also pretty to look at. Which one of those facts was more important to the slew of ladies attending her events, Adalia had never been able to discern.

What none of the ladies realized was that Logan and all of his men had lost a foot or part of their legs in the war. Specially made boots hid the fact well, and for all intents, made their injuries moot. The only tell each of them possessed was a slight limp—and only if one watched closely. As long as they didn't need to run, these men excelled at their jobs.

Adalia smiled at Cassandra, thankful her friend had ushered the last of the night's guests into the first rays of the hazy morning. "Do what?"

Cassandra's slippers stepped lightly across the foyer, not a touch of her inherent grace waning after the long night on her feet. She slipped her hand around Adalia's shoulders as they walked up the stairs to the main drawing room. "How you are able to take the money so sweetly from the little old dowagers is remarkable."

"The sweeter I am, the more hope it gives them for next time. And you know as well as I, that most of them are far cannier with the cards than they would have us believe."

"True, but you are far tougher than I could be, as all I can do is imagine that will be us in forty years, delightful old dowagers with gambling our only solace in life."

Adalia chuckled. "Except I have no margin to be that delightful old dowager if I allow the lot of them to fleece me today. I am more desperate than you, Cass. Your husband supplies you with a healthy income, whereas I fear I will need to protect my pennies until the end."

Cassandra squeezed Adalia's shoulders, her pretty mouth upending into a concerned frown. "Still no word from Theodore?"

"No. I am beginning to fear the worst. Even though I do not wish my mind to go there."

"I think you are right to worry. Even with his wanderlust, it is far past time that he should have returned. Is it possible he has not received your letters about Caldwell's death? That the title is now his?"

"Yes, but even without the letters, he should have come home by now. He said this trip would take six months at the most."

"Have the solicitors started to look into the line of succession?"

"Not yet—or not that they have told me. But it has been two years since Caldwell died. I am sure they have begun the process, no matter my wishes."

Weaving through the empty card and hazard tables scattered in the drawing room and the adjoining ballroom, Adalia stopped, turning to her friend. It had been another long night, and she didn't have the energy to think on her missing brother. Not without breaking down into tears. Not that Cassandra would mind. Her friend had an unusual capacity for empathy and support. But Adalia didn't want to burden her. Not tonight. "You should take your leave, Cass. It has been an exhausting night."

"Yes, as should you. I am exhausted, and I don't run the place as you do. Nor do I go home and then manage to care for twins."

"Josalyn and Mary are my joy—you know I would do anything for them." Adalia took the scolding with a slight shrug. "Still, you should go. I will finish with the ledgers as the maids clean."

Cassandra's eyebrows arched. "And then you will leave and rest for a spell?"

"Yes."

"Will you be safe here alone? I am happy to wait. I did see Mr. Trether corner you earlier."

"Cornered, yes, but I managed to escape his tentacles with relative ease." Adalia flipped her fingers, dismissing her friend's worry. "Logan has already sent one of his men with the evening's proceeds to the bank. There is nothing in the house to steal at the moment, and Logan is downstairs. I am as safe as I ever will be."

"Logan mentioned to me Mr. Trether had several of his men outside the house tonight." Cassandra's bottom lip slipped under her teeth.

"You spoke to Logan about him?"

"I did. Logan did not say much, as is his way, but that he mentioned Mr. Trether as a threat at all is troubling. You do have to admit it is worrisome, especially after your last several altercations with Mr. Trether and the bruise he left on your arm. Logan has been fuming about it since it happened. He went so far as to call Mr. Trether dangerous." She shook her head. "I do not think Mr. Trether means to respect your decision to reject his proposal. He wants this house, Adalia. By any means necessary. You included."

Adalia's nose wrinkled. "That is a disgusting thought. He does not want me, Cass."

"He does. Aside from the fact that you are desirable, you are what makes this place so successful. He knows it and wants all of that."

The hairs on the back of Adalia's neck spiked. Mr. Trether was a problem. Once he had bullied his way

into viewing her ledgers, the man had started to salivate. Cassandra was right—he meant to take over the Revelry's Tempest. And Adalia's multiple refusals to him for a stake in the house—or, heaven forbid, marriage—had only made him more aggressive with his demands.

Adalia shrugged, shaking off the trepidation. Mr. Trether would not cow her. She couldn't afford to let him do so. "Mr. Trether cannot do anything but accept my refusal—not if he would like to stay in the good graces of society. That alone will keep him above reproach as he cannot afford to lose his connections to the wealth and desperation he has tapped into amongst the *ton* through me."

Cassandra offered a sideways nod, half agreeing and half resisting Adalia's logic. "I do hope you are correct. Regardless, he and his men have been gone for hours, so I suppose that is not a worry to dwell upon at the moment." She gave Adalia a quick hug. "As long as Logan is here I will escape then. Aside from Mr. Trether, this has been an inordinate amount of fun, as always."

"Thank you, as always." Adalia gave her friend a wide smile. "Without you and Violet, I could never do this."

"Hush. You know we are always here for you."

"I do, and I do not know how I managed so finely in having friends such as you."

A kiss on the cheek and Cassandra disappeared into the drawing room and down the front stairs.

With a sigh, Adalia moved through the ballroom as the two maids continued to clean the mess the night's attendees had managed to make. Members of the *ton* were not the most careful partakers of wine and treats. And if a glass or ten smashed to the floor during the night—no matter to them.

Past the hazard tables at the rear of the ballroom, Adalia veered to the door in the right back corner. It led to a small room, the one she used as an office—and a place to escape—during the gaming nights.

The white paneled door blended in with the tall wainscoting and Adalia opened it, stepping into the room before she realized a man sat behind her desk, leaning back in her chair, his left leg propped up wide atop his right knee.

She jumped with a squeak, not recognizing the man and ready to slam the door closed and bolt.

"Lady Pipworth, please, wait." The man sat straight, his foot thumping to the floor as he stood.

She stopped, the voice vaguely familiar, and stared at the man's face.

It took several seconds for the face to register.

Theodore's friend. The one from the funeral. *What was his name?* She never had bothered to recall.

She glanced over her shoulder at the maids who hadn't even noted her slight screech. They were close by, and Logan was only a scream away. She was still safe—mostly.

Warily, she stepped fully into the room, but left the door ajar behind her. "Mister…sir, I must ask what you are daring to do in my office, sitting behind my desk."

His head instantly cocked to the side, his look searing into her. "You do not recall who I am, do you?"

She waved her hand in front of her. "Of course I do. You are Theodore's acquaintance. The one that so rudely approached me at my husband's funeral. Just because you knew my brother does not give you free rein to stroll into my home and hide in corners, sir."

"I thought the Revelry's Tempest gaming nights were open to all members of polite society."

"Yes. *Polite* society. That you are not, sir."

"You know this because…?"

"Because of the funeral—because of this." Her hand swung manically in the air. "Because this is my office and you have no right to be in here."

His harsh look shifted to perplexed as he watched her hand flit about. "Because I waited until you were not busy to talk to you?"

"You snuck in here and waited until you could pop out of a dark corner and scare me half to Hades."

"I assure you, Lady Pipworth, I did not skulk into a corner to surprise you. I thought it generous of my time to wait until your guests of the evening had departed to speak with you. I ended up in here merely because I grew tired of the abundant foolery afoot."

He was *judging* her guests? Judging her affair? The hairs on the back of her neck spiked. "Sir, my brother's friend or not, you go too far with your presumption that I welcome a chat with the likes of you. Especially when you think to walk into my home and judge my guests—judge the entertainment."

"Entertainment?" The side of his mouth twitched. "That is what you call these games of chance? Do you realize how many fortunes were lost here tonight?"

She stepped forward, slamming her hands onto the desk, leaning forward. "No one asked you to be here, sir. I do attempt to keep the supercilious, pious ogres out of my home, and it appears as though I failed on that account this night."

There was not the slightest reaction to her insult. Not a raised eyebrow. Not a frown. Not a curdled forehead on the man's face. Without her brothers around, she was out of practice with her barbs.

His look staid, he stepped around from behind the desk, stopping next to her. She hadn't realized he was this tall. The world had been askew at the funeral with the black veil in front of her eyes, and in the back shadow of her office he had not appeared the good head and a half taller than her that he was. And broad in the shoulders. His height did not come at the expense of a wiry frame. Solid. Most likely strong.

For the first time since stepping into her office, a spike of fear cut into her gut.

Just as she was about to open her mouth to yell for Logan, the man leaned past her and clicked the door to the office closed. Without the light from the ballroom, his face fell into the dark shadows, only the dim light from two sconces illuminating the small room.

"You still do not know who I am, do you, Lady Pipworth?"

Her eyes flickered to the doorknob as she assured herself Logan would still be able to hear her if she screamed. She set her spine straight, as tall as she could manage without rising onto her toes, and met his look with a glare. "No. I do not recall."

"I thought not. I am the Duke of Dellon"

"The Duke of Dellon?" Her eyes grew wide. "The One-Faced Duke?"

She blurted out the nickname so quickly she didn't consider the boorishness of speaking it out loud in front of the man. She had only ever heard of the Duke of Dellon in passing, as he spent little time at society's functions. If she recalled correctly, he earned the name because he didn't show emotion. One face. That was all he offered the world.

And she couldn't for the life of her recall Theodore mentioning the duke was his friend.

His face remained composed, offering only a mere blink at her rude words. Adalia decided the nickname was fitting.

"Yes." His countenance remained unmoved, but his stare managed to shift its intent, searing into her, expecting.

Her jaw shifted to the side, unnerved by his stare. He didn't need to move his face. Even in the shadows his eyes were enough. "And you think I would like to retract calling you an ogre now because I know who you are?"

"Yes."

Adalia gave herself a shake, ire seeping back into her chest. The man had entered *her* office. Sat down behind *her* desk. And now he wanted *her* to apologize? She smiled sweetly up at him. "I do not wish to retract a single word, as every one of them was honest, and I will not lose integrity merely because you think to stare at me. But do tell me what you are here for, your grace, and be done with it."

He sighed, his hand motioning to the chair behind her. "Would you like to sit?"

"This will be quicker if we stand. What did you want to speak with me about?"

His head cocked slightly to the left, again puzzled, as he looked at her. "I am here to again offer my assistance in your time of need."

"Time of need?" Her fingers tapped along the edge of the desk. "My, you are a presumptive one, your grace. How have you come about the belief that I require assistance—*again*?"

His hand lifted, pointing toward the ballroom through the door. "The Revelry's Tempest, my lady? Opening a gaming hall in your ballroom? This is not becoming of a lady in your station, and you need to cease your operation."

"A lady in my station? My grace, you know nothing of my situation."

"Enlighten me."

Her arms crossed in front of her. "I am a widow attempting to keep the Alton estate solvent until Theodore returns from the Caribbean—and foremost within that goal is the necessity to keep food in the bellies of my nieces."

"Your oldest brother's children? There are two?"

"Yes. Twin girls."

"Then you must realize you do harm to the name of the very title you are attempting to protect by turning your home into a gaming house."

"This is the Pipworth dower house—the scandal attaches to my late husband's name. Not to my brother's title."

"You believe that?" His eyebrows drew together. "And you do all of this to protect the Alton estate?"

Adalia glared at him. Why was the man so perplexed by this? Her knuckles rapped onto the wood of the desk. "It is called loyalty, your grace. Apparently you do not understand

that. And yes, I will do whatever I have within my power to protect my family's legacy. And the one thing in my power that will generate funds is this house and these gaming nights. So no, I will not be ceasing my evenings of gaming here."

"But I am willing to offer you my assistance."

It was Adalia's turn to be perplexed. "Why? You don't know me. I don't know you. Why do you want to help me?"

"As I said months ago, your brother, Theodore, asked me to watch over you."

"Yes, you did say that at my husband's funeral. But I did not believe you then, your grace, and I do not believe you now."

"And yet he did." He nodded, his face reverting to the solemn, unmoving look. "Before he left for Caribbean waters, Theodore asked me to watch over you. I agreed."

"No." Her head shook. "Theo would not have done that. And why would you agree to such a thing? And why would he have even asked such a thing of you—Caldwell was alive and I was betrothed when he left. I needed no such thing as another man to watch over me."

The duke shrugged. "I agree. But regardless, Theodore asked, and I agreed. I made the vow believing I would never have to act upon it. I wondered at his state of mind, but if you remember, he was grieving over the death of your brother, Alfred, and he needed that assurance for you before he left. I believe Theodore did not trust your late husband, my lady."

"True. Theo never cared for Lord Pipworth." Her eyes narrowed at him. "But why did I know nothing of you until the day of my husband's funeral? Where were you when Caldwell died?"

"You married quite quickly after your eldest brother died—the news of his death reached me well after you were married. I would not intervene upon a marriage. Your husband was alive. He was the one responsible for you. But as no one has acted in that capacity in the ensuing months since his funeral, I believe I must be the one to implore you to stop the nonsense of this gaming house."

"But why now? I have been operating the Revelry's Tempest events for three months now."

He exhaled, his look finally diverging from her face to look at the white wall paneling over her shoulder. "Frankly, I did not expect you to make a success of it."

She guffawed, a smile cracking her face. "You thought I would fail?"

He met her eyes. Something flickered in his dark brown eyes—actual emotion. He did not care that she laughed at him.

But only that stray glimmer in his eyes gave evidence to his thoughts as his voice stayed even. "I did believe you would fail. You did not. I looked through your books. So instead I am here to insist you stop this nonsense."

"You rifled through my ledgers?" Her eyes whipped to the leather volumes on her desk. Incredulous, she could do nothing but let loose an angry chuckle. This man overstepped so many bounds and was so far removed from her reality—and what he could do to control it—it became all the more laughable. "You would insist?"

"I do."

"You realize, your grace, that you have no bearing over my time and actions whatsoever?"

"I still must insist." He gave a curt nod for emphasis, and his stare shifted again. Searing her. "You will stop hosting these…little gaming evenings…forthwith, Lady Pipworth."

She jumped a step forward, her neck craning so she could meet his piercing stare with her own. "You tyrannical, overbearing fiend. You cannot just accost me in my office and demand that I bend to your wishes. I don't even know you. I don't even know if you and Theo were ever truly friends."

She poked her right forefinger at him, almost touching the cut of his impeccably tailored black tailcoat. "For that matter, Theo never once mentioned you to me. What game do you think to play with me, your grace? Do you own a gaming hell that has had its business dented by my little affairs? Is that what you are about? You think to do me under by using my brother against me? Steal from my coffers? Take over my business?"

His eyes dropped to her flung-out forefinger for a long second before he met the fire in her gaze. "The number of conclusions you have just jumped to in thirty seconds is astounding, Lady Pipworth."

"I can concoct more, if it will rid me of your presence."

"Your imagination does impress, my lady."

Her hand went to her forehead, rubbing it. "Your grace, I have been a breath away from calling for my guard since I entered this room. It has been a long night, and I still have much more to do. My restraint is now gone."

"Then I will leave you to your accounting." He nodded to the ledgers on her desk. "Good day, Lady Pipworth."

Without another word, he stepped out of her office.

Good riddance.

# { CHAPTER 3 }

Josalyn tucked under her right arm and Mary tucked under her left arm, Adalia tightened her holds on her nieces with the latest bump of the carriage. She had heard horror stories of travel by stagecoach, and the tales she had heard did not do the reality justice.

At least they were inside the stagecoach and not sitting atop, one small jostle away from slipping off the carriage. Stuffed onto a hard-backed bench between one plump fishmonger with the smell to match, and a tall, skinny man with sharp elbows, the two days inside the stagecoach had been grueling. Protecting the twins from every hard jolt of the carriage. Keeping them calm. Holding her reticule tight from the boy—not even thirteen—who had been eying it since she and the girls had wedged themselves inside the tight quarters.

Adalia had not let herself sleep a wink in the past two days, and she was currently losing the battle against her heavy eyelids.

Her thumb and forefinger slipped past the drawstring of her reticule, fingering the letter folded inside—the entire reason she was stuck in this atrocity of travel with the twins. She would take it out and read it again if she could move her arms, but she would not give up the precious space she had captured by wedging her arms around the girls. They were finally asleep, dead weight against her torso, and she meant to keep it so.

The coach turned onto a new road, smoother, the bumps more rhythmic, and it lulled Adalia even further into drowsiness. The weight of her determined eyelids overcoming her will, her eyes slid closed against the last remnants of her struggle to stay awake.

Into blackness, and the frantic barks of Hazard at the back gate instantly filled her head. Sitting on the iron bench between the foxgloves and daffodils, Adalia looked up from scanning the *Times* to find their wolfhound jumping, clawing with desperation at the rear gate to the mews.

At the exact moment Adalia realized Hazard would only be that frantic for one reason—the girls were in trouble—the dog backed up and ran at the fence, clearing it with a lumbering leap.

She looked around, realizing the girls were no longer in the back garden. No longer digging around, placing shells under the wall of evergreens along the alley. Jumping to her feet, Adalia ran to the back gate after Hazard.

"Auntie Ada, Auntie Ada, Auntie Ada." The cries echoed down the alley in front of the mews before Adalia could get the gate latch open. She craned her neck out past the long line of tall evergreens to find Josalyn running, terrified, toward her. "He has her—he has Mary, Auntie Ada."

Adalia ripped the gate open, breaking into a full sprint down the alley, following the vicious growls she could still hear from Hazard. In the next instant, she was at the edge of an alley a block away, just in time to see Hazard jump on the man that was dragging Mary between the buildings. The bastard and Mary went flying, landing on the ground hard. By the time Adalia got to Mary, Hazard was fully on top of the bastard, attacking, the man screaming, trying to ward him off.

Her heart pounding, terror seizing her, Adalia picked up Mary and ran out of the alley before she whistled back to Hazard. Carrying Mary, Hazard on her heels, she sped back to the townhouse, snatching Josalyn's hand along the way and dragging her with them.

Running. And running. And she couldn't run fast enough.

*Clunk.*

Her head slammed into the wood behind her and Adalia jerked awake, her heart hammering, fear choking her just as it had two days ago.

Coach. She was in the stagecoach. The girls were right next to her. Safe.

Her eyes landed on the boy crouched in front of her, his creeping fingers only a hair away from her reticule.

Her foot quick, Adalia kicked him in the gut just as he realized she had awoken and he was about to get caught attempting to steal.

With a grunt, the boy fell back, landing in the lap of the man that had taken his spot on the middle bench. The man shoved him off, and with a grumble, the boy sat on the floor of the coach, smashing himself in between legs, feet, bags, and two other children sitting on the floor.

Awake. She needed to stay awake.

Her fingers tightened around the top of her reticule, crunching the paper within. If the near abduction of her niece hadn't struck the fear of Hades into her, the letter inside her reticule had.

She had found the letter on the silver salver in the foyer after she had gotten the girls settled in their room—Mary valiantly attempting to be brave after what had happened, Josalyn openly crying about nearly losing her sister.

Had Adalia seen the letter earlier, maybe, just maybe, Josalyn and Mary wouldn't have been terrorized so.

Passing it three times before she glanced at her name scrawled across the front of the letter, it wasn't until the fourth passing that she paused to look at it close enough to recognize the handwriting.

Theodore.

Theo had finally sent a letter. Finally, after all that time.

Her hands had trembled as she broke the seal and unfolded it, so violently she could barely complete the task to get to the contents. Had she known what was inside, she might never have opened it.

*My Little Sprite,*

*I am journeying to you at this moment, but I am writing this letter as assurance in the event my actions do not unfold as I have planned.*

*If I do not return to you, alive, in a week's time, I can surely be counted amongst the dead, and I apologize that you will learn of my death in this letter. Mourn for me, but do not do so until you and the twins are safe.*

*The three of you are in imminent danger, and you must trust no one. No one. Not a friend. Not a business associate. Not a servant. Not your coachman. No one.*

*I do not exaggerate. Do not think to defy me on this, Sprite, for I will surely come back from the grave to haunt you.*

*I need you to trust no one. No one, except for the Duke of Dellon. Get to the duke, as he is the only one that can assure safety for you and the girls.*

*I stress this because I know how you think, dear sister. I beg you, do not question, do not wonder, do not make excuses for why or how I am misguided or could be wrong. Do not. I am dead, and the duke is the only one that can keep you and the girls safe. He is currently in residence at his country estate. He will know what to do.*

*Think of me with kindness. You were and always will be my beloved sprite, Adalia.*

*Forever yours,*
*Theodore*

She had just finished reading the letter a third time over in the foyer, trying to comprehend it—trying to reason against the words just as Theo had known she would—when a knock had come on the door. Her head had been down, concentrating on the letter when her butler had opened the door. A man in uniform. Grave face. He had talked to her butler in hushed tones. Hushed tones she had heard perfectly.

Theodore's body, found in the rookeries, his throat slashed.

Her head clunked back against the hard wood of the stagecoach as it hit a rut, and Adalia swallowed back a sob that had lodged in her throat. Her look fixated on the top of the would-be thief's head now sitting by her boots as she tried to stop the welling tears.

Theo had been right. Now was not the time to mourn. Now was the time to get the twins to safety. To the duke.

Taken alone, she would have ignored the letter, or at least taken Theo's message with a healthy dose of caution, but she would not have acted upon it—as Theo knew she wouldn't, even as he begged her to do so.

But the letter and the man reporting Theodore's death had arrived in the exact hour that Mary had been abducted. If not for Hazard and his fierce protectiveness of the girls, she would have surely lost Mary.

A ripple of horror shook through her body.

She was awake again, as awake and as frantic as she had been in those minutes two days ago after reading the note and hearing of Theo's death—when she had torn through the house, gathered the girls, and left without a word to any of the staff.

Terrified, she had paid the fare and boarded the stagecoach with the girls, bringing nothing but the clothes on their backs and a sack of coins for the journey.

And the letter.

Now they were almost there—she just had to stay awake until Dellington, where his grace was in residence at his ducal estate.

Awake. She had to stay awake.

Only a few more hours.

Mary grumbled in her sleep, stretching her little body against the clamp Adalia had around her. Adalia tried to loosen her hold, but could tell by the way Mary still wiggled against her arm that she didn't succeed in the effort.

She could not let go of them. Not until they were safe.

In another hour, the stagecoach slowed at the edge of the small village of Dellington. They disembarked, and the coach rolled onward before Adalia and the twins had even taken two steps away from the wheels.

Looking around through the dust kicked up by the horses of the stagecoach, Adalia found only one lone woman carrying a basket of rushes, walking along the tiny lane that weaved through the village.

Holding the girls' hands, she held them slightly behind her skirts as she approached the woman. "Excuse me, miss, can you please tell me in which direction the Duke of Dellon's estate is?"

The woman balanced the wide basket into one arm, setting the other arm straight to point down the lane past Adalia. "Tis two miles that way, then it be the only lane to yer left. A mile more from there."

Adalia glanced back over her shoulder, peeved at herself. If she had known that fact, she would have had the driver of the stagecoach drop her and the girls off two miles back.

She considered for a moment on asking the woman if there was someone with a wagon that could deliver them to the estate.

But no, Theo said trust no one. And she would not chance harm coming to the girls—no matter how innocent the woman looked. She looked back to the woman, nodding. "Thank you."

The woman shifted the basket in her arms and continued her slow amble along the lane.

Adalia sighed, turning in the road, exhaustion smothering her body, her limbs, and nearly sending her to her knees. The ground looked inviting. Only a few rocks to brush aside. She could just curl up, sleep for a few short moments.

*No. Just a bit farther.*

She tore her eyes from the dirt, looking up along the road.

Three miles with two seven-year-olds.

This was not going to be enjoyable.

# { CHAPTER 4 }

Adalia jerked awake, fear thundering in her chest.

The twins. Where in Hades were they?

On her back, she searched around her. She was on a settee, one leg long on the cushion, the other stretched down to the floor. The room was dark—a big room.

For that matter, where was she?

The duke. The Duke of Dellon's home. His castle. His drawing room. She had made it into there, sat down on the settee with the girls. The last thing she remembered was the comforting feeling of the three of them being safe—finally—and then…nothing.

She jumped to her feet, her eyes starting to adjust to the darkness, and she spotted the door. Fumbling with the knobs, she flung the double doors wide and light hit her—not bright daylight, but just enough to blind her dry eyes for a moment and give her pause.

Darkness lined the far edges of the hallway in front of her—it was nighttime—and where were the girls?

"Josalyn, Mary?" she yelled down the corridor, panic seizing her. "Mary, Josalyn? Girls?"

*Thunk.* She turned to the sound at the end of the hallway and ran toward it, desperate.

Laughter. She heard the laughter—the giggles—before she reached the room at the very end of the hall. The corridor growing darker the deeper she went into the castle, she focused on the light spilling from the open doorway of the room ahead as unyielding terror made her limbs shake.

Sliding to a stop in the hallway, she looked into the room, frantic to see the girls.

The giggles grew louder.

Adalia froze.

She recognized him, even from the backside. The Duke of Dellon.

He sat, both arms stretched out in front of him on a table, pieces of paper under his splayed hands. Josalyn was on his right, Mary on his left, and both of the girls were giggling uncontrollably, tracing his wide fingers on paper.

Then she saw all the paper. Scraps and tears and pieces of it all over the floor, the table. Strips tucked into every opening of the duke's dark tailcoat.

Paper in what looked like the shape of a chicken sprouting out of his collar to peck behind his ear. Small white sprinkles of paper dusting his head, stark against his dark hair. A creamy white paper snake trailing out from the other side of his collar, sliding down his back. A monkey hanging off the back edge of his cravat.

Paper animals all over his body.

Mayhem.

She had to shake herself once, twice, at the scene before she could react.

She clapped her hands. "Girls."

Both twins' eyes went wide as they dropped their pencils, looking up to Adalia in the doorway. Their lips drew inward, identically and in unison—caught doing exactly what they knew they shouldn't be doing.

Adalia stepped into the room as the duke turned in his chair, and she had to stifle a laugh—she couldn't afford to waver on her stern look directed at the girls.

The man looked ridiculous. What she had been able to see from the backside had only been a tiny part of the picture. Animals, every size and shape imaginable, stuck up and down his lapels, an entire zoo of creatures living on his chest. A snowy blanket of paper balls covered his lap.

And in the middle of it all, his face, blank, looking at her.

At least he wasn't angry. Or so she hoped. She guessed she wouldn't be able to tell one way or another with him.

She clapped her hands together again. "Girls, I am mortified by your behavior. Whatever are you thinking? We do not waste paper like this. Aside from the fact that this is not how we are proper guests in anyone's home."

Tears instantly swelled in Mary's eyes, and seeing it, Josalyn skipped in front of Adalia, looking up at her with wide, pleading blue eyes. "But, but, we are so sorry, Auntie Ada. Sir Duke asked what we could do with paper and we showed him. And he didn't stop us."

"Yes, well, the duke is unfailingly polite to his guests." Adalia crossed her arms, leaving one finger out to point to the chaos. "The best apology is to clean all this mess up as quickly as possible."

Both girls turned, dropping to their knees and scooping up paper shreds from the floor, dumping them on the table. They stood, pushing the mess to a big pile in the middle of the table and turned to Adalia to measure their success.

Clean, by a seven-year-old's standards.

Adalia wasn't quite done with them. She nodded to duke. "And the duke."

"But—" Josalyn whined.

"No. Him as well."

Both girls sighed, arms heavy with defiance as they began to clean all the little balls of paper off of him. One by one, they plucked the paper animals from his body, setting them onto the table and smoothing them with the utmost care.

Their masterpiece ruined. Even if it was a zoo on a duke.

A pang of guilt sliced through Adalia's ire. But she held tight to her censure. There was proper behavior, and then there was adherence to the proper behavior Adalia prescribed to. She knew her own bounds of propriety often stretched thin the meaning of the word. But decorating a duke like a bizarre paper zoo doll could in no way be considered proper.

The last animal, a giraffe, Adalia guessed, landed on the top of the pile of animals. The girls' downcast faces were almost unbearable.

Simultaneously, the duke lifted his hands, his fingers under each of the twins' chins. "They were done so well, I would like to keep the animals, if it is agreeable to the two of you?"

A heartbeat of wide-eyed silence, and then both girls broke into giggles, nodding their heads.

"Excellent," the duke said. "Do you both remember where your room is at the top of the stairs and to your right?"

"Yes, Sir Duke," they said in unison.

"Good. Will you please go up there and ready yourselves for bed? I have a maid searching for some nightclothes for you. She should be in there to help you."

Mary looked to Josalyn, and Josalyn looked to Adalia. "Auntie Ada, will you come up with us?"

"I will—"

"She will just as soon as I have had a chance to talk to her." The duke cut her off, drawing the girls' attention. "Do not fret, we only have a few things to discuss, and then she will be up. It will not take long. Go now."

Satisfied, the girls clasped hands and walked past Adalia toward the door. It wasn't until that moment that Adalia realized they were dressed in different clothing than what they had worn on the journey.

Watching them exit the room, she waited until she heard their footsteps on distant stairs before she turned to the duke.

"The girls, they are in different dresses."

"The clothes they appeared in smelled of fish."

"Yes, there were some characters on the stagecoach. We were next to a fishmonger for two days."

"You took the stagecoach?"

"We did." Adalia studied him. He still had speckles of the paper in his dark hair. She pointed at them. "They did miss a few scraps in your hair."

His right eyebrow lifted, and he dropped his head forward, shuffling his hands through his dark hair—short, more so than fashion dictated, but most practical without the pomades her late husband had been fond of—and setting free the tiny paper balls. "It was snowing at the zoo."

Adalia couldn't swallow her chuckle. "So it was a zoo. I had guessed. They have been learning about foreign animals recently and are especially fascinated by the African ones."

The duke stood, brushing the stubborn pieces of paper off the front of his tailcoat, and then thought the better of it and stripped off his coat, snapping it hard and sending paper flying. "Their ability to tear the paper so precisely was impressive."

"Yes, well…little fingers." Adalia eyed him, slightly taken aback that the removal of his dark tailcoat made him look even broader than she thought him. Usually, a man in a linen shirt and waistcoat looked much less imposing, but not this man. A wide chest that tapered down with his black waistcoat—he held no fat around his belly like her late husband had.

Her look lifted to his face. Handsome, with a strong jawline, neat nose, and canny brown eyes. Yet still he was a blank. No expression.

She still was not sure if he was angry about the entire scene he was forced to just be in with the girls, or if he was taking it with good humor. She hoped for humor, but since she had not seen the slightest smile from him since she walked into the room, she was preparing for the worst.

"I apologize for their behavior." The last of the paper fluttered to the ground and Adalia moved to plant herself in front of him. "The girls, they have always liked to tear paper into shapes—but I do not let them do it with fresh paper—only with old correspondence that has served its purpose."

"I am not upset with them, if that is what you are wondering, Lady Pipworth."

"Oh. But this waste—this perfectly good paper now ruined."

"Was a perfectly good way to entertain them while you were asleep." Draping his tailcoat along the back of the chair he had been sitting in, he looked at her. For the first time since she had met him, his eyes held the slightest glimmer of curiosity. "Come. Let us sit at my desk."

"You do not appear surprised by our presence here."

"I have had several hours to grow accustomed to your appearance."

He started walking to the far side of the room where a heavy, wide desk of the darkest walnut sat. Adalia had initially assumed this room to be his library, with the three walls—interrupted only by a wide hearth—full from floor to coffered ceiling with row upon row of leather-bound volumes. It must be his study—or possibly it served both purposes.

"Yes, can you tell me how that happened—my falling asleep?" Adalia followed him across the room, scooting onto the lone, simple wooden chair at the front of his desk. He waited until she was seated, and then sat behind his desk, his posture stiffly erect. "I only remember being shown to your drawing room, sitting down, and then in the next moment I was awake and came in here."

"You fell asleep on the settee before I appeared in the drawing room. The girls were awake, so we left you. We toured the castle. They were inquisitive. I showed them their room. They told me—Josalyn, primarily—of your journey here. We ate dinner. Then we came in here."

Adalia's jaw dropped. She had missed all of that? "How long was I asleep?"

His left hand went to the top of the desk, his pinky absently tapping the wood. "You slept a long time—five, six hours."

"I was awake for a long time." She inhaled a deep breath, shaking her head. Unforgivable, she had let her guard lapse, let the twins be in danger. No matter how safe she had felt, she should have stayed awake. Should have verified the duke's willingness to assist them.

"So I gathered. Josalyn's version of the trip here was that of a fun adventure. I imagine the reality was more arduous?"

Adalia shrugged. They were alive. Unharmed. It didn't matter what it had taken to get there.

"I saw you walking up the drive with one of the girls on your back, Lady Pipworth. How far did you carry them?"

"Just from the village where the stagecoach deposited us. I traded off between carrying one at a time. They were very brave when they had to walk."

The duke's head tilted slightly, and he set his other arm on the desk, leaning slightly forward. "Why did you not ask for a ride from the village?"

"I…my…my…" Not able to force the words out past the sudden lump in her throat, she reached down for her reticule, still dangling securely from her wrist. Opening it, she pulled free the now crumpled note from Theodore. Carefully, she set it on the desk between them, smoothing it flat before nudging it in front of the duke.

He scanned the note quickly, his look hard when his brown eyes lifted to meet hers. "This is what sent you here?"

The lump still heavy in her throat, she swallowed, forcing it down into her chest so she could spit out her words quickly. "Yes. And they found Theo's body in the rookeries." Gripping the edge of the desk for stability, she fought back the threatening sob with a quick breath. Now was not the time for tears. "And Mary was almost taken only minutes before the note and the news of Theo's death arrived."

"So that was true?"

"Yes."

"The girls told me the story—how their wolfhound saved them. It was fantastical and I was not sure if it was real or not."

"It was. It is why we took the stagecoach. Why we walked. My brother said trust no one. No one until I reached you." She leaned toward him. "I have reached you, your grace. My life has just been shattered and I don't know why. So I want to know why we are in danger. Why Theo would have sent me this letter, why he would send me to you, and you alone."

The duke opened his mouth, then shut it as he sighed, leaning back in his chair. "I do not have an answer for you, Lady Pipworth. The only communication Theodore sent me was a day ago when a cryptic note arrived from him. It said he was invoking the vow he withdrew from me years ago."

"Which was what, exactly?"

"To...look after you. As I have told you in our previous meetings."

Her eyes narrowed as she studied him. "You paused. What did he truly ask of you?"

"I did no such thing."

"You did. I both saw and heard the pause quite distinctly."

"No." He shook his head, his look dismissing.

Adalia scooted forward on her chair, the side of her ribcage hitting the front edge of the desk. "I have spent the last four months studying hiccups in mannerisms at the gaming tables—and untold years before that studying my brothers for the very same thing. And you just hiccupped, your grace." Her forearm went long against the edge of the desk as she pinned him with a stare. "Why?"

"Your mind is as fantastical as your nieces' minds are. You saw an imagination, Lady Pipworth, not a hiccup."

Adalia knew exactly what she saw in him, and now he was denying it.

Yet questioning him was not going to get her any answers. Hiccup aside, she still needed to gain his assistance.

She retreated from the desk, settling her hands in her lap. "Someone has threatened the girls, your grace. I do not know who, and I do not know what to do. Theo told me to trust you, and I trust him. So I ask you, your grace, for your help to keep them safe. At least until I can determine what the threat is."

"What about you, Lady Pipworth? Who will keep you safe?"

"Me?" Her head tilted to the side. "Why, I will keep myself safe."

"You are not worried on your own safety?"

"I would be a fool not to be worried. But my main concern is for my nieces. They were the ones that were attacked, not me. And I have not a clue as to who would do such a thing to them. You must understand, your grace, that they are my heart, the only ones left of my family, and I could not bear it if they were harmed in any way." She offered a small smile. "Can I depend upon your assistance?"

He stared at her as his elbows went to the arms of his chair, his fingers clasping under his chin. The unnerving stare. The one he had used in her office at the Revelry's Tempest.

She resisted a squirm. He could stare at her all he wanted, just as long as he agreed to keep the twins safe.

"Frankly, Lady Pipworth, I have my hesitations."

# { CHAPTER 5 }

Hesitations?

Adalia blinked, her head snapping back. "Which are?"

His stare did not crack, only drew to a point, skewering her deeper. "The first time we spoke after your husband's funeral, Lady Pipworth, you called me a vulture."

Her hand flew to flatten on her chest. "No. I would never."

"You did—though not to my face—you waited until you had turned from me to chat with your friend." His forefingers flipped upward together, tapping on his chin. "If I recall correctly, your words were that you did not expect a vulture to descend so quickly."

She bit her tongue, nodding. She remembered quite clearly she had said the words to Violet and there was no excuse for them. "Can I plead that I was deep in grief at the time and could not hold my tongue?"

"Is it the truth?"

"No."

"Then do not plead it."

Her lips drew inward, stalling for a long second. "I do apologize for that. On hindsight, I understand you were attempting to hold to your vow to my brother. I do not truly imagine you are a vulture—or if you are, you have questionable choices in carcasses."

His left eyebrow quirked. He apparently did not understand her quip, or understood it quite well and did not find it humorous.

She stifled a sigh, beating down upon what she truly wanted to say. Contrite, apologetic—she would do whatever was needed of her to extract the promise from him to keep the twins safe.

He cleared his throat. "My other hesitations—"

"I had hoped it would be just the one."

"It is plural."

This time the sigh escaped. Her earlier relief at the security of being in the duke's home was waning. This was not going nearly as well as she had hoped for—or planned upon. Especially when the duke was the only option available to her at the moment to keep the twins safe. "Please, pray tell."

"In our second meeting you called me a tyrannical, overbearing fiend. But that was only after you called me a supercilious, pious ogre."

A blush tinged her cheekbones, her mouth going dry.

Damn her brothers.

No fine young lady of the *ton* should have ever been exposed to as many creative barbs as she had in her youth. A contrite frown framed her words. "I did. You were attempting to remove me from the only source of income I have to keep the Alton estate solvent. I cannot apologize for defending my livelihood and for protecting the estate from ruin. Though I did not need to express myself so… enthusiastically."

His forefingers went back to tapping his chin. "Why is keeping the Alton estate solvent so important to you?"

"The girls. My loyalty to our family. I do not want my brothers' memories tarnished. They were so much

more than numbers on a ledger. None of them could have
predicted the mines were to fail."

"But your brothers are dead. What does it matter
now?"

Her eyes blinked hard at his callousness. "What does it
matter? They are my family. They are the girls' family—their
father, their uncles. I will not see their memory ruined. Not
if I have breath and the will to stop it."

The duke waved his hand, seemingly to dismiss all
silly notions she had of loyalty and love with a swish of air.
"All that said, Lady Pipworth, you have been very clear in
your opinion of me, when all I wished to do is offer you
assistance. So I must conclude I am not the one you need
help from."

His hands dropped, folding across his waist. "I can
arrange to have one of my carriages bring you and your
nieces back to London, or to the Alton estate in Derbyshire,
if you prefer."

Stunned, she stared at him, for how long, she wasn't
sure.

Theo had said this was where she was supposed to
come. So she came.

And for what?

To have her past rudeness thrown in her face? To
believe she was safe and have it ripped away from her? To
believe her nieces would be protected from a threat she
could not identify, and then tossed out to unknown wolves?

*No.* She did not just stay awake for two nights and two
days straight, to find out this blasted duke was not about to
help her. To help her nieces.

Her voice went fatally calm. Maybe she had misheard him. "So you are thinking to not help me?"

"That is correct."

"Yet you gave a vow to my dead brother that you would do so." Her words were even, challenge dripping from every syllable.

The words hung in the air, filling the cavernous space, echoing louder than any words ever had from the thousands of tomes along the walls.

Slowly, the duke leaned forward, his palms flattening on the desk, and he stood, glaring down at Adalia. Belying his blank face, his stare could have seared through a hundred warriors. "You are daring to call my honor into question?"

She looked up at him, knowing she had finally forced the man to show the smallest modicum of emotion. A small victory. "Yes."

"Do you think that wise?" Voice crushingly brutal, he leaned forward even further, his fingers curling on the wood of the desk.

She swallowed a "no" as her chin jutted out. "Yes. A vow is a vow, and I mean to hold you to your word."

Holding her breath, for an agonizingly long moment Adalia thought he was going to reach out and choke her. Or slam his fists onto the desk. Or lunge at her. Or pick her up and toss her out the front door—or a window.

But he did none of those things.

"You think to hold me to my vow?" He said the words with eerie composure, his face settling back into blankness. So odd, it made her question her own demand. Made her question the wisdom of holding him to his vow.

She shook off the sudden worry. This was for the twins. If anything, what she just saw in this man was the undeniable ability—raging through him—to protect anything he held dear, such as his honor. And if she could get him to hold the twins dear, then they would be safe.

She met his brown eyes. "Yes. I am demanding it."

"Then I bow to your needs. I must adhere to my oath." He nodded, pushing off of the desk as he sat on his chair, his stare never veering from her. "Earlier, Lady Pipworth, you pointed out my unnatural pause when I spoke of my vow to your brother."

"Yes?"

"You were right. I did pause—hedge. For offering you assistance was never truly my vow to him."

"You lied? What was your vow?"

He paused again. And this time it was obvious, long and drawn out to torture her. That, she could see.

Finally, he opened his mouth. "Your brother made me vow to marry you, should it become necessary."

Adalia sprung to her feet, her hands slapping onto the desk. "What?"

The duke nodded, the distinct tightness of his mouth making no secret of what he thought about the prospect.

She shoved off from the desk, backing away, her hands waving in front of her. "Well, no, your grace. No. That is not necessary. Not necessary at all. This instance has no cause for such extreme measures."

"I think your brother would disagree."

"No, your grace. No, I think he would quite agree with me on the matter." Her head bobbed frantically up and down as she moved backward. "I think he understood that I already had one husband chosen for me by my eldest brother, and that was a failure on all measures. I do not need another husband chosen for me by another one of my brothers. They have proven to be inept at it. So no. Most certainly not. Theo must have been drunk as a wheelbarrow when he extracted that vow from you. It is inconceivable. Utterly ridiculous. It is not going to happen."

The duke sighed. "You are done?"

"Spectacularly foolish on all sane accounts."

Both of his eyebrows cocked in question.

Having backed herself halfway across the room, she stopped, nodding with a tight smile. "I am done—no—wait—yes—I am done."

His head tilted slightly to the side, waiting several seconds for her to blurt about again. She managed to keep her mouth clamped shut.

"I made a vow to Theodore, Lady Pipworth. And he has invoked that vow—from the grave, no less. So I do intend to keep it. It is what is needed in this situation. You are the one that demanded it of me."

"No. Not fair. What is needed? What is needed is for you to keep the twins safe. That is what is needed. I give you full authority to swap out the specific vow to marry me for a vow that you will keep the twins safe. That will do much better. I am sure Theo would approve—I know he would."

"Would he approve even more of me keeping all three of you safe?"

Her lips went tight, pursing into a bunched frown.

"Exactly. And the most logical way to do that is for me to marry you."

Adalia's mind scrambled, searching for any miniscule thread to attach argument to—anything to remove this mad thought from the man's head. "But you—this is not fair to you, your grace. You must have a slew of ladies that would gladly misplace an arrow into my back if they thought they could become your duchess."

"What would have you believing that, Lady Pipworth?" His hand swung in small circle in front of him. "Do you see a line of ladies waiting outside my door? Do you imagine there are even any at all within twenty miles of my estate?"

"But surely in London?"

"I do not care for London, the season, and all the nonsense it entails. I am in London for parliament, only because it is necessary. And I attend only the functions that need my presence. Everything else in the city has no bearing on my needs."

"That is all you care about? What is needed?"

"Yes."

Her head slanted. He said the one word so adamantly, so perfunctorily, it was as though he had never once imagined anything past what was needed. Never let himself aspire to an actual want. Only needs.

His hands settled on the desk, his pinky methodically tapping the wood once again. "I do have the need of a wife. The need of an heir. And I do need to satisfy the vow I made to your brother." He nodded, more to himself than to Adalia. "So a marriage between us fulfills three of my needs quite succinctly."

She watched him, slightly dumfounded at how cold the prospect sounded coming from his lips.

Her brothers truly were dismal at choosing men for her.

Her eyes drifted downward to the desk, settling on the tip of his now still pinky. At least Theo had one part right in the Duke of Dellon. She had planned to never marry again, but if she was forced to, she preferred a husband that was cold—and nothing more.

Cold—from beginning to end—she could handle.

Never anything more. Never wanting. Never longing.

Cold she could handle.

Her look lifted from the desk to meet his gaze.

His brown eyes watched her. No curiosity in them, no desire—nor was there any displeasure or antipathy. They were just…blank. A yes or a no from her, and she couldn't imagine it would matter one way or another to him.

Maybe she could manage this.

She needed to ensure safety for the twins, and if she had discerned anything of the Duke of Dellon in the past minutes, it was that he would be dependable. He would adhere to what was *needed*. He would regard the twins as family, and their protection would then become a need. And a need he would serve without fail.

"You would protect the twins?" she asked.

"As they were my own."

She paused, taking a long moment, her tongue slipping out to moisten her lips. "Before I agree, you must know there is a chance I may be barren. I was married for eighteen months and there was not the tiniest hint of being with child."

He did not succumb to the slightest blink at her admission. "I am not fearful of the possibility. My title only

demands that I make the effort. My concerns on the matter
do not go further than that."

She exhaled the breath that had lodged in her chest.
She had no more barriers, real or imagined, to erect. She
gave one slow nod. "Then, yes—I agree to marry you, your
grace."

Without reply, he stood, walking around the desk and
past Adalia. It wasn't until he was across the room that he
stopped and glanced back at her, surprised she was not
following him. "Then I have much I need to attend to, Lady
Pipworth, and you are no longer required. I will show you
to your chambers." He moved to the door.

Her hands curled against her skirts.

Why had she done it? She had three brothers. She
knew better.

Never question a man's honor.

Especially honor that was attached to a fiendishly
tyrannical, overbearing, supercilious ogre.

# { CHAPTER 6 }

Adalia stared out the window in her bedroom, watching the bright three-quarters moon dance above the treetops of the forest that lined the duke's main residence. The midsummer heat had not dispelled, and not a wisp of a breeze made it through the open window. Even if she wanted to, she doubted she could sleep with the warmth a stifling cocoon about her body.

The duke had been gone for four days, traveling to London for the special marriage license, and Adalia was starved for normal conversation. That she was even considering her encounters with the duke "normal"—and yearning for them—was testament to the madness slipping into her mind.

Mary and Josalyn kept her busy enough during the waking hours, but long after they had gone to bed, the evenings would stretch into long, silent hours where the only thing to occupy her mind was worry.

Cautious, the duke had cleared the house of all extraneous servants, keeping only the core needed to run the estate until he returned. Of those servants, all had been with the ducal estate since before the duke was born.

She could not fault him for the heed, but it had left her with not a soul to chat with, for the staff was oddly quiet. Avoiding her at every turn. Slowly scurrying away on creaking elderly legs when she approached. Almost as though they had been instructed to not approach her or the twins, except when necessary.

The moon not moving near fast enough up into the night sky, Adalia sighed. She needed fresh air, or she would never get to sleep.

Slipping on the simple yellow muslin dress that had appeared in her room days ago, she made note to request it to be dyed black. She had been in black since her husband died, but only for proper appearances. But now with Theo's death, she needed to be in proper mourning, for her heart actually held true sadness.

Out of her room, Adalia moved through the castle's dark corridors, slivers of moonlight showing the way, and walked outside into the night by way of the main rear entrance that led to the gardens.

She paused at the edge of the gardens, taking in a deep breath of the fresh night air. It had been days since she'd been outside. She had kept the twins inside the castle since arriving, the sense of uneasiness after Mary had been attacked holding fast in the pit of her stomach—and only exasperated by the duke's absence.

Looking over the gardens closest to the castle, she could see that square plots, ten wide and eight deep, had all been taken over by the needs of the kitchen, a variety of beans and squashes and vegetables trailing upward on trellises. Beyond them, the neat rows of vegetables led into a wall of tall evergreens. From the angle out the window in her room, Adalia could never see what existed past the top of this particular evergreen hedge.

Curiosity piqued, her boots crunched along the crushed granite path between the plots of vegetables as she aimed her feet toward the arbor gate in the middle of the hedge. Her fingers flaking off bits of rust, the gate creaked as she slid it open, the sound scratching the stillness of the night.

She looked back over her shoulder, counting the windows from the left on the third floor. Five in, and that was the twins' room. Their window was open, and she would be able to hear if they called out to her.

Stepping through the arbor, Adalia lifted the gate as she closed it to minimize the noise, and then turned to survey the land in front of her. Whereas the kitchen garden possessed straight, even lines, in this garden, wide boxwood-lined sections curved gracefully along paths, intersecting and weaving without reason.

The scent hit her instantly, even though she could not see the plants near her.

A rose garden. An elaborate, sprawling rose garden that must have, at one time, held thousands of plants.

The scent was there, but as Adalia walked along the winding path, she realized the remnants of the rose bushes were struggling against the ravages of rogue weeds choking them out. Roses still remained, proud in the mess, still producing blooms. But it was only a matter of time before they would succumb to the onslaught of weeds.

By the time she drifted down to the far edge of the rose garden, her heart had been slightly saddened by her stroll. At one point in time, this garden had been glorious—the bones of the past splendor still evident. But neglect, for whatever reason, had taken the beauty and battered it down, leaving only a mess in its wake.

Humming interrupted her thoughts, and she turned to the sound, finding a lone man in simple clothes walking up the hill from the stables.

He didn't see her in the night shadows of the garden—that was evident, as he wasn't avoiding her as all the other staff had done.

Not wanting to surprise him before he was upon her, she called out, "Hello, sir."

The man jumped, searching the landscape until he spotted her waving at him.

"Aye, good eve, m'lady." He quickly turned and started walking in the opposite direction.

Adalia hissed out an exasperated sigh. She'd had enough of this avoidance nonsense. She rushed after him. "Excuse me, sir. Please stop. Please."

He took a few more steps before slowing. Hesitantly, he turned back toward her, pulling the hat from his head to clutch it between his thick hands. He was old—as old as the rest of the staff, but solid, any creaks in his bones held off by his fast walk. A white shock of hair ruffled up straight from his head, glowing in the moonlight. "I meant no interruption, m'lady."

Adalia closed the distance between them, coming to a stop only when she knew she would have his full attention. "I am quite done with the foolery of everyone in this place running from me on sight, sir."

He blinked hard, looking over his shoulder, his fingers on his hat tightening. "Ye be what, now, m'lady?"

"I am done with this avoidance. Who are you, sir?"

"The stable master, m'lady. Valence." He glanced over his shoulder again towards the castle, his weight shifting back and forth on his feet.

"I apologize for waylaying you, Mr. Valence—"

"No mister, m'lady. Just Valence."

"Valence, then. Is it not late to be in the stables?"

He shrugged. "There be a mare due to be foaling within days. I was checking on her progress before I bed down. That be all, m'lady?"

He was going to bolt, she could see it. She took a step closer. "Forgive me, Valence, I do not mean to keep you—but no, that is not all. Tell me why all the staff is as you—avoiding me as you just tried to do—as you are clearly still itching to do?"

For a moment, Adalia thought her question would make him turn and run.

But then the deep etched lines on his face crinkled somewhat, a cautious smile coming to his thin lips. "It's what we do, m'lady."

"Avoid me? But I have only been here four days, sir. Why would you avoid me?"

His head shook, his smile widening. "Ye misunderstand, m'lady. We avoid his grace. And ye are one and the same by extension of yer upcoming nuptials to his grace."

Her eyebrows drew together, fully perplexed. "Why in heaven's design do you avoid the duke?"

Valence shrugged, his busy feet relaxing to stillness. "We have since his parents died. Ordered to do so, though I never thought it be right. Little boy in that big castle. Nothin' but a 'yes, your grace,' we be allowed. Lost me post once, 'cause of it, 'cause of talking to the boy—then ole Pauly up and cracked his back on a horse, so I got me post back. Never talked to his grace after that. Only a nod. I do what I need to, that be all."

"When did his parents die?"

He bit his lip, weathered teeth gnawing, struggling for memory. "Don't recall, m'lady. His grace be a wee one, though, when it happened. Two, maybe three. Walkin', but not much more if I 'member with me ole brain."

He glanced over his shoulder again and Adalia could sense he was ready to excuse himself. She reached out, touching his arm. He jumped and looked at her with a crooked white eyebrow.

"Wait, please, Valence, just another moment to explain this to me. I would like to understand. The staff does not speak to his grace?"

"No. Them be the orders back twenty-five—bugger that—thirty years past now. No staff could talk to 'im 'cept his solicitor guardian, and the governess. And she was a cold wench, that one. Don't 'magine she talked to that boy 'cept to be scoldin' him. Don't know why. It just be what it be."

Adalia nodded, both horrified and curious by what Valence was telling her. "That must have been quite stark for his grace, growing up like that."

"Not be our place to question it, m'lady. But, yes, I 'magine ye be right on that. What started was ne'er changed in the years. Still be so."

Adalia dropped her hand from his arm, a tight smile on her face. "Thank you. I think I do understand the avoidance now, but I do want you to know, Valence, that I am not his grace, and I need not be avoided."

He inclined his head, his scruff of white hair swaying toward her. "That is kind of ye to offer, m'lady."

"Oh, and I do enjoy an exhilarating ride, Valence. How is the stable?"

That drew a wide smile from his face. "We do have several fine mares—thoroughbreds that itch to get out far more often than they do, m'lady. His grace does keep a fine stable."

"Excellent. I look forward to meeting those mares soon."

"Good eve, m'lady."

Adalia watched him walk up around the far end of the gardens to the castle. His steps were quick, belying what she imagined his age to be. If he had been in employ when the duke's parents had died, he had to be well past fifty.

She looked to the border of low boxwoods on the lower side of the rose garden, fascinated by what she had just learned.

No one on staff talked to the duke. Hadn't for the past thirty years.

Walking along the lower border, her fingers brushed along the ragged tops of the boxwood hedge, their singular scent filling her nostrils. She speculated on what it had been like for the duke growing up, but knew her imaginations had no basis in reality, for her own reality was so very different. Her parents had died before she ever knew them—the same as his—but she had always had someone next to her to talk to. Her brothers, always. And many in the Alton staff had always been like family to her.

Silent. Lonely.

She could imagine nothing as atrocious.

Walking from the stables, Toren saw Lady Pipworth in the moonlight. Strolling along the lower boxwood border to the rose garden, her face was tilted up, moonlight casting a glow about her head as she looked to be pondering the stars. Her red-blond hair hanging loose down her backside, it was the first time he had seen it free, not piled in tight knots at the back of her head.

Her left hand lifted, her slender fingers diving under her hair to the back of her neck as she turned into the path winding up through the rose garden. She twisted her hair with one hand, the long waves wrapping around her wrist and onto her forearm. Letting it unfurl, she settled it to drape forward over her shoulder.

The simple muslin gown, almost white in the darkness, floated with an ethereal airiness about her, while hugging her curves in the appropriate spots. She was slight, but surprisingly strong—as he had witnessed when he watched her carrying one of the twins up the long main drive days ago.

The sight of her in the moonlight gave him slight pause, and rarely did anything give him pause—slight or otherwise.

If this was the woman he was going to marry, at least she was pleasing to the eye. He would have no trouble bedding her.

He wondered if she would be as cantankerous in bed as she was outside of it. The woman was predisposed to it—he should have known from what Theodore had told him of her years ago.

Theodore. Maybe that was why. Being raised by three brothers, there had likely been little opportunity for her to become anything but naturally contrary. It was a wonder she was as refined as she was.

She was raised loud and boisterous. He could imagine nothing as atrocious.

Never did he envision he would have to work so hard to convince a woman to marry him. He had presumed he would ask, and the woman would say yes. Quick and efficient.

But Lady Pipworth had made it arduous, and he didn't care for tasks that took longer than they should.

He sighed. He imagined Lady Pipworth was about to make a lot of things arduous for him.

Damn his vow to Theodore.

But he would stand by it. Theodore deserved it.

A pang of guilt swept him. Would Theodore approve of the lies Toren needed to tell his sister?

Fur brushed against his fingers, nestling under his hand, and he looked down. The great beast of a wolfhound—Hazard, the twins had called him—looked up at him. He had gathered the dog from the Alton townhouse in London to bring him to Dellon Castle. If Josalyn's story about the grey-white dog had any truth to it, the wolfhound would be the best protection available for the twins.

The dog caught sight of movement—Lady Pipworth strolling up the pathway—and it only took a moment before it went tearing toward the rose garden.

Its lumbering size uncanny in its speed, the wolfhound reached her before Toren could lift his forefinger and thumb to his lips and whistle.

She turned just before the dog reached her, a shocked screech escaping as the dog lifted onto its hind legs, knocking her down and out of Toren's sight.

Hell. He sped into the garden, only to find the blasted dog pinning her to the ground, smothered garbles coming from her.

He lunged, grabbing the wolfhound by the scruff and yanking it off of Lady Pipworth.

The dog yelped, struggling against him, but Toren refused to free him.

Then the laughter reached him.

Lady Pipworth sat up, laughing. "Stop, your grace, let him go. No need."

Toren looked down to her, relieved to see her face hadn't just been mauled. Scooting closer to the wolfhound, she threw up both of her hands, scratching the wiry fur along the dog's neck as its long tongue bathed her face.

She fell into a fit of laughter again.

He loosened his hold on the furry fold of skin he had grasped. Still unnerved, he kept his hands at the ready. It took a full minute of Lady Pipworth laughing and the dog licking every inch of her face and neck for him to believe the dog would not attack.

Finally, she looked up at Toren as the dog's tongue worked over her cheek. "How I suffer so. It is no small feat to be loved like this. Even if it is a dog. You did not need to yank him off of me as you did."

Toren offered his hand down to her, and she took it, letting him pull her to her feet. "That hound outweighs you by a number of stone. I thought he was crushing you—if not eating you."

She laughed, leaning down to gather the edge of her skirt, and she lifted it, wiping dog slobber off of her face. "Thank you for bringing him back with you. However did you get him to follow you?"

"I brought Mary's shawl with me to London. From that story they told me of him, I guessed he would follow that scent to the ends of the earth to find her."

"You would be right." Face wiped, she let the edge of her skirt drop and rested her hand on the top of the wolfhound's neck. "The girls will be beyond ecstatic Hazard is here. They were so distraught at leaving him, but I did not know how to manage him while travelling in the stagecoach."

Toren motioned toward the castle. "Shall we go in, or did you want more time out here? I did not mean to interrupt."

"No, it is fine. Worry has me and I could not sleep, that is all."

They started moving upward along the path, their boots crunching along the crushed granite, and within three steps, Hazard had wedged himself between the two.

Adalia chuckled, her fingers scratching the dog's ears. She looked over at Toren. "I just discovered this garden tonight. It must have been magnificent in its prime."

Toren scanned the flower beds. Even in the moonlit shadows, he could see the monstrosity of weeds choking out the remnants of the roses. "I would not know. I never saw it in its prime. It was my mother's garden."

"Your parent's died when you were young?"

"Yes. Before I could remember them. My mother shortly after I was born. My father when I was two."

Lady Pipworth nodded, her gaze going to the gravel path before them. She looked to say more, but remained silent.

Several more steps, and her look jumped up to him. "Why did you not have it kept up? The flowers?"

"It serves no purpose in the running of the estate."

Her delicate eyebrows drew together as she looked at him. "Beauty serves no purpose?"

Toren shrugged. Beauty had never been necessary to his life, and after the long ride back to Dellon Castle, he was not interested in a philosophical discussion on the purpose of beauty. "No."

Her look at him twisted, and for a long moment she stared at him strangely. So much so, he was at the brink of saying more when she shook her head, directing her attention to the gate and arbor in the evergreen hedge they approached.

"All went well with the archbishop?"

"Yes. We can marry tomorrow."

Was that the slightest cringe on Lady Pipworth's face? It flickered away so quickly, he couldn't decide if it was real or imagined.

"The girls are very excited I am to marry you." She noticed a leaf stuck on her shoulder from her roll on the ground and she brushed it off. Angling her back to him, she pointed over her shoulder down her back as she pulled her hair to the side. "Is there more?"

"A few." He reached over the wolfhound's head and flicked free the few dried leaves sticking to the muslin.

"Thank you." She set her hair to her backside. "The twins think you quite their gallant knight. Slaying all evil. Perfect for the princess-roles they've adopted."

"I have slayed nothing for them as of yet."

"Yes, well, you managed to make them feel safe in the hours you spent with them."

"Mary too?" His eyebrow cocked. "She is so quiet. Josalyn does all the talking for them."

They reached the arbor and Toren opened the gate for her. Hazard made sure he was second through it.

She waited for him as he closed and latched the gate. "You can tell the twins apart already?"

"Yes."

"How?"

Toren turned to her. "Josalyn has the small freckle directly in front of her left ear."

Lady Pipworth's eyes went wide, crinkling at the corners as she smiled at him. The light of the moon lit her face, making it almost glow. "That is the smallest thing—you are right—but it is the only physical difference between them."

*Beauty—her beauty—actually had purpose in the world—offering joy to others.*

*Fanciful.* The odd thought that had randomly struck him was nothing but fanciful. He instantly disregarded it, wiping it from his mind.

He motioned toward the castle and they resumed walking, Hazard still stubbornly between them.

"They also laugh differently," he said. "Josalyn has more of a chuckle, and Mary has much more of a chortle."

"A chortle and chuckle, whatever is the difference?"

"Well, Josalyn's is more like this." Toren mocked a laugh, attempting to send his pitch high in a titter. "And Mary's is much more like this." He let three sharp bursts fly, sending spurts of air to vibrate the cords in his throat.

Toren looked at her. Lady Pipworth stared at him, her mouth appearing to strain into a straight line.

She cleared her throat. "I am not positive I heard the difference. Could you repeat that?"

Toren did so, his throat itching after his repeated imitation of Mary laughing.

Lady Pipworth's giggle pierced the air. Within a second it turned into body shaking laughter, so much so she had to stop, bending over, her hands on her knees for support as she gasped for breath between cackles.

"You were teasing me." He wasn't quite sure what to do with her. She was laughing, yet appeared quite distressed, her body spasming in fits. He'd never seen anything quite like it. Pat her back? Hold her upright? She was clearly having trouble breathing, and tears were streaming down her face.

She looked up at him, words breathless as she tried to drag air into her lungs. "Yes. Forgive me." Her head shook as she lifted one hand to wipe the tears from her cheeks. "Neither of those laughs sounded anything like either one of the girls. But it was an admirable try in mimicking them."

The smallest smile lined his lips. "I don't sound like a seven-year-old girl, do I?"

That sent her into another quaking fit of laughter. It passed, and she managed to pull herself upright. "No, and

I am glad for it. I do wonder if I could be married to a man that laughed like a tiny girl."

"We are not officially married yet."

"No, so it is good and proper we got that out of the way before we became so." Her hand flat on her chest, she took a deep breath, her smile still beaming at him. "But I am happy you are able to identify the twins. For as close as they are, they both do like their independence from the other. Not everyone can do that—in fact, very few can."

"It merely took concentration on details."

"Yes, and I have seen that you are observant of details." Lady Pipworth waved her hand in the air and started walking to the castle once more. "Thank you. I have not laughed like that in a long while. It felt good."

"That felt good?" He fell into step beside her. "You appeared as though you were in pain."

She looked at him, her green eyes incredulous. "Have you never laughed until you cried?"

"No. What would be the purpose?"

Her head tilted to the side as she glanced down at the path and then back up to him. "We are very different, you and I. Are you positive you would like to marry me? I do not think I am what you envisioned in a wife."

He met her eyes, trying to read if she was reconsidering her decision to marry him. He didn't particularly want to have to convince her once more that marriage would be the best action in the situation. The twins and her safety depended upon it, whether she understood that or not. "The decision has already been made and I am committed to it, Lady Pipworth."

She shook her head, a wry smile lifting the side of her mouth. "I daresay we will have a time of it."

*I hope so.*

The words popped into his head. Fanciful, even as he thought them.

There was no doubt Lady Pipworth was a strange creature and would madden him to no end. That her contrary nature would be hard to control.

But her smile when she was laughing. The way her look twinkled, stolen bits of the sun sparkling in the green of her eyes.

*Fanciful.*

And fanciful had no purpose.

# { CHAPTER 7 }

Adalia sat in the enormous bed, small in the uppermost corner, the line of her right leg even with the side of the mattress. Her new husband had asked her to wait for him here once she was ready.

So there she sat, every minute passing becoming more and more overwhelmed by the width of the bed. Curious when she had entered the duke's chambers by the adjoining door, she had stretched herself long on the bed in both directions. Lying both ways, from the tips of her toes to the tips of her fingers, she could not touch edge to edge.

Why anyone would need a bed so big flummoxed her. Not sure what to do with the size of it, she had curled up tiny against the mahogany headboard, the cerulean blue coverlet pulled up past her chest. Right by the edge, for she didn't want to have to awkwardly crawl out of the middle of the bed once they were done.

It had been long—too long—since she had entered his chamber. She ran a forefinger under the high neck of her white cotton nightgown, wondering if she had misheard her husband. Maybe he had wanted her to wait in her room to consummate their marriage.

Her look flickered around the spacious chamber. Two wingback chairs and an ottoman by the fireplace. One bureau with a simple design of rosewood inlaid walnut. Heavy blue silk draperies along the outside wall of windows. A side table with two full decanters—one of amber liquid, the other of red—and two glasses atop. This bed. A bedside table on each side. That was the extent of furnishings in the room. Only the necessities.

She jumped as a doorknob across the room suddenly creaked a half-turn—from the entrance she assumed led to his dressing chamber.

The door opened and the duke walked into the room.

Her breath caught. Bare skin, with just a sheet wrapped around his waist. She wasn't prepared for the sight of him. His full, wide chest she had not just imagined—it truly existed, and was even more sculpted than had been hinted at under his clothes. Lean cords of muscle ran along his stomach, disappearing beneath the white sheet tight to his skin.

She swallowed, quickly realizing her mouth had gone completely dry and she had nothing to swallow.

He stopped in the middle of the room the moment he spied her in the bed. "There you are. You are ridiculously small in that bed."

"I feel ridiculously small in this bed."

He nodded, his face a blank.

Blank, just as it had been the entire day. Just as it had been throughout the wedding ceremony. Blank.

She snuck a fortifying breath, forcing a bright smile to her face. "Your grace, before we move onto…" Her words petered out on her dry tongue as she looked to her lap.

"What is it you would like to ask?"

She glanced up at him, surprised he had moved a few steps toward her. His bare skin grew even more commanding the closer he came. Her eyes dove again to her lap, her fingers picking at the blue coverlet. "You knew

Theo, so you also know how casual he was—with everyone. He called you Dell, didn't he? I remembered only a few days ago of a friend he spoke of called Dell—was that you?"

His brow furrowed. "Yes, that was me."

"He concocted that nickname on his own, didn't he? No one else has ever called you that?"

"Correct. You know your brother well."

"Yes, and I miss it—him—he had a charm that let him do anything." Adalia drew air in deep, her chest rising high. "I miss the warmth of it, all my brothers. And I have a request."

"Yes?"

She lifted her eyes from her busy fingers to meet his look. "Now that we have wed, will you please call me Adalia? Or Ada? I do not care which. My brothers always used it—or some variation—depending on how annoyed they were with me at the time."

He scratched the back of his neck. "I do not know—"

"Please?" Her fingers curled into the coverlet. "I will continue to address you as your grace, if you wish it. But my name. It hurts my heart that I have not heard it with the low rumble of a man's voice in two years and I miss it."

"Yes, I will do so." His hand fell from the back of his neck. "But I have no name for you to call me in reciprocation. Theodore called me Dell, though I never turned to it."

A frown set into her face. "There is none?"

"None that I would answer to."

"Your given name? Toren? I heard it during the ceremony."

He shrugged. "Aside from your brother, no one has ever called me anything other than 'your grace.'"

"No one?"

He shook his head. His brow had stayed creased, and she could tell he struggled to understand this need of hers. But if she was to take to bed with this man, she wanted something—anything—that could bridge past the blankness in his eyes, no matter how factitious.

Her head slanted to the side, imploring. "Please, can I try 'Toren'? If I say it often enough, maybe it will eventually bend your ear."

"Possibly."

Her eyebrows arched in question.

"Yes. If you wish it, then I bow to your needs."

"Thank you."

He gave her a quick nod, his eyes running over the lump of her body under the covers. "I am too early? I expected for you to be ready. Shall I come back?"

"Yes—no—I mean I am ready." Her eyes dropped to his bare chest. Flustered by the expanse of his skin, her look slipped down to her hands as she rubbed the coverlet draped over her legs. "Is there something wrong with me?"

At his elongated silence, she glanced up.

He stared at her, eating her appearance, calculating. "No. I assumed you would be wearing less clothing."

Her look jerked downward to her chest. The top of the fat, white row of ruffles on her nightgown scratched the bottom of her chin. Less clothing? This was what she always wore in bed. "This is not right?"

He shrugged. "It is not wrong. But why are you wearing it?"

She looked up to him. "I have always worn this during intimacy."

"You have?"

"Yes."

"Over your whole body?"

She shrugged, her finger slipping under her collar to scratch the back of her neck, which was quickly becoming heated. She hadn't been prepared to actually discuss what they were about to do. "Well, the bottom is pulled up under the sheets, of course."

He nodded. "I understand."

He didn't move, standing rooted to the spot in the middle of the room, steps away from the bed. He stood and stared at her. The stare that pierced her.

It only made the flush along the back of her neck drift upward, filling the tips of her ears.

"So…" Her eyebrows lifted at him in question when she could stand the silence no more.

As if jabbed in the gut, he suddenly gave himself a slight shake and took three steps toward her. His long strides swallowed the remaining distance and he stopped by the edge of the bed. His scent wafted to her nose with the movement—cedar and leather with hints of cinnamon and spiced liqueur—like he was made of the earth, drew his strength from it.

He cleared his throat. "May I be direct, Adalia?"

"Yes."

"Are you a virgin?"

"No. Of course not." Her cheeks flamed red, her arms lifting to tighten around her belly. "I was married. We consummated the vows. Lord Pipworth attempted to bring me with child three times."

Toren's eyes narrowed. "You only copulated three times? I know the answer, but tell me again how long you were married?"

"Eighteen months."

He visibly winced. "Was sex…unenjoyable, difficult?"

"No. Neither. It was not anything after the first time. It was just…" her eyes flew to the fire burning in the hearth as she searched for the right word, "…there. My husband much preferred his mistress. He remarked upon it every time." She looked up to Toren's face. The tiniest flicker of something flashed in his brown eyes, so fast, Adalia barely noticed it, much less could determine what it meant.

He took another step toward the head of the bed, his thigh brushing the side of her leg through the coverlet. His gaze had gone hard, pinning her. "May I be direct again, Adalia?"

She hesitated. She hadn't cared for his first questions in the bedroom, and she doubted she wanted any more of his directness. Her lips drew inward with a shallow breath, but she lifted her look to him, meeting his brown eyes. "Yes. Please do so."

"I need something very different than your late husband."

"Oh. What?"

"I need you naked." His words were even, the depth of his voice rolling around her, factual. "I know exactly what my body needs in this act to come to completion, and it needs you naked. It needs you climaxing around me. Your body contracting, tightening in waves, surrounding my cock."

She gasped, her hand flattening fat ruffles onto her chest. Those words—demands she had never imagined coming from his mouth. Demands she had never imagined would be directed at her.

"You…ah…you need me to…climax?" She had to force the last word out of her arid mouth. For all that her friends had lauded such a thing, her own pleasure had never been part of sex for her. Never.

"I do, Adalia." Toren's fingers flickered at his side, almost as if he wanted to touch her leg. But he didn't. He wouldn't. That would be an emotion—a want—and Toren only did what was needed. She already knew that of him. "I need you naked, standing in front of me. I need to be able to learn what your body responds to for that to happen. Where to touch you. How fast. How hard. It is very difficult to discern anything under mounds of heavy cloth."

Her look fell to the bump on the coverlet where her toes pointed up. "So you would like me to strip?"

"Yes. And stand from the bed. It is not particularly cold in the room. We can stand by the fire, if you would like."

Adalia attempted to swallow again. No. Heat was not her problem at the moment. Heat was pouring from her, every pore, looking for escape, pooling in areas on her body that had never quite felt like this with her husband.

Correction. Her *late* husband. She was in the room with her new husband, and she needed to remember that fact. She had to do what was necessary.

Trying to quell the shake in her fingers, she folded back the coverlet from her lap. He stepped away from the bed to give her space, and she swung her legs down, dropping to her toes.

Silently, she turned her back to him and pulled her hair forward over her shoulder.

Without request, he loosened the weave of ribbon that held her nightgown tight to her neck, unthreading it down her back between her shoulder blades.

The fine hairs on her arms spiked as he tugged the fabric downward, letting it slip to the floor. Her body tensed as the nightgown puddled around her bare feet.

Toren settled his warm hands on her shoulders and spun her in place.

Before she was forced to turn fully to him, Adalia let her eyelids slip closed.

Facing her, his hands repositioned on her shoulders, his thumbs settling lightly into the swooping dips behind her collarbone. He stopped her movement, the silence heavy in the room as her shuffling feet stilled.

This was the moment. This was the moment he would grunt. Scrunch his face. Close his eyes. Not open them during the act. Pretend she was someone else. Not look at her until he was done and he could remove himself from her.

She braced herself.

She had suffered this before. She could again.

"You are beautiful, Adalia."

Her eyes flew open. She had not been prepared for the comment.

A slight smile had carved into his face. "I realize what I said about beauty last night. It serves no purpose. But this—your body—there is a definite need for it in this world."

She stared up at him. Traces of the blank look still etched his face, but his eyes—his eyes continued to take in her body, appreciating, almost admiring. But no. That could not be for her.

Her look fell to his chest. No. Not for her body—breasts too small, nothing on her backend to grip, no cushion along her midsection—she had heard her faults over and over from her late husband.

Her arms lifted, ready to hide what she could from his gaze.

His hands snapped down, wrapping around her wrists to still her movement. "Whatever truth you are hearing in your head at the moment is not the truth I see before me, Adalia."

She looked up, meeting his eyes. "I—you don't know—how do you presume to guess at what I am thinking?"

"I can see you creating argument against my words. I could recognize that look of yours in our second meeting. I know it is in your contrary nature to argue with me, but on this, I will not hear it."

He moved a step closer, the bare skin of his chest almost touching her nipples. "I am not your late husband. And whatever he thought of you, that was his business, not mine. And it is no longer yours. Your body is beautiful, Adalia. And that is the only truth you need now believe."

His gaze locked on hers, and she could not form the smallest word on her tongue. She nodded, realizing that she needed to breathe. Air into her chest.

His grip on her wrists released, his hands going to her shoulders again as he began to steer her backward across the room. "Come, by the fire. I need the light."

Stopping by the hearth, the heat of the flames wrapped her body. She glanced back to her nightgown piled on the wooden floorboards, both wishing for its comforting cover and glad to be free of the suffocation of it.

She closed her eyes. This was what her husband needed. He had been direct. So she would strive to give it to him.

Toren moved around her, and she heard the feet of the chair scrape along the floor behind her.

"Adalia, this chair."

He waited to speak again until she opened her eyes and looked over her shoulder at the chair he had shifted behind her. He had angled it so the arm of the chair was behind her backside.

"The chair is here for support should you need it."

She looked up at his face as he stepped in front of her again. The expressionless cast of his brown eyes had returned.

"Can I touch your body?" The words were low, seductive, belying his blank look.

She nodded.

The tips of his fingers, delicate, almost like a feather, traced the line of her collarbone, dipping down to her breasts. He bent, his lips languidly following the path of his fingers across her skin.

Before Adalia could fully take in the sensation of his lips, of the warmth spreading across her skin, her nipple slipped into his mouth.

Her knees buckled. Throwing her hands back, she caught herself on the arm of the chair before she fell, not that she imagined Toren would have let her slip. His hands wrapped around her waist, holding her body to him as his tongue, his lips, enveloped her nipple. Her skin went taut, her nipple hardening as he tugged, his teeth raking over the delicate skin.

He pulled away slightly, still clutching her body, as he slipped down to his knees. "That. You liked that?"

"Yes." The word came out much stronger than she imagined her airless lungs could produce.

He nodded, the tip of his nose brushing along her skin. "Good."

Moving downward, his lips went lazy, tasting her skin as his dipped down past her ribcage. Her stomach drew inward with a gasp, the caress both tantalizing and tickling.

"You are ticklish."

The tips of her fingers dug into the arm of the chair as the slight stubble on his chin dragged across the delicate skin near her hip bone. "Yes. I always have been."

"It is good to know." He murmured the words without pulling away, the wet heat of them sparking her skin to life in an entirely new way.

"Do you like it?"

"Yes." The word was not nearly as strong this time, as her body had begun to respond in foreign ways. Pangs shooting from deep inside her belly downward. The folds between her legs starting to throb, pulsate. This—this she had never felt with her late husband. Never anything of the kind.

Toren dipped backward, resting on his heels for a moment as he took in her body. The blank look was gone. His brown eyes had turned ravenous—but with an odd glimmer of control about them.

It lasted a moment before he moved forward, setting his fingers on the tips of her toes. Circling, the pads of his thumbs moved upward along her calves, and his lips met the long bone of her shin, nipping at the skin. His fingers dove around her legs to the delicate area behind her knees. A gasp, and her knees buckled again, her hold on the chair slipping.

He smiled into her skin.

"Ticklish here, as well." A statement, not a question. Not that she could have answered.

He moved up her thighs, his tongue carving a line to her inner thigh.

"This. Do you enjoy this, Adalia?"

She swallowed, desperate for words to form between gasping breaths. "It…it makes me…makes me want you to not stop…go higher."

A chuckle left him, hot, steaming onto her skin.

Heaven help her. This was what her friends had talked about. Relentless pounding in the folds between her legs, shoots of need deep inside of her that begged, angry, to be taken a hold of and commandeered into submission.

"That, I can accommodate, Adalia."

His arms ran up the outside of her thighs, his left hand shifting around to her backside, gripping her in place as his right hand dove inward, his thumb slipping down the center of her folds. She screeched, the touch both rewarding and torture.

Slowly, his thumb circled, taking the hard nubbin and teasing it into a voracious, pulsating beast. His tongue followed and she buckled forward, her fingers gripping the back of his neck. His tongue sending her mind into black, swirling fits of pleasure, he slowly dipped his thumb into her, stretching her, searching.

And then he nudged a spot. A glorious, evil, divine spot deep in her body that sent her trembling, screaming.

He nudged it as his tongue slipped around her nubbin, his lips clamping about it, pulling. His grip on her backside tightened, almost to pain, yet it only sent her nerves into a fevered pitch as her hips swiveled, begging for more.

"That Adalia? Too hard?"

She pulled herself from a moan that had taken over her chest as her hands went back to grip the chair again. "I don't think there's anything you could do to my body that I wouldn't like, Toren."

He chuckled. "I like that answer."

His thumb flipped deep within her, dragging out slowly as his palm ground against her.

"And I think you will like this even more."

He was pulling from her, even as he was stroking, bringing her to a pinnacle, her body standing on a precipice she couldn't name, feared, and needed to go over at the same time.

*Needed.*

She needed this.

Now she knew what Toren was talking about.

"More, Toren, more."

"Hold, Adalia."

Torture, pure and simple. It had been his plan all along.

She opened her eyes to him, surprised to see him standing again, for his hands were still clamped to her body. His sheet was gone, his shaft long and hard and reaching for her.

He set his tip on her entrance, bracing her hips a second before he slid smoothly into her, filling her, letting her body adjust to him.

The mangled mew that escaped her throat drew a slight growl from him, and he withdrew, leaving her body.

He paused, taking a moment to wedge her fingers from their grip on the chair, and he wrapped her hands around his neck. Lifting her, he set her onto the arm of the chair.

His next stoke was not gentle. He slammed into her, reaching deep, forcing her entire world to shift.

Her fingers dug into his shoulders. "More. That. Like that."

"Damn, Adalia." He did as she commanded. Pushing, demanding her body stretch for him, succumb to his need of her.

She climaxed. Screaming, fire in her veins. Her body twisted out of control, and it was exactly what he needed.

Growling, his body exploded within her as she shuddered around him, grasping for anything solid she could hold onto as she left her body.

Spinning waves fought through her body, one after another after another.

He held her until she sank down to earth, her senses gradually returning with each slowing heartbeat.

Unburying her face, she pulled her head from his chest, untangling her arms so she could look up and find his eyes.

"I do enjoy what your body needs of mine. Can you do that again?"

# { CHAPTER 8 }

Toren laughed.

This, he had not expected. He could tell from the first moment he saw Adalia that she was not experienced in bed. How she held her body. Slightly rigid at all times. Not with the ease of a woman that owned her own body through and through.

But she had not shied in the slightest to his tongue. And her body was very, very good at giving his body exactly what it needed.

"Yes, we can. But you must give me a few minutes."

She bit her lip, her green eyes glowing at him. A few minutes apparently not soon enough for her.

He chuckled, freeing his arms from her body. He grabbed her hands, pulling her forward to slide off the arm of the chair. It was upholstered, but still, the bar of wood had to have been digging into her flesh. Not that she looked like she minded. She looked, quite frankly, like she would sit in that exact spot for the rest of her life if it meant she would get to enjoy what just happened again and again.

Motioning her to the chair, he went over to the side table by the window, pulling free the stopper in the brandy decanter.

He looked over his shoulder at his new wife as he set rim to glass. "I would not normally ask this of a woman, but you are…unconventional…because of your brothers and how you were raised."

Tucking her feet underneath her on the wide chair by the fireplace, she looked up at him, her gaze cautious. "In what way?"

Curious that she didn't scurry for the cover of a sheet or that monstrosity of cloth she was dressed in earlier. She sat, naked, the fire enough warmth for her body.

"Do you drink brandy?"

She laughed. "Fair enough. No, actually, I do not. I tried it once long ago when Theo slipped me one too many drams in a night. I thought I had far too much to prove, so I sipped and sipped and sipped away. It turned out Theo got everyone exorbitantly foxed that evening so he could finally win the bulk of the wagers."

"Wagers?" Still gripping the thin neck of the decanter, he turned fully to her.

"We would have grand nights of gambling—baccarat and hazard and whist and piquet—my brothers and I." She settled her forearm along the arm of the chair, leaning toward the fire. Smooth and languid, her body had shed much of its inherent rigidness. "Except Theo never won, and it drove him insane. Alfred and I were very good at recognizing tells. And Caldwell bullied his way to wins. So Theo finally got his win that night, and while my two older brothers fell to the brandy and slept, I was left with my head over a chamber pot."

Toren cringed. "The bugger—that sounds like something Theodore would concoct."

"Yes—exactly." She smirked. "But he received his vengeance in full—he had to tend to me vomit after vomit—it went on for six hours. The stench was atrocious and he had to wash it from my hair. Justice was more than served." She shook her head, her nose wrinkling. "So no, I do not drink brandy."

"Claret, then?"

"Yes, please."

Toren turned to the table, pouring her a ruby red glass of wine. Grabbing her glass and his own of brandy, he walked back to the hearth, handing her the claret. He sat on the wingback chair opposite her, stretching out and crossing his legs on the low ottoman between them.

Her gaze dropped to the fire as she sipped the wine. He took a swallow from his own glass, studying her. She had angled her arm in front of her breasts. Modesty creeping into her consciousness. He didn't care for that.

She looked at him, her eyes traveling in a careful line from the fire to his face, avoiding everything below his neck. "How did you know Theo? I do remember him mentioning you with the name 'Dell' but only in passing. I still don't understand how or why he would have asked this of you."

"Asked me to watch over you—marry you?"

She nodded.

Toren took a sip from his glass, then set it to balance on the top of his thigh. His palm went up to sit atop the rim of the glass, forefinger tapping along the edge. "I do not have an answer for you, Adalia. He never told me the why. What I can tell you is that Theodore was my friend—my only friend, truth of the matter."

A disbelieving smile crossed her face. "Surely not your only." Another second, and the smile slipped from her face. "You only have one friend? And it was Theo?"

"Had." Toren nodded. "And yes, Theodore was the only person I considered a friend. He was also the only person

I knew at school, or as an adult, that did not approach me with an ulterior purpose at the ready. The ducal title is the reason for my interactions with all people. It always has been. What they need of me. What I need of them. Everyone in my life has always either been paid to be there, or had hopes of some gain."

"Why—" She coughed, her hand flying up to cover her mouth. It took her a moment to recover, a sip of wine helping. "Why, that is awful, Toren—pure and through."

"It is a reality that I have always lived with." He shrugged. "I hold no ill will to the fact, as I came to terms with it long before I knew any different."

She took another sip of claret, still clearing her throat as she nodded. "I can imagine why Theo was your one friend then—he always cared so little about titles or power—or money, for that matter. Only about his next adventure. Only about the fun—or trouble—he could manifest."

Toren's eyes glazed over. "Yes. Never once did Theodore ask me for a favor in all the years I knew him. He only asked that I participate in life with him."

Adalia smiled, nodding. "Theo was infectious, wasn't he? He did not think there was such a thing as a bad idea. He would do anything—and he never plotted with regard to any caution. I imagine you did help him with that?"

His cheek lifted in a half smile. "There were a few scrapes I extracted him from. But he never asked for the help—never for a favor, save for this one." He flipped his forefinger in a circle above his glass.

"Me?"

"Yes. And my vow to him was the only favor I have ever granted where I did not gain something in return."

"A truly benevolent act on your part?" Her eyebrow cocked, grin lining her lips. "What could have ever possessed you to make such a magnanimous promise?"

He heard the light sarcasm in her voice but did not bow to it. Instead, Toren's voice notched lower. "Theodore was my only friend. It was the only thing he wanted of me. So I knew you were the most important thing to him."

Her breath caught, and he could see how his words had cut into her. Opened a wound he had not intended to poke.

A broken smile reached her lips. "For all of Theo's wild ways, he loved me best of all. I knew that." Tears welled in her eyes, glistening in the light from the fire. "He was supposed to come home. Not in a box."

"I agree."

Her eyes dropped to the fire, her lips pulling inward as she fought tears. Admirably, they did not spill from her lower lashes.

After taking a long sip of her claret, she looked to him. "I fear I have lost all taste for nudity this evening."

Toren inclined his head. "I understand."

Adalia unfurled her legs from their wedge on the chair, and she walked across the room, setting her glass on the bedside table as she picked up her nightgown. She didn't put it on, holding it instead in front of her body.

Walking back over to him, she stopped by the chair he sat in. "Do know that I did enjoy what you did to me tonight, and I…I hope it continues."

"Beyond the bed chamber?"

Lines creased her forehead. "What do you mean 'beyond the bedchamber'?"

Toren shook his head, standing so he could look down at her. Now was as good a time as any to tell her. "We are married, yes, but I do not want to encourage emotions between us that will do neither of us any good."

She exhaled through a relieved smile, meeting his look. "If you think I mean to fall in love with you, Toren, I assure you, I have no intention of doing so. I wish you no harm."

"Harm? How could that possibly harm me?"

"Everyone I have ever loved, save for the twins, is dead. Everyone." Her words held no sadness, only resigned acceptance. "That is a lot of death that swirls around me, and I would rather not add you to the list."

"You think you are cursed?"

"I am not willing to prove it any further." She offered him a smile, her fingers curling tight into the ruffles of her nightgown, the only barrier between their nudity. "I am willing to bear your children, Toren. Nothing more. Though I hope we are amiable. Which should suit you well, as I don't believe you wish for anything more than that from me."

Relief cut through him. If Adalia was truly being honest with him, he could not have hoped for a more appropriate wife for his needs. He gave silent thanks to Theodore on that accord. "On that, you are correct, Adalia. I do not wish for anything more than an affable marriage. It pleases me we are in accord on the subject."

She gave him one nod, tightening the fabric in front of her across her chest. He wondered how she was going to clutch it to her backside when she exited.

"Excellent. Sleep well, Toren."

He inclined his head to her, taking the last swallow of brandy from his glass.

She turned, walking toward the door that joined their chambers. Toren watched her move away, noting she didn't bother to wrap the nightgown around to her backside. Her long red-blond hair in waves swung slightly with her steps, the tips of it brushing the top curve of her buttocks. For some reason he could not name, the very fact that she did not fully hide from him pleased him beyond measure.

She stopped at the door, turning back to him. "Forgive me, Toren, but curiosity has gotten the better of me."

His eyebrow cocked. Curiosity in a woman was never good.

"Why is it that you do not want me to love you?"

"I cannot return the love."

Her eyes drifted downward and she nodded, more to herself than to him. Her look shot back up to his eyes. "Why not?"

Toren needed no time to prepare an answer. He'd had this conversation before. The words came from him, practiced and impassive. "I do not know what love is, Adalia. I know what I need in life. But love—that is something I am not capable of."

"Because of how you grew up?"

"What do you know of that?"

"I have gathered that you grew up with one cold governess and one indifferent solicitor that served as your guardian and watched over your assets. A very lonely upbringing."

He eyed her, attempting to piece together who she had been talking to. "I was raised as appropriate for a boy in my position."

She didn't argue his statement, but her head tilted to the side, and her astute green eyes went calculating. "Just because you were never loved, Toren, does not mean you aren't capable of it."

"And just because I was never loved, Adalia, does not mean that I yearn for it."

She exhaled, nodding, and slowly turned to the door, exiting his room.

Yes. They were, indeed, very different.

# { CHAPTER 9 }

"You are sure the girls will be fine?" Leaving the stables, Adalia looked over her shoulder at the retreating castle.

"Adalia, not a soul makes it onto my estate without me knowing," Toren said from his large brown steed next to her mare. "I have four men standing guard, and the maid that is watching the girls is very skilled with the rolling pin she keeps in her apron. I have seen her whack the overly saucy third footman many times with it."

She looked at him, frowning. "You are trying to make me laugh so I do not worry."

"True. I do want your concentration on where we are going and not back on the castle. And you must remember that beast of a hound is with the girls. He will attack any threat long before any one of those people I mentioned lifts a finger."

"Hazard is not a beast. He is a puffy sweet soufflé." Her head swiveled. Fields to her left, a deep forest straight ahead, pastures to her right—and each of them stretching as far as the eye could see. "But this will take hours, Toren. Your land is so vast."

"Exactly. And that is the advantage I need you to have. I need you to know this land in case it ever becomes necessary. Where the trails are. What they lead to. We will be doing this for several days—more if you cannot pay attention the first time we travel through it."

"Days? But you just said we are all safe here."

His eyes went to the sky. "I did. But I want you prepared, as well. I have yet to discern what the exact threat is—why Mary was taken—the danger Theodore believed you all to be in. Why he took the extreme measure of sending you to me. I cannot plan for every eventuality, and making you aware of the land around you is a last resort you should never need, but I want you to have it for your own sense of peace. Can you understand that?"

"Yes. Fine." She lifted her hand off the sidesaddle's pommel and flitted it in the air. "I will stop my worry. Or at least not speak of it."

He gave her a sideways glance, shaking his head.

Down the rolling hill behind the stables, Toren directed the horses to the middle of a long stretch of trees. "There." He pointed forward. "This is the main trail through the woods. There are more in and out, and we will get to those, but most of them lead to or from this trail. This is the first choice—the quickest area to escape to with the girls should it be necessary. Most of the horses in the stable have been on it, and can move fairly quickly through it in the dark, so Josalyn and Mary should have little problem guiding their horses."

The trail wide, their horses remained side-by-side as they stepped from the bright summer sunlight into the cool shadow of the trees.

"Toren, the girls do not know how to ride."

He glanced at her, eyebrow lifted. "Well, they must learn. They are far past old enough."

Her head shook so emphatically her small bonnet shifted, almost slipping from the crown of her head. "No. I do not want them harmed. I will not allow it."

His body bobbing in ease with every step of his horse, Toren stared at her. For long seconds he said nothing.

Stare at her all he wanted, Adalia wouldn't yield on this matter. She would not allow the girls to go near horses.

Toren opened his mouth, his words calm, reflecting the cool serenity of the woods surrounding them. "To learn how to ride properly will ensure the girls are not harmed, Adalia. I have an excellent stable of fine, gentle mares. And several docile ponies that would be perfect for them to learn on. They will not be injured."

Her look whipped to him. "Absolutely not, Toren. I said no. No. My brother Alfred died from a horse. So, no. I do not want them anywhere near the stables. Anywhere near the horses. I cannot have them at risk."

His jaw clamped shut, and his look swung forward, silence falling over them.

Adalia gave an imperceptible sigh, her eyes busying themselves with watching the passing bark of the trees closest to the trail. At least he wasn't fighting her on it. The entire time they had spent together thus far had been riddled with more contrary conversations than she could ever remember having with one person.

Was that what Theo had seen in Toren? A man that would drive his sister to Bedlam with his converse opinions? Had Theo thought it would be funny to toss the two of them together? She wouldn't put the notion past her brother.

She looked at Toren, studying his profile. His brown eyes remained forward, his face gone to blankness. Yet even with that blasted emotionless look, she recognized he was handsome. Strong features, with a hard jawline that lent itself to impenetrable aloofness, if the assessment stopped there. But his eyes, his mouth—when they weren't a mask of indifference—softened his face, making him almost approachable. A peculiar attractiveness she could not deny.

Especially when his lips were on her bare skin as they had been the previous night.

"Why did Theo trust only you?" The question blurted out of her mouth, startling herself.

"He trusted only me?" Toren looked at her. "That is an assumption. I think your brother trusted a lot of people."

"No. In his letter—he said very clearly that you were the only one I could trust. The only one." Her hand tightened on the reins as she looked to her mare's silvery mane reflecting rogue rays of sunlight through the tree canopy. "Not even my friends, and my friends are beyond trustworthy."

"Your friends are women. They are in no position to protect you and the twins."

"Yes, but Theo had scores of other friends." She looked at him. "I am just curious as to why you were the one he sent me to."

Toren shrugged. "It is a mystery to me as well. Though, if you were him, trying to protect a sister—or the twins—who would you have chosen?"

She looked past Toren, considering his words.

She would have chosen the strongest, most connected, wealthiest, smartest, most honorable person she knew. Someone with unfailing integrity. Irreproachable valor. Someone that was unattached and would have the time and energy to devote to eliminating the threat. That's who she would have chosen.

Her gaze landed on him.

Buggers. She would have chosen Toren, or someone exactly like him.

Except maybe someone that also had the capacity to care, as well. Yes. That would have also been a nice addition to the necessary qualities.

But certainly not the most important thing on the list.

"My brother was a smart man, wasn't he?"

The corner of Toren's mouth quirked, though his face stayed mostly blank. "Yes. And clever beyond words—he kept that well-hidden from most."

Toren pulled up on his horse, pointing to his left. "This is the first branch in the trail. It goes west and will follow the stream that runs through these woods. It doesn't split off and it eventually emerges near Dellington. It is the quickest way to get to the village."

Adalia looked at the parting in the trees that she had almost missed, then craned her head backward, searching for distinctive markings around the break in trees. "How far to the village?"

"A little less than two miles."

She nodded, spotting an odd clumping of three fat stumps just before the opening. That would do.

Toren nicked his horse along and looked to her once her horse was beside his. "I also wanted to come out here so I could talk to you away from the girls. I did not want them to overhear anything that may frighten or upset them."

A chill went down her spine. "What did you want to discuss?"

"My trip back to London. I arranged for Theodore's body to be delivered to the Alton estate in Derbyshire for burial."

The words stole her breath. It took long, silent seconds for her to steel herself enough to look at him and speak. "Did you see him, his body? Did you verify it was him?"

His chest rose in a long breath as his eyes flicked to the side. "I did."

"You paused. What are you not telling me, Toren?"

He met her eyes. "I did not pause, Adalia. This is not an easy topic and I do not wish to bring you any more heartache."

"No, you did pause. Now please don't argue it. What are you not telling me?"

He looked away from her, heaving a sigh. The horses took several steps before his gaze centered on her. "Theodore was not…whole…it had been a severe beating and—"

"No. Nothing more." She cut him off, only able to stammer out the few words before she had to stop and swallow the bile that had rushed to her throat. Her head bowing, her eyes closed as she fought the waves of revulsion running though her body. The onslaught of dizziness—exasperated by every step her mare took—threatened to make her slide from her sidesaddle.

*The pommel. Grip the leather. Don't let go.*

Long minutes passed before she could crack her eyes open, but she could not lift them, could only concentrate on the white tips of her horse's ears. "How could you tell me that?" Her voice a raw whisper, she could not look at Toren.

"I did not want to. And I attempted not to. I apologize. I do not profess to know what I can and cannot say to you,

Adalia. I did not realize it would distress you as much as it did."

Her chin bumped into her chest as she drew a steadying breath. "Thank you for…attending to Theo. I had to leave with the girls so suddenly that I did not have time to do so, and it was weighing upon my soul. I would like to visit his grave at Glenhaven soon."

"Of course. As soon as it is safe."

She managed to lift her head, looking at him. "When will it be safe?"

"I do not know." His eyebrows drew together. He was choosing his words carefully. "I go under the assumption that Theodore knew of the danger you three were in, so I am retracing what his last steps were in London, hoping for a clue as to who would have attacked the twins, and why."

"Have you found anything?"

"Not as of yet. But I have a team of Bow Street Runners attempting to piece together what his final days were. What ship he stepped off of, where he had been, why. What he was doing in the rookeries. That he didn't seek you out immediately once he set foot on English soil is telling. He thought the threat the utmost importance."

"You will tell me if there is news from the investigators?"

"I would prefer not to. I believe the less you know, the safer you will be."

"Do not even attempt that argument, Toren." Her hand waved in front of her. "Do you see where we are— what you are showing me and why? You yourself said the more knowledge I have, the better. This is no different."

His hand lifted, his gloved fingers rubbing the back of his neck. For several breaths, he didn't answer her. Finally, he sighed, his look going to her, his brown eyes searching her face. "I will tell you. But I will guard against words that may distress you."

She nodded.

That he agreed to that much was a victory in itself.

~ ~ ~

Past his chambers, Toren walked along the hallway, fat bricks of grey stone to his right, the warmth of plaster and paint to his left. He stopped, turning to the stones, brushing his finger along the dusty mortar.

He had always appreciated being able to see the bones of the castle. But now with two little girls running about… maybe the stones weren't appropriate.

For that matter, maybe they were. What did he know of little girls?

Add it to the list of items to ask his new wife.

Toren turned from the stone wall and moved to the open doorway of Adalia's chambers. Her back to him, Adalia sat inside, tucked up to the delicate rosewood writing desk by the tall windows. Her pinky tapping on the desk, her head tilted up as her attention shifted to the window.

Pausing at the threshold of her room, Toren stared at the back of her head. Her hair had been swept into a simple knot, freeing the back of her neck to the air. He liked that spot on her. The exact center of the divot along the back of her neck that sent her skin to prickle. He was amazed he had discerned as much about her as he had the previous night, but she held little—nothing—back in the bedchamber.

Immediate trust born of marriage. Confidence in him from the start. Whether that was wise of her or not.

A pang of guilt struck him, a frown carving his face. He'd had to do it. The lie that would keep her safe.

He rarely—never—lied. The truth was always simpler, harsh though it could be. He had never once been afraid of the truth.

But this. This he had to lie about. He had no choice.

His look centered on the back of her neck, as the nettlesome debate on the wisdom of his decision gnawed on the back of his mind.

Her right hand lifted, dipping the tip of a quill into an inkwell.

No.

It spurred him across the room, his hand grabbing her right wrist before she set nib to vellum. Ink splotched across the paper.

"Toren? What?" She looked up, peeved.

He released her wrist. "Who are you writing?"

"My friends, Violet and Cassandra." She pointed at the one letter, already sealed and sanded and propped against the box of inks in front of her.

"No. Absolutely not." He plucked the finished letter from the desk.

"Why in heaven's name not? They are my dear friends and they will be dreadfully worried on me. We left London without a word and they—"

"No."

Her mouth clamped shut, her head snapping back.

"Do you want to be safe, Adalia?"

"Well of course, but these are my friends." She reached for the letter in his fingers.

His elbow jerked back, holding the letter out of reach. "Do you want the twins to be safe?"

Her glare deepened. "Telling Violet and Cass that I am safe does no harm."

"Do you want the twins to be safe?"

"Yes." The word hissed from her teeth.

"Then no. No one can know you three are here. No contact with anyone until I determine what Theodore was doing in the rookeries. Until I determine what the exact threat is."

"And just when will that be, Toren? I don't think you understand the extreme worry this—that I disappeared with the girls—will be causing my friends."

"They will survive."

She slapped the quill onto the desk, her mouth clamping shut.

At least she managed to resist calling him an overbearing ogre. He could see the insults were brimming on the tip of her tongue, but she held them back.

Again, because she trusted him—so quickly it was near to foolish on her part.

"Is that alone why you came in here?" Her words clipped, she was dismissing him.

He set the sealed letter onto the desk in front of her. "I will tell you when you can send it. And, no, I actually have a request of you."

"Yes?"

"I was hoping to have you talk to Mr. Fredrick, my head gardener. I know nothing about roses, but it appeared as though the rose beds sparked an interest in you and I thought we could revive the rose garden. I asked him to meet me in the study in a few minutes to discuss the plans. Perhaps you can help?"

The tight line of her mouth relaxed as the whole countenance of her face softened—so much so that it made him blink. Curious. He had never seen anger leave a person so quickly.

"I would enjoy that. Very much so." Not quite a smile, but acceptance. He would take it.

"Good." He started to step away from the desk, but then curiosity stopped him. "What is it—that odd look upon your face?"

"Nothing. You came in here and took something away from me." She swiveled on her chair to fully face him. "But then in the next instant, you offered something to make me happy. I am just not sure what to do with that."

"You don't want to be happy?"

"No—yes—of course I do. I am an entirely happy person. I always have been. Life has just not encouraged it in recent years." Her hands lifted, palms flipping upward as a hesitant smile crossed her face. "So this, the roses…it is kind. That is all. It was unexpected, so I thank you."

His lips drew inward, his brow creasing as he gave a slight nod. He started to move away from her, but her voice stopped him before he stepped into the hallway.

"Toren, I promised Josalyn and Mary we would play cards this evening. Would you like to join us?"

"I…"

"Four would be optimal for whist."

His knuckles rapped softly onto the wood of the doorframe as he looked at her. "You are teaching them whist? Are they not too young?"

"Not by far. They can hold the cards, Toren. I learned when I was five and Theo had to hold my cards for me."

"I generally avoid games of chance."

"Please? It will save me from playing two hands and partnering with both of them simultaneously."

Her green eyes so enticingly hopeful, Toren had to nod. "I will join you."

~ ~ ~

Laughing, Adalia watched as Hazard squeezed in between Josalyn and Mary just as they scampered through the door of the library. Three-wide, they got stuck in the doorframe, much to their instant delight. Hazard yelped, wiggling forward, and the girls broke free in fits of laughter.

"Good night, my dears, you both played very well tonight. I will check on you soon," Adalia called out after them.

Mary grabbed the doorknob, closing the door. "Good night, Auntie Ada."

Adalia tapped the stack of playing cards in her hand on the square table, her look going to Toren. He had leaned back in his chair, his left ankle slung up over his right knee. The white of his muslin shirt interrupted only by the dark of his waistcoat, he looked relaxed, his sleeves rolled slightly, shirt open wide at his neck. Even more relaxed than he looked naked, if that was possible.

"Remind me to never play against you," he said, threading his fingers together behind his head.

"I strike fear in your heart?"

"Yes." He smiled. "Or at least to never bet against you. I fear I ruin all the progress you make with the girls. If they follow my example, they have long lives of losing ahead of them."

She laughed, shuffling the cards. "No bets? Even if it was for something worth winning? Something valuable?"

"Valuable?"

She looked up at him with no control over the wanton smile that invaded her face. "Such as my clothes? We are currently alone."

He laughed, a low rumble that warmed the already toasty library. "That. That I do not think I can refuse." He sat up, flicking his fingers toward the cards. "Deal, then. Even though I know I will regret this. It is comical how good you are and how bad I am."

"Each trick, one item?" Adalia shuffled the cards, starting to peel them out, one by one. "I used to play so often—I realized tonight how much I miss it. I rarely get to play at the Revelry's Tempest anymore, since it became so busy." She looked up at him. "You will get better, I imagine."

"I doubt it."

"Why?"

"I do not have the demeanor for it. I do not care for risk, for guessing at the duplicity of those around me."

"But that is half the fun. Who has what. Their tells. Trying to outwit those around you, which is even more fun when you know your opponents well." She set down the stack of cards in the blind, picking up her hand. "That burst of giddiness when you catch someone bluffing—my heartbeat speeds just thinking on it."

"You embrace all of it so fully—your brothers raised a peculiar woman."

She shrugged with a grin. "They did their best."

Toren leaned forward, lifting the edge of his cards to note them, and then he fanned them out across his stomach as he leaned back in his chair. "Tell me of your late husband's family."

He tossed the king of spades onto the table.

She glanced at him above her cards. "You would like to probe into my past?"

"I want to make sure I know of any possible enemies that would harm you or the girls."

After flipping out the ace of spades, she slid the trick toward her. "Your waistcoat."

She waited until he shrugged out of his waistcoat before laying the jack of spades. "You think Pipworth's family could have had something to do with Mary being abducted?"

"I think nothing until there is evidence." He followed suit with a queen. Buggers. Not in the blind. "Your left slipper."

She flicked off the heel of her slipper with her right toes and exhaled, flipping her fingers in the air. "No. They are harmless. They are angry—at my late husband, and by extension, me—but they are harmless. I understand that they now realize how very much of the fortune was spent on his vices. Vices that had nothing to do with me."

He nodded. "Can you think of anyone else that would want to harm you—harm the twins?"

"No. Goodness, no." She shook her head even as Mr. Trether's face popped into her mind. She instantly dismissed the vision of him. Mr. Trether was handled—he wanted the Revelry's Tempest, nothing more. And he most certainly had no intentions to harm her, much less the twins. "There is no one."

Six tricks went by, various items of clothing disappearing. While Toren had quickly been relieved of his shirt, both boots, and stockings, Adalia had managed to only lose her other slipper.

His forefinger tapping the edge of his cards, Toren looked at her. "Did you enjoy your late husband, Adalia?"

Though the question should have given her pause, Adalia had long since removed from herself all emotion regarding her first husband. She shrugged. "I held Pipworth in esteem for a while. At least from afar. That was until we were married."

"Marriage was not what you had hoped for?"

Adalia's card hand dropped, her look meeting Toren's. "My eldest brother, Caldwell, chose him for me. Pipworth was a dear friend of his. We married months after Caldwell died. I do not know if it was obligation upon Pipworth's part. I imagine so. Regardless, we spent very little time together."

Toren nodded, his look starting to sear into her. "He had other pursuits?"

She lifted her cards, methodically collapsing and spreading them out evenly in her hands. Again and again.

Her tell, and she knew it—her brothers called her on it each and every time. But Toren didn't know it. Not yet.

She cleared her throat. "Pipworth had a mistress with much more rotund assets than what I possess. That was the direction his pursuits were focused. She was his main vice. He did everything with her. I imagine he loved her."

"Why do you say that?"

She collapsed her cards into her right hand, avoiding his eyes. "He jumped into the Thames to save her after a horse bumped her off a bridge. He must have loved her in order to do so. And he did save her. He saved her and then drowned himself."

She fiddled with the top right corner of her fore card.

Toren leaned forward, laying a nine of hearts on the table between them. "You have suffered disappointments, Adalia—far too many for one so young. Yet from what I have seen of you, it has not become you. I find that admirable."

A compliment? That did give her pause. She looked up at him, a smile curling the tips of her mouth. "Yes, well, thank you. But my friends are the admirable ones. They have not allowed me to lose the person I am."

She laid down her queen of hearts, her smile widening. "And now, Toren, I will need you to please remove your trousers."

He stood, tossing the remaining cards in his hand onto the table. The devil grin that crossed his face made her momentarily question the poor plays of his hand. He inclined his head to her. "Then I bow to your needs, Adalia."

She smiled.

She liked those words. Liked them beyond all others.
Words that could very well make her happy.

# { CHAPTER 10 }

Adalia stepped out into the bright sunlight from the rear entrance of the castle. Summertime did this land well—the ducal estate alive with green fields, busy sheep, birds tweeting from sun-up till sundown. Alive. The entire place felt alive, and that spirit had taken root in her soul, lightening her heart more and more each day.

Eight nights in Toren's bed didn't hurt with that in the slightest.

A blush creeping up her neck at the mere thought of how he had twisted her body the previous night, Adalia searched the close-by gardens and fields, looking for Josalyn and Mary. Toren's ancient butler had said Lucy, the young maid turned into nanny for the girls, had brought them out to the gardens.

Adalia started down the garden path, aiming for the expansive rose garden beyond the evergreen border since the girls had discovered the joy of digging small creatures out of the rose beds.

The heat creeping along her scalp not abating, her mind remained consumed with her husband. Nights with Toren were the least of her concerns. Nights with him had made her feel, of all things, normal. Normal in her body, and all it had ever yearned for. He had requested her to join him, night after night, without fail, and Adalia had begun to find her mouth watering for his bedroom hours before the twins went to bed.

There was never a thing she could not ask him about—ask him to do—that he did not contemplate with good will, and he had never refused her. His body was hers to explore, and she had taken to the opportunity with gusto. That his body was a molded specimen, worthy of stone and chisel, had made the nights all the more delicious.

For a man that could not love, Toren had an amazing capacity to make her feel. Right down to the curling of her toes. Again and again. And again.

Two rabbits sprinted in front of her, diving under the evergreen hedge. Fat rabbits that had surely been snitching Cook's parsnips again.

She smirked at them as their white tails disappeared. Cook would not be happy.

Opening the gate to the rose garden, Adalia heard Mary's laugh floating in the air, and her head tilted to the sound. Toren was right—her laugh was more of a chortle.

Shaking her head to herself, she went through the gate expecting to see the girls up to their elbows in dirt.

Instead, her heart stopped.

They weren't in the dirt of the rose beds.

On ponies.

Both of them by the stables. Both of the girls on ponies, riding.

Her feet started running before her mind caught up to the sight. The girls so high. So high off the ground and so easy to falling.

She couldn't scream, couldn't do anything but run.

Through the rose garden and halfway to them, Josalyn spotted Adalia running toward her. Her niece squealed in excitement, her hand coming up high and waving, pride shining so bright at her accomplishment that Adalia thought she would burst into a thousand rays of sunlight.

Laughing, Josalyn waved again, her whole body lifting from the sidesaddle. The pony turned.

In the next breath, Josalyn missed grabbing the reins and slipped to the side.

Her little body dropping.

Slow.

Time stopping. Falling.

*Thunk.*

The sound of Josalyn's body hitting the ground overtook Adalia's world.

Her feet sped, a thousand deals made with the devil before she skidded to her knees at Josalyn's prone body.

Gasping for breath. No breath, no breath.

Gulping air that didn't reach her lungs, her hands shook, terrified to touch Josalyn. Yet they managed to land softly on her head, her fingers wrapping into her niece's blond hair.

She tilted Josalyn's face to her. The girl's eyes remained closed, her body motionless on the ground, her arm twisted grotesquely behind her back.

Adalia lifted her into her arms, clutching Josalyn to her body. A scream stuck in her chest. Stuck below the gulps of air she gasped.

She looked up to see Toren, frozen, standing next to Mary and holding the reins of the pony she was on.

At the sight of him, air flooded into her chest, a tornado of horror. "How could you do this, you bastard?"

The scream echoed across the lands, stilling all sound.

Whimpers cut into the dead air, Mary's face contorting as she stared at her sister on the ground. Toren jumped at the sound, swiftly lifting Mary from the speckled pony and setting her softly to her feet on the ground.

Swaying back and forth, clutching Josalyn tighter, Adalia heaved another breath and found sound again in her lungs, her face contorting at Toren. "You bloody bastard."

"Auntie." The sound, muffled, vibrated against her chest.

Adalia yanked Josalyn away from her chest—from the terrified clutch she had her gripped in.

Josalyn blinked, looking up at her, confusion filling her sweet blue eyes. "Auntie, why are you yelling?"

Adalia let out a garbled screech, her fingers tightening into Josalyn's hair as her body nearly collapsed.

Josalyn smiled up at her, still confused. "I was riding, Auntie Ada. Did you see me? I was good. Very, very good. Uncle Toren said so himself."

Tears flooding down her cheeks, Adalia gasped for breath after breath, straining to believe that Josalyn was alive, smiling up at her. That it wasn't a dream. Wasn't a hallucination. She smothered Josalyn to her chest once more, the air lodged in her lungs unable to move.

She only gave Josalyn space once the girl began to squirm. Room to breathe, but Adalia could give her no more than that, keeping her hands on Josalyn's shoulders, not willing to free her niece just yet.

"Did you see?" Josalyn asked again, the earlier pride still beaming bright.

"I did, sweetheart. I did." Adalia nodded, her hands running down the sides of Josalyn's face. "Does anything hurt?"

"Just where you are squeezing me, Auntie."

A monumental feat, Adalia forced her fingers to unclench from Josalyn's shoulders.

Josalyn looked around. "Where did my pony go? Uncle Toren said Sparkles could be mine. I named her. Mary got to choose first, but she didn't choose Sparkles and I wanted Sparkles from the start. I don't want to lose her before I even have her."

Adalia looked up out of the tiny bubble that her world had just been reduced to, her eyes squinting in the light.

Birds still chirped. Sheep still ambled across the fields. The breeze still rustled the leaves of the forest beyond the stables. She pointed. "There. She is over there, Josalyn, nibbling on grass."

An enormous smile split across Josalyn's face. "I want to ride more. It was fun, fun, fun, Auntie."

"No." Adalia had to swallow back the screech that came with the word.

"No? But, Auntie Ada, I was quite good at it. Did you not see? You said you saw." Josalyn wiggled the rest of the way out of Adalia's grip and sprang to her feet. No cracked bones, not even the smallest flicker of pain in Josalyn's face.

"I did see." Adalia had to cross her arms, tucking her hands under her elbows so they didn't escape and snatch Josalyn again.

Josalyn may be fine, but she was not. Far from it.

"No more today, sweetheart," Adalia said. "We will talk about it tomorrow. Are you sure you are steady on your feet?"

"Of course I am, silly Auntie."

Adalia tried to smile, but knew it didn't make it to her lips. She inclined her head toward the castle. "Then you and Mary go inside and ask Cook for some lemonade. I believe she was having lemons squeezed earlier today. And sit, please. At least for a few minutes."

Mary ran the few steps to her sister, grabbing Josalyn's hand, and the two of them ran up the long hill to the castle, their light skirts swinging merrily behind them.

On her knees, Adalia watched them as she collapsed downward onto her calves, her legs slowly splitting under her until she sat on the ground.

It wasn't until the girls had long since disappeared into the door of the castle that her breathing slowed to normal and her body no longer felt like every muscle would fail her if she tried to move. Slowly, she managed to gain her feet, her boots shuffling in the dirt, and she turned to her husband, venom twisting her lips. "I will not lose them, Toren."

"Adalia—"

She ran at him, shoving him as hard as she could in the chest. "How could you? Alfred died when his skull was crushed by a horse, Toren. My brother dead by some stupid beast that could not control itself and now you set them on top of those beasts? How in the bloody hell could you?"

Only losing one backward step to her power, he grabbed her swinging wrists. "Calm yourself, Adalia. They have been persistent, both of them. Day after day pestering me about riding. I was no force to deny them."

"No force to deny them?" Her forehead scrunched, incredulous as she grunted and wrenched her wrists free from his grip. "That is no excuse, Toren. They are *little girls*. They do not control you. You control them. You are a bloody duke, and you cannot control two wee girls?"

He opened his mouth in retort, then clamped it closed.

Her eyes went to slits. "What? You have something more to say on the matter?"

He stared at her, his face almost blank. Almost.

But she could see it. Fire in his eyes, leaching out to crack his carefully crafted indifference.

"What?" She thwapped him in the chest again with open palms. "What?"

He snatched one of her flailing wrists and turned, dragging her with him down the hill and toward the stables.

Running to keep up with his strides, she tried to pry his fingers from her wrist. The clamp just grew harder.

He yanked on her. "The girls are watching, Adalia, their heads hanging out a window and I'd rather not have this argument in front of them."

She craned her neck, looking backward to the castle. Two little faces, eyes wide, staring down at them.

Avoiding the main stable, Toren veered, stalking into the smaller side stable that housed mares when they were foaling. A stable boy, pitchfork in hand, jumped at the sight of them.

"Go." Toren growled, and the boy dropped the pitchfork, running from the barn. "Door." Toren yelled after him, and the boy quickly slid the heavy barn door closed.

He stopped in the middle of the stable, spinning her to him.

Adalia yanked her wrist free, red blurring her vision. How dare he? He had absolutely no right to his anger. Absolutely no defense of his idiotic, tyrannical actions.

She shoved him again. "What? You cannot possibly have more to say."

His mask now shattered, fury palpitated across his brow. "Yet I do, Adalia. I do have something to say. I brought the twins out here so that they would learn to ride properly. So that they would not sneak out here and try for themselves without supervision. I could see how close they were to that very thing—I came upon them plotting that very escapade."

"No, they would never—not when I told them expressly that I forbid it. Never."

"And that was exactly what drove them."

"What?" Her head shook. "What do you know of it?"

His head tilted back, eyes to the roof of the stable as his hand ran through his dark hair. His look dropped to her. "I know because I did the exact same thing when I was a year younger than the twins. My guardian, my governess forbade me to ride until I was sixteen. Sixteen. It was what killed my father, after all. Tossed from a horse. They did not wish a repeat of that tragedy under their watch—the last in the Dellon line, done in by a skittish horse. So I know—I know because I was them, Adalia."

His fingers slipped around to the back of his neck, rubbing. "Only I snuck out to the stables and stole a pony. Saddled it myself. Except I did not know how to attach a saddle—no one had ever taught me. But I was determined.

Determined—just like the twins are. Only when I fell, I broke my arm."

That gave her pause, his words only half sifting through the blood pounding in her ears. "What? You broke your arm?"

"Yes. And then I had to have my bone set." His jaw shifted forward, his voice dropping. "Do you know how much pain setting a bone is to a six-year-old?"

She exhaled, taking a full, slow breath before answering. "I can imagine."

His look veered to the left, settling on the saddle bench in the empty stall next to them.

She eyed him, her ire abating. "You suffered it alone, didn't you?"

"I managed."

In that instant, her heart fractured slightly for the long past boy Toren once was.

No one to hold him. No one to wipe away his tears. No one to assure him all would be well. Just pain. Pain he'd had to live with alone.

But it gave him no right. No right at all.

That same pain could have just been Josalyn's.

Her eyes closed. Josalyn's body on the ground. It was too close. Too close to…Adalia had to cut her own thoughts. She couldn't think on that possibility.

She opened her eyes, her gaze centering on him, her voice shaking. "The twins, Toren—you cannot supersede my wishes just because they are enchanting little sprites."

He met her look, his brown eyes earnest. "I will abide by your wishes, as long as you promise me you will consider easing the walls you have erected around them. You are trying to keep them too safe, Adalia."

"There is no such thing."

"There is. Believe me, there is. It will only do them harm, and they will resent you for it eventually."

"That is not true."

"Tell me, Adalia. How did your brothers raise you? Were you locked in a cage? Suffocated by rules? Sheltered at every turn? Did they ever say no to you?"

Her arms clamped together over her stomach. "That is different. My brothers didn't know the first thing about raising a girl."

"Exactly, and they could have made very different decisions regarding your childhood. But look at how strong you are now."

"I am not strong—not when it comes to them." Her head dropped, the toes of her boots kicking at the straw dusting the ground. "I...I cannot lose them, lose the girls, Toren. They are my everything." Weak, she could not keep her voice from quivering in pain with the weight of the possibility.

"The best way to ensure that doesn't happen is to give them the knowledge they need to make their own decisions, become their own people. Let them make the mistakes when you are there to catch them. To hold them. To make sure they know they can survive anything."

He stepped to her, stopping right in front of her, his finger going under her chin, lifting her look to him. "Let that be the legacy of your brothers—their father, Adalia. Your brothers managed to raise you proud and independent and loyal and intelligent. Your nieces no longer have their

father or their uncles to do that for them, so instead, it falls
to you. Continue their legacy."

She stared at him, her lower jaw shifting to the side.
"You are attempting to sway me on the matter with pretty
words—I did not know you had the ability to do so."

He chuckled. "Neither did I."

"It won't work. I am still too furious with you."

His head tilted to the side, the calm façade back in
place on his face. "But you must recognize the need the girls
have to be set ever so slightly free?"

He wasn't going to stop. Again with the needs. Always
with the blasted needs.

She growled, frustration lifting her hands to ram him
in the chest again. "And that is the only thing you care
about—needs, needs, needs—what everyone needs."

He shrugged, neither stopping her motion nor
continuing to argue the point.

Frustrating to no end.

She was not done with the argument, and it had
already been settled in his mind. Settled by the logic of the
almighty *need*. "I am so sick of needs, Toren. Letting needs
govern everything. There are other things beside logic to
guide a person."

"Such as?"

"Wants—desires—what about the fire in your gut that
overrides the logic of needs? What about anger that spurs
you into action—that tells you to your core what should
be?"

He gave the slightest shake of his head. "Anger and
desires are not always guided by the best thinking, Adalia. It
is best to avoid them. Logic needs to control action."

"The best thinking? No. But logic in one's head does not make a life complete." She stared at the calm lining his eyes. He was dismissing her. Dismissing the possibility of how half the world actually worked—with passion.

How could she make him understand this? Needs were not the only thing in life—far from it. Her palm suddenly thumped onto her chest. "Then explain desire. Desire has the ability to speed my heart—spike a tingle down my spine. Desire can do that when a paltry, logical thought in my head cannot."

His mouth quirked into a frown. "What are you talking about, Adalia?"

"I am talking about you understanding that life cannot be ruled solely by this." She tapped her own temple, and then stepped in, closing all space between them as she looked up at him. The anger still running rampant under her skin pushed her voice nearly out-of-control. She had to make him understand this—understand her. "Don't tell me that when I am pressed up against a wall, and my naked flesh is pricking under your hands, and you slide into me, pounding, that those moments are not desire, Toren. That they are guided by logic and need."

"You play a dangerous game, here, Adalia."

"No, I am making a point."

"Which is?"

"That your logic cannot always control your desire. That you have no more control over your desire than any lesser man."

"I emphatically disagree, Adalia."

"Do you?"

"Yes. Why do you insist on pushing this so?"

"Because you refuse the notion, and that makes you unequivocally right in your mind. So I want you to admit you stoop so low as to feel such a thing as desire. Feel something you cannot control with logic. Admit that your body craves mine. I freely admit to wanting you, Toren." She pushed herself closer, her breasts pressing into his coat. "That I want your fingers trailing into every swell of my body. Your tongue circling my nipples, your teeth teasing them into hardness. That I want your shaft long and hard reaching the deepest parts of me. That I want you to control every moan I make. That I want to beg. That I want you to beg."

Her eyes narrowed at him. She could see him fighting it, his jawline pounding with every beat of his heart. She could feel him fighting it, the rock-hard bulge in his buckskin breeches straining for freedom, jabbing into her belly.

"Admit it, Toren." She swiveled her hips against him. "Desire rules you just as much as it does me. Only I know what to do with mine—that I openly desire our bodies together, it makes it that much sweeter when it happens. I get to anticipate. Imagine. It makes me feel, and that is just as valid as your logic. Even more so."

She took an abrupt step backward, air rushing between them.

The last vestiges of his control slipped from his face. "Admit it, Toren."

He rushed her in one step, picking her up and crashing her against a stall wall. Her back flat against the wood slats, he kept one hand under her backside, both supporting and trapping her while his other hand came up to her neck, holding her still as his mouth captured hers.

His lips, his tongue demanding access, shocked her.

He had never kissed her before.

For all that his lips and tongue had explored every part of her body, he had never kissed her. Never.

The fury of it sent a tinge of fear down her spine. Fear that only lasted a second before being overtaken by a craving that commandeered her body—a vice that demanded satisfaction.

She opened her lips wide to him, letting him plunge, plunder, taking the essence of her. His hand shifted along her neck, his fingers slipping up deep into her hair to cradle the back of her head, controlling the angle of her mouth.

His teeth raking against her lower lip, claiming it, he dragged her to the left against the wall, setting her on top of the flat plank capping the adjoining half wall of the stall. The movement freed his hands to dive downward, shoving her skirts upward and freeing the fall of his breeches, yet his mouth refused to break contact, giving her no reprieve to breathe air.

He slid into her hard. His skin under her skirts hot, pulsating. She had shoved him way beyond his boiling point and unleashed something primal that had only one mission.

Take her. Make her body his.

And she loved it. The brutal strokes, dodging the line between pleasure and pain. His mouth on hers, exhausting every bit of air she managed. His scent, filling her head. Her fingers buried into the back of his head, she gripped his dark hair for balance. Thrust after thrust, her backside lifted off the ledge with only his hands gripping her hips to hold her solid against the onslaught.

Without warning, without build, her core shattered. Harsh and raw, it shot unyielding shocks through her body that she had not prepared for. Ravaging her body in carnal waves that she could not control. Over and over her body shuddered, her screams swallowed by his mouth.

Swallowed, until he sped, the growl building from deep in his chest. One final, savage drive into her body, and he shuddered violently, his grip wrapping around her waist.

His lips withdrew from her mouth, his face burrowing into her neck as each shudder of his explosion shook his body from head to toe.

His breathing finally slowing, she untangled her fingers from his hair. Her own gasping breaths had quelled, but her words remained breathless. "A dangerous game indeed, Toren. I would call that a game I just won."

He chuckled into her neck, his breath hot and steamy on her skin. "I think that would qualify as a draw, as I am just as much a winner."

"Desire has its place?"

"Possibly, Adalia. Possibly."

Victory. At least one.

# { CHAPTER 11 }

"I was thinking a fire eater today."

Toren took an inordinate amount of joy in watching the twins' blue eyes grow wide.

Josalyn hopped in her chair. "A fire eater? What is that, Uncle Toren?"

Half of his face lifted in a grin as he leaned to his right toward her along the small round breakfast table. "I am not entirely sure, Josalyn. I have only heard of them—I have never seen one. But presumably, a fire eater eats fire."

"But however do they do that? Is it a dragon?" Mary asked from across the table.

"I imagine he opens his mouth and in goes the fire." He shifted to the left to lean toward Mary, mocking big, smacking bites with his mouth. "And then he chomps it down."

Mary giggled. "Oh, yes, please. Let us do that today, Uncle Toren."

A hesitant smile on her face, Adalia set her fork down along the edge of her plate. "Where have you produced a fire eater from?"

Toren looked to her as he sat straight in his chair. "There is a gypsy troop that is traveling through Dellington. The fire eater is their main performer. And now that the rain of the past week has let up, they plan to perform today."

Adalia's look flickered to Josalyn and Mary, her eyebrows drawing together as her gaze landed on him. "In Dellington? Do you think that wise?"

Toren knew exactly where Adalia's mind was spinning. For as much as his wife lauded the necessity of passion and anger and joy as the meaning to life, none of those things extended to the girls if there was the slightest modicum of danger afoot.

But he had gotten her to agree to let the girls learn to ride in the past fortnight. That had been a monumental feat in itself. Both Josalyn and Mary had been quick learners on their ponies, and were already quite steady on their sidesaddles.

He glanced at each twin. They stared at him, eyes pleading. He met Adalia's hard gaze. Using the twins against her was questionable, but he was not above it. "I do think it wise. I think we have two boisterous squirrels that are dressed up as little girls that need to get beyond the borders of this castle before they explode."

"Yes. Oh yes, me," Josalyn chimed in, her head bobbing up and down. "I am a squirrel, Auntie Ada. I need to go. I truly do."

"Yes, me as well." Mary put her fingers to her mouth, nibbling at an imaginary acorn, giggling. "A crazy squirrel I am, and I need to scurry about."

Adalia laughed. The smile stayed on her mouth, but her green eyes held worry as she looked at him. "You are positive it will be safe?"

"Yes. Not a soul knows you and the girls are even here at Dellon Castle. And there has been no indication from London of anything out of the ordinary. Other than your friends, no one has been beating down the door at the Alton townhouse, looking for you. Your butler has been assuring everyone inquiring about you that you have retired to Glenhaven House in Derbyshire."

His fingers tapped on the white linen cloth atop the table. "All that is aside from the fact that I will have an appropriate number of men with us in Dellington."

She wanted to resist, he could see that. But then her look drifted down to the twins. Their pleading blue eyes were all it took.

She sighed. "Fine. Fire eater it is."

~ ~ ~

The fire eater wasn't a him, at all. It was a she.

And she was magnificent. Ball of flame after ball of flame, she ate fire from a long stick—most impressive, as long as one ignored the patches of her scalp by her temple where hair had been scorched off.

The rest of her long, dark hair pulled back in rows of tight braids, she danced and swung and ate fire for an hour with the twins enraptured every single one of those minutes.

Walking away from the gathering at the edge of the village where the gypsies had set up camp, the girls bounced along between Toren and Adalia, their cheeks flush with excitement.

Closest to Toren, Mary grabbed his hand, tugging on it. "Uncle Toren, how does someone learn to do that—swallow the fire?"

He shrugged, looking down at her, reflecting her wide smile. "Travel with a gypsy troop and apprentice it, I imagine."

"Do not put ideas into their heads, Toren." Adalia's sharp tone made him look at her above the twins' heads.

"But it does sound like a wonderful adventure, Auntie Ada," Josalyn said. "To travel and eat fire in front of all those people—can you just imagine the fun—a true adventure."

Adalia shot him a scathing see-what-you've-done look, and then glanced to Josalyn, nodding. "A great adventure, indeed. The lands and the people you would meet. But you would also have to sleep in that tiny wagon. Did you see that behind the fire eater? I do not imagine it is nearly as comfortable as your big bed."

"I could be happy in a wagon, Auntie Ada."

"I am sure you could be, Josalyn. But you are still too young for such adventures. You must remember to bring this topic up again when you are sixteen. Maybe then we can consider fire eating as a possible course for you."

"Me too, Auntie Ada, me too," Mary chimed in.

"Of course, sweetheart." Adalia's arm went around Josalyn, squeezing her to her side. "But until then, you are sticking close to my side, for I could not bear to be without you two, agreed?"

"Yes, Auntie Ada." Both girls sang out their agreement.

Toren watched her profile as she chatted with the girls. The smile came so incredibly easy to her face—especially when she was with the girls.

But he knew how to make his wife smile in his own way. And he had found himself unwilling to go without her in the past weeks. Ever since the argument in the stables, night after night, he found he could not deny himself her body.

Every night, his body started aching for hers before the sun disappeared from the sky. The anticipation of her skin bristling under his fingertips and the soft moans vibrating from her chest had driven him to distraction night after night.

Having a wife was far more beneficial than he would have ever guessed.

A rogue tendril of hair fell from her upsweep to tickle her cheek, and she brushed it aside, her green eyes catching him.

Her lips parted, her hand going to her throat.

"Parched?"

"I have been since we started watching the fire eater." She shivered. "Just watching her I was smacking my tongue."

Toren chuckled, looking ahead on the main road into the village. Some villagers had set up makeshift booths, capitalizing on the opportunity of more people traveling through to the area to see the show.

He pointed ahead to a robust woman hauling a heavy pot to a ledge. "There, I can find lemonade for the girls, as well as something for us before we move back for the puppet show and then maybe we can visit the fortune teller."

The girls squealed in agreement.

Adalia looked ahead, her fingers going above her brow to shield her eyes from the sun. "Perfect." She looked around, her eyes landing on a shaded, grassy knoll aside the milliner's shop. "I do regret forgetting a parasol. Shall we come with you, or can we wait in the shade?"

"I believe I can manage the feat." He loosened his hold on Mary's hand, and she ran around to Adalia's free hand, grabbing it before they veered off to the left.

Minutes later, Toren had procured three goblets, two of lemonade and one of ale, balancing them in his hands as he was looking at the selection of hot pies. The girls would be hungry soon—as was he.

A scream, muffled, floated through the air, not enough to give anyone around him pause. But it rang like a bell in his head. Adalia.

Dropping the goblets to the ground, he tore up the main road, whipping around the corner of the milliner's shop to the grassy knoll. Empty.

His eyes frantic, a breath passed before he saw the edge of a skirt fly through the air behind the building.

Sprinting up the hill and around the back of the shop, he found Adalia wildly swinging a knife. The knife landed, cutting into the upper arm of a blackguard that had Josalyn tucked under his arm, the girl kicking and screaming.

The knife hitting flesh wrecked her momentum and made Adalia stumble. Seizing the second, the man swung, smacking Adalia brutally across the cheek.

It sent her flying to her knees, the knife spilling from her hand.

*Mary.* Where was Mary?

Toren spotted her in the next instant, cowering around the far corner of the building, watching—terrified, yet not willing to run from her sister.

Without another breath, Toren attacked, snatching the bastard's arm and twisting it behind his back before the man even saw him coming.

*Snap.*

An insane fury took a hold of his body, and the crack of the man's bone spurred Toren to twist it even further.

The blackguard wailed, dropping Josalyn to the ground as he tried to free himself from Toren.

Toren would have none of it, twisting harder, shoving the man to his knees, inflicting as much pain as he possibly could.

Yet it wasn't enough.

He went for the man's throat.

"Your grace, we have this."

His fingers wrapped around the man's neck, squeezing.

"Your grace. Your grace." Words he barely heard, muffled and miles away.

He squeezed harder.

Tugging, someone tugging him away.

No. Someone yanking him away.

"Your grace." The yell in his ear made Toren pause.

He looked up over his shoulder only to see they were surrounded by four of his men, one of them pulling him away from the bastard that had grabbed Josalyn.

Where the hell had they been a minute ago?

His hands flew wide, fingers stretching straight as he shoved off from the bastard.

Toren jumped to his feet, kicking the man in the ribcage as he went past him. "Get this filth to the gamekeeper's cottage."

Two of his men picked up the blackguard, dragging him with no kindness past the next building and out of sight.

Adalia had crawled across the ground, grasping a sobbing Josalyn into her arms, shielding her from everything, whispering in her ear as her hand stroked the girl's blond head.

Toren ran to Mary, picking her up and balancing her on his side, her arms tight around his neck. He moved to Adalia, stopping in front of her.

"We need to leave."

She looked up at him, terror etched in her face. "You... you said we were safe."

"I was wrong."

# { CHAPTER 12 }

The girls were finally asleep, their hiccupped breathing the last remnants of their tears. Hazard lay between their beds on the floor, his ears nervously perked, as they had been since they had arrived back at the castle.

Toren listened to the sounds through the open door, soft murmurs that held promise of a better day tomorrow, before Adalia stepped out into the hallway and clicked the door to the twins' room closed.

Her fingers shook on the doorknob, the first slip of the steely façade she had worn since gathering Josalyn in her arms.

Calm, comforting, she had let nothing but the warm presence of reassuring safety show in front of the girls.

Toren, on the other hand, had been a raging oaf. Furious beyond the pale on the journey home, pacing in the girls' room as Adalia had tried to soothe them to sleep.

It wasn't until she caught his eye with her glare, pointing to the door, that he realized he was doing the girls more harm than good by staying in their room. So he had continued his pacing just outside their chamber, watching the three of them through the crack he had left open in the door.

Her hand leaving the brass knob, Adalia stretched her fingers wide, shaking them in attempt to still the quake as they dropped to her side. Her head down, she took five steps around and past Toren before she stumbled to the side, catching herself on the stone wall of the hallway.

He was to her in one stride, grabbing her around the waist. For an instant, he thought she would fight his touch, shove him away as he deserved.

Instead, she fell back into him, her body turned to jelly, all strength deserting her.

"I failed you—them." The words, a low, brutal whisper, dragged from his throat.

"No." She lifted her arm, motioning down the hall.

Biting his tongue, Toren set his arm around her waist, walking her down the corridor, every step she took a monumental effort. He turned into his chambers, bringing her to a chair by the fireplace and setting her down.

She slumped back in the wingback chair, looking up at him. Where her body failed her, her eyes did not. Alive with vehemence, her look pinned him. "No, you didn't fail us, Toren. Do not think that. You were there when we needed you."

"No. I should have been there from the beginning. My men—I told them space—but it was too much." His head shook, his lip snarling as his look landed on the flames of the fire. "That you had to pick up a knife and—" His gaze whipped to her. "Where in the hell did you even find a knife, Adalia?"

"The milliner—I saw it on his front table as we went up onto the knoll. I was chasing them in circles—I was the squirrel and they were my nuts and then I was at the bottom of the hill and they were at the top and then…" She gasped a breath. "Then he grabbed Josalyn and I was by the knife so I took it and ran after him."

"You are a fierce protector, Adalia."

"I am nothing of the sort." Her voice went soft. "I could not protect them—not on my own."

The last thing he wanted to do was be still, but he forced himself to sit down in front of Adalia. Sinking onto the ottoman, he leaned forward, his hands sliding over her knees through her skirts. "You saved Josalyn from being stolen, Adalia. You made it so difficult for him to take her, that you stalled him long enough. It was all that was needed."

"Yet I was worthless. Worthless at the one time I needed not to be. I thought...I thought I could do more in that situation. I thought I was stronger—I always imagined I could do more." Her head shook, eyes closing. "But I couldn't—I couldn't protect them any more than a fly could."

His fingers lifted, running along her cheek that had been struck, and she jerked away at the touch, not opening her eyes. The skin along her cheekbone was already yellow, quickly turning into a blue-black swath marring her flawless skin.

All he wanted was for her to rail at him—scream about how he had failed them.

Not this. Not this defeat that had swallowed her.

Her mouth opened, yet her eyes remained closed. "You didn't fail us, Toren—I let this happen. I never should have allowed us to go. Never should have felt so safe I thought playing on some grass under a tree was a good idea. I have been lulled into this sense of security here, so much so that I have let my guard erode. Idiotic, when we still don't know what the threat is, what Theo was warning me against. So

I don't blame you. You never could have known. But I—I should have been more careful."

*Hell.* He wanted to tell her. Needed to tell her. Tell her the truth about his own damn imbecilic lies.

He was almost certain of where the threat had come from. And the truth would undoubtedly ease the torture she was heaping upon herself. But he had to keep this lie.

He had failed her. More than she would ever know.

"Open your eyes, Adalia." His fingers went under her chin, tilting her face to him.

Her eyelids cracked open, her look wary as it met his gaze.

"You need to stop. You do not give me way to skirt the blame on this, just to blame yourself. I am the one that suggested we go to the village. I am the one that walked away from the three of you, leaving you vulnerable. I am the one that has not taken this threat as seriously as I need to. And I will not allow you to flog yourself on the matter."

"You have not taken this threat seriously? But the note. The missive from Theo."

"Yes. And I thought I gave it grave enough weight. But I did not heed the warning properly." His hand dropped from her chin, curling into a fist. "No more."

Her eyes closed to him, her head shaking. "That man—he found us in the village, Toren. How did he not make it onto your land—get to us sooner?"

"No one moves onto my land that has not been thoroughly scrutinized. It has always been so. A blackguard like that would have never made it past my gamekeepers. They track everything on Dellon land." He stood, his fist thumping onto his thigh. "And I intend to find out where in the hell that bloody miscreant came from."

His boots shuffling past her skirts, Toren stepped away from the chair.

She jumped to her feet, grabbing his elbow and making him pause. "Wait. Where are you going?"

"My men are holding that blackguard at my gamekeeper's lodge. I am going to get some answers."

She nodded, worry plain on her face. "Toren…be careful."

He afforded himself a moment to look down at her. But his eyes could go nowhere but to her bruised cheek. He touched the bruise, the slight scab forming on her skin at the apex of her cheekbone. The image of her getting smacked to the ground flashed into his mind. Her body flying through the air. Thudding to the ground.

He held onto the image, held onto it tight, not letting it dissipate from his mind. Held onto the rage that swelled in his chest, spinning, demanding freedom.

He didn't agree to her request. Just turned and walked out of the room.

Careful, he was not about to be.

He needed to break some bones.

~ ~ ~

The doorknob creaked, and Adalia slapped the stack of playing cards onto the small table. Dismissing the salvation of them—they had kept her hands busy for the last three hours—she jumped to her feet and ran across the room.

Toren stepped into his room, closing the door behind him just as Adalia reached him, planting herself in front of him.

She quickly scanned his body. His black tailcoat and cravat long gone, his dark waistcoat and white linen shirt were unusually rumpled. Pink tinged his knuckles—from what she didn't want to guess—but aside from that he looked perfectly fine.

Her breath exhaled in a hiss, expelling air that had held firm in her chest since Toren had left.

"You are unharmed?" Her hands went to his sleeves, searching his arms beneath the linen.

Toren's dark head cocked at her. "That is your first question? You are not curious what I learned?"

"Of course I am, but not if it comes at the price of injury to you."

He twisted his hands upward to grasp her probing fingers. Setting her hands off of his arms, he stepped around her, unbuttoning his waistcoat.

"I am unharmed," he said, his words clipped.

She followed him across the room as he peeled off his waistcoat and then sat on one of the wingback chairs by the fire. Adalia went to her knees in front of him, lifting his foot and starting to tug off his tall black boots. "What did you learn?"

Toren stared down at her for a long moment, his face gone to its customary blankness. "The man said they knew where you and the twins were because the matter of the special license by the archbishop was leaked."

"It was? But you said that would remain a secret until it was determined that the twins were safe."

"I was assured it would be. And I will be paying the archbishop another visit the next time I am in London."

She yanked on his boot, falling back onto her heels as it freed from his foot. She looked up at him, a frown settling onto her face. "Then it is common knowledge that we are married?"

"Apparently."

She nodded, her frown deepening as she set his left boot aside.

"That upsets you?"

"No." She picked up his right foot, tugging on the boot. "I had just hoped I would be the one to share the news with Violet and Cass. I know the worry they must have been under as to where I have been, and then to learn that I had run off and gotten married without telling them would surely upset them."

"I am positive they will understand when you explain the situation."

"Yes." A final tug, and the right boot was freed. "And now I can write to each of them since it is no longer a secret."

Setting his right boot in alignment with the other, her hands settled into her lap as she looked up at Toren. His mask of indifference wavering, his brow had creased as he watched her movements, his look much akin to the rage he had been in when he had left for the gamekeeper's cottage. "What? What is in your face, Toren? You are still angry?"

"You are worried that your friends haven't gotten a letter from you."

"Of course I am. They love me and I would not want them to worry about me."

"You should be worried about yourself, Adalia."

Uneasiness settled into her chest. She pushed herself up to her bare feet, tightening the belt of the pale blue silk robe she had wrapped around her. Taking a step backward, her arms crossed in front of her ribcage. Terrified at what he had to say, she still managed to force the one word from her throat. "Why?"

Looking up at her, his brown eyes shot through her, his jaw shifting to the side. "That blackguard admitted to working for a Mr. Trether."

Her arms clenched around her torso as the blood drained from her face. "Mr. Trether?"

"Yes. And I had hoped I would not, but I can see by your face you know the name, so do not try to deny it, Adalia."

*Blast it.* Not Mr. Trether. No. Impossible. He wouldn't have tried to harm the twins. And Theo would not have known of him. Would not have known to warn her against him. Would he?

Toren sprang to his feet. "Stop moving, Adalia."

Unaware she had even been shuffling backward, Adalia stilled her legs, her head shaking.

He closed the distance between them, his stare piercing her. "Tell me who the hell this Mr. Trether is to you, Adalia."

Staring at his chest, she could not look up and meet his eyes. Not when all of this had been her fault. Her fault from the beginning. And then Theo had somehow gotten involved…and killed…her stomach started to roil. "I…I made a deal with the devil."

"You what?"

Her head still shaking, trembles ran up and down her
body, chilling her. She attempted a deep breath to steady
herself, but it couldn't make it past her throat. "Months
ago—when I first opened the Revelry's Tempest—I
underestimated how much money I needed in my bank
to start the gaming house. Mr. Trether was recommended
to me by an acquaintance as a man that would front me
funds—I was in danger of losing my only means to support
the twins and the Alton estate, so you must understand
how very desperate I was. I met with him and he looked
respectable, well-mannered—indistinguishable from the
*ton's* elite. I thought he was something very different from
what he is. I should have known I was making a deal with
the devil."

"So Mr. Trether is a moneylender?"

"Not just any moneylender—Mr. Trether is notorious
in the rookeries for his establishments—gaming hells—I did
not know it at the time I agreed to his deal. And it wasn't
until much after that first transaction that I realized his
ways and his…his intentions."

Toren's brown eyes narrowed at her, the crease in his
brow deepening. "What sort of intentions did he have?"

"The kind that keep me indebted to him. I could
have paid him back the total sum plus interest in the
second week after the loan, but he refuses to accept the
last payment. I did not understand what game he played
with me. But Cass knew—Logan knew. They said he was
dangerous only I didn't listen. And he had gotten aggressive
in approaching me, in how he wanted to control me.
Control the gaming. But I never thought he would…" Her
hand covered her mouth as bile chased up her throat. "I

never imagined he would threaten the girls. Never. They are just little girls—why would he do that?"

"If he had one of the girls would you have done anything he asked of you?"

Her eyes flew wide, her face blanching. She slowly nodded.

"What did he really want of you, Adalia?"

"He wanted the Revelry's Tempest...the money, the house makes so much...and he wanted me."

"Did he hurt you, Adalia?" Toren's question chiseled through gritted teeth.

Her breath quivered into her lungs. "A bruise, nothing—"

"Hell—he bloody well bruised you, Adalia?"

"I thought it was nothing—Logan stopped him. And it was right after he proposed and I refused him. He was furious and he grabbed me and Logan was the only reason he stopped—he instantly calmed and apologized, but I should have known then he would not stop until..." She swallowed a sudden sob. "Cass warned me—she knew he was dangerous, but I put him off time and again so I thought that was the end of it."

"Dammit, Adalia." The mask of indifference completely dissolved from his face, Toren grabbed her shoulders, slightly shaking her. "Why didn't you tell me of this before?"

"Had I ever thought..." Her hands fought their way to her face, rubbing her eyes, settling on her temples. It all made perfect sense. Mr. Trether had said in their last meeting he would force her to listen to him—do as he bade. She owed him and he would own her, willing or not. She had just never imagined he was this dangerous—that he would go this far—that anyone would. To try and take a child—the man was the lowest of the low. "I thought he was handled, Toren—an annoyance, nothing more. I never imagined—"

"You don't trust me?"

She looked up at Toren. Fury simmered behind his brown eyes. "I know Theo said I could trust you, and I would have told you, but…"

"But what? You trusted me enough to marry me, but not to tell me of this?"

"I trusted Theo in sending me to you—not you, Toren. Those are very different things."

"Bloody hell, Adalia, those are not different." His fingers dug into her shoulders. "Have I not done enough over the past month for you—for the twins—to make you trust me?"

"You have—you have." Her hands slapped down onto his upper arms, gripping muscle through his shirt. "By everything you have done you made me trust you and I love you for it."

*Hell.*

The thought slipped out of her mouth before she could censor it.

She had planned to never speak the words, never fully acknowledge them to herself. It was easier that way. Simpler. But even with her adamant skirting of the truth, she had known it for weeks now, ever since their argument in the stables.

Toren only drove her insane for one reason. She loved him.

His hands snapped from her shoulders as he jerked a step backward, his face contorting. Shock. Horrification. She wasn't sure. Whatever played out on his features, it wasn't good.

"No. I did not just say that," she blurted out, waving her hands between them.

"You didn't mean it?"

"No—I mean yes—I meant it. But I know—I know how you feel and I never wanted to see this look on your face. I never was going to tell you, because, well, you…" Her voice trailed off, unable to finish her thought.

Because he wasn't capable of love. Because he would never return the sentiment to her. Because she had fallen stupidly, foolishly in love with a man—once again—that would never love her in return.

She had travelled this path before, and she knew the pain involved. So, no. She had never intended to tell him.

He turned away from her, his hand running through his dark hair, his voice grave. "Adalia, you know I cannot return the sentiment. I do not know how."

"Forget I said it, Toren."

Damn her tongue. Damn her heart for leaping past her mind. She had never wanted to put him in this awkward position—never wanted to push him for more, for he had done everything within his power for her and the twins, and that was enough.

Her look trained on his profile, she took a step forward, wanting to reach out and touch the side of his shoulder, but she held her hand firmly at her side. "Please, just forget I uttered the words. I am not asking or expecting anything of you—you have done more than enough for the twins, for me. Forget you ever heard my words. I never meant to say them."

His chin dropped as his look went to the floor. "I did not want this complication, Adalia."

"I know. You were very honest with me. And I was honest with you when I said I was of like mind on the subject. It is just…these last weeks. It changed. I changed. I did not intend it to happen. Please, I beg you to just forget it, Toren."

He shrugged, looking to her. The expressionless mask had fixed once more onto his face.

Adalia moved in front of him, desperately grasping at anything that would change the topic. "What I did want to tell you was thank you."

His eyes lifted to look over her head, avoiding her gaze. "For what?"

"I did not get to thank you properly earlier for saving us." She lifted a hand to slip it along his waist, sliding closer to him. "It is horrible of me—and I blame my brothers for my lack of squeamishness—but when I heard the crack of that man's arm under your hands, his wail, I felt no sympathy for him. I only felt a surge of…pride…"

"Pride?" His brown eyes lowered, meeting hers.

"Yes. I know that is another one of those unexplainable emotions you take no stock in." She slipped her other hand lightly around his waist. "Pride that you were my husband. That you would break a man like that for me, for the girls. I know I should not be so callous—so unrefined. But it— your brute strength—quite frankly, it made me wish we were alone in your room."

His eyebrow cocked. "Are you attempting to seduce me, Adalia?"

"Possibly. I am appreciative. And we are now alone in your chambers." Her hands slipped from his waist, entwining around his arms until she could thread her fingers along his. "I have been quite fixated on these amazingly quick hands of yours since Dellington."

The wariness dissipated from his gaze, his brown eyes starting to smolder.

Exactly what she needed in the moment.

She stepped into him, brushing her body against his. Not giving him a moment to wonder at her actions or to question her further. She could not let her humiliation at the slip of her tongue build any further. And this was the best way to move forth.

For both of them.

If he couldn't return her sentiments, he could give her this. His body on hers. His hands, his mouth commandeering her senses.

This, he was willing to give her. He had proven that, time and again.

And this would be enough.

She accepted that.

She *had* to accept that.

~~~

His arm fully asleep, dead weight under Adalia's sleeping head, Toren's cheek scrunched as he tried to shift without waking her.

If he didn't get blood flowing back to his fingers soon, he feared losing the whole limb. She hadn't left the room after sex, as was usually her way. As he preferred it.

But he couldn't blame Adalia. The whole day had been exhausting. And the five different, inventive ways she had just shown her appreciation to him and his body had only exasperated her fatigue.

Not that he minded in the slightest. Adalia and her tongue were very good at showing appreciation. So much so that he wished there were a few more bones to break in front of her, if what he had just experienced was his reward.

She jostled, mumbling nonsensical in her sleep. A waft of her honey-scented hair escaped, reaching his nose, and his eyes dipped to the top of her head.

Adalia loved him.

Her own words, whether she had meant to say them or not. He had warned her against it at the beginning, and she had agreed that love need not have a place in their marriage.

They had both agreed.

Little good that did.

Toren had tried to put it out of his mind, her words. She had said to forget she spoke the sentiment. But she hadn't promised she would fall out of love with him. And he had no intention of being unkind to her in order for that to happen.

Yet he didn't want to encourage her love. He didn't want to have to bear the expectant look from her if she ever said it again. The hopes he would be dashing, time and again. He couldn't love her, yet he didn't want to see her in pain because of his own inadequacies.

*Inadequacies?* Since when had he considered his lack of feeling as an inadequacy?

He had always enjoyed the detachment it gave him from people. It made him smart when it came to his estate and investments. Smart when it came to parliament. Smart when it came to choosing how to conduct oneself.

His lack of feeling was an asset, not an inadequacy. He had to remember that, just as he had always been taught.

A pain shot into his shoulder, spearing through the dulled muscles. He had to move.

His stomach muscles tightened under her arm flopped along his stomach, and he raised his shoulders from the bed, lifting Adalia with him. Cradling her, he attempted to slide her off his immobile arm onto a pillow.

Her temple almost touching the pillow, she suddenly jolted upright, frantic, tears streaming down her face. He sat up next to her. It took her a long, frantic moment to orientate herself to him in the low light of the coals glowing in the fireplace.

"Oh. Oh." Soft murmurs escaped her as she wiped tears from her cheeks. Her eyes went down to his bare upper chest, and her palm ran haphazardly across his skin, brushing wetness away. He hadn't even felt the warm tears pooling on his skin until she had pulled away. "Oh. I am sorry."

"You need not be. What has brought tears to your sleep?"

Her look dipped from him as she concentrated on quickly brushing the last streaks of wetness from his chest. Tears continued to drop into her lap. "It is no bother."

He tilted her chin upward. "Tell me."

Her head shaking, she scooted away from him on the bed, her words a rapid whisper. "Everything tumbled around me in the end. Real—they were real in my dream, I could feel them. My brothers. Touch them again. Truly touch them. Hug them. Laugh with them. It was real. I could feel it. They were all around me and I was warm—safe. And then it tumbled away. But it was so real, and I was happy and they were right with me."

"And then you woke up?"

"Yes. And they are not real, even though I felt it. Knew they were with me. It just seemed so real." Turning from him, she reached the edge of the bed, her bare feet dropping to the floor as she reached for her robe on the foot of the bed. Tugging it onto her shoulders, she swiftly stood. "I apologize. You do not need this emotion ruining your sleep and I do not wish to burden you with this. I do not allow myself to think of my brothers when awake."

Wiping tears that would not cease, she started to walk away from the bed. She only made it two steps before her legs buckled. Stumbling backward, she caught herself on the edge of the bed. Sinking, she sat, her shoulders trembling as she curled into herself.

Toren moved across the bed, setting his hand on her shoulder, partly to hold her up, partly to offer awkward comfort.

She hid her face from him. "I thought I was fine to leave. Afford me a moment, please. Just until I get my legs under me." Her voice cracked in a sob she desperately attempted to suffocate.

His fingers tightened on her shoulder. "You feel the loss of your brothers very deeply, don't you?"

She nodded, still trying to control a sob, her hands pressing over her eyes. "I loved them."

"Why have I never seen this…this sadness in you before?"

Her shoulders lifted with a deep breath that sent a tremble through her body. It took a long moment before her hands lifted from her eyes and she wiped her cheeks with her palms. Her voice shook as she forced words. "I do not think of them during the day—the girls are so resilient—they have suffered their grief over their father so well. Their mother died in childbirth, so they do not remember her, but Caldwell—they remember their father. I do not want to send them to tears, which is what happens if I think on my brothers and then they see me crying. So I do not do that to them. I cannot do that to them. I can control myself so they can move forward. So I hold it in until nighttime, when I am alone in my bed. It is not every night—but in my dreams—I cannot control anything in my dreams."

Toren stared at her back, her long red-blond hair falling in waves atop the silk of her robe. He didn't understand this. Logically, he understood what grief was. Understood that it destroyed weak people. But he didn't think Adalia was weak. He *knew* she wasn't weak.

Yet there she sat in front of him. A crumpled mess that could not even walk.

And he wanted to make it better for her. Needed to make her not cry. Not suffer this.

She took a shaky breath. "I will leave."

"Why?"

Her right hand went to her face, her fingers pinching the bridge of her nose. "I need to cry and you need to not witness it. So I will leave."

"Wait." His hand shifted into a clamp on her shoulder. "If you need to cry, Adalia, I do not mind it. And I…"

She looked over her shoulder at him, her green eyes rimmed in red, tears still glistening in heavy droplets on her dark eyelashes. "Yes?"

"I think I would prefer to hold you as you do."

Her fingers dropped from her nose, her eyebrows cocking in confusion. "You prefer to hold me while I cry?"

"Yes." The word came stilted from his mouth, almost embarrassed. It was clear he had no idea how to give her comfort, even though, at the moment, he wanted nothing more in the world than to be able to do so. He swallowed, attempting words again. "If it will help you, Adalia. Grief such as yours does not seem like it should be suffered alone."

"I have been alone since Caldwell died."

"But you are no longer alone. I am here."

Her look drifted from him, settling on the sheets behind him. "Do you not need your bed empty to sleep?"

"I can make an exception, Adalia."

Her eyes lifted to him. For a long moment, she just looked at him. Confusion, mingled with sadness. His chest tightened. Had he put that despair into her eyes, or had her dream?

Finally, she nodded.

He drew her back into the middle of the bed, settling her head onto the crook between his chest and shoulder, his

arm wrapping around her back. It would likely send his arm into painful sleep once more, but he would suffer it.

If it helped her, gladly, he would suffer it.

# { CHAPTER 13 }

A blackberry poised on her lips, Adalia watched as Toren shut the breakfast room door behind the girls as they scampered out, and then he gave a nod to the footman by the side entrance to the room. The footman silently slid out the side door.

They were good at that—Toren's servants—silent to a fault, disappearing and appearing with only a nod or a pinky twitch by Toren, and never saying a word. How long did it take to train them thusly?

She popped the blackberry into her mouth just as Toren strode back across the room to her. The easy smile he had worn while the twins were with them had vanished, and the room was now empty except for the two of them. Toren's face had gone suspiciously blank, and she had come to understand that rarely meant anything good.

He sat down across the small round table from her, his fingers not moving to pick up the fork and continue his half-eaten breakfast of eggs and sausage. His brown eyes scrutinized her with such deliberateness that she had to swallow hard to move the blackberry down her throat.

She wiped the corners of her lips. "You have something to tell me? Is it about Mr. Trether—did he accept the satisfaction of the debt that you had delivered? Please tell me he accepted it—and that you threatened him to no end, as well. For him to so brutally want the Revelry's Tempest that he would be a danger to the twins—the man deserves every lick of hellfire that will come his way. "

Toren offered a slight nod, his countenance unchanged. "He did accept it. Both the money and the threat. You are now married. The Revelry's Tempest is closed. The matter *should* be done."

Her eyes narrowed. "But it is not?"

"I do not know yet."

"Why not? When will you know?"

"Money drives some men. Vengeance drives others. I do not yet know where Mr. Trether lands on that spectrum." He paused, clearing his throat. "Mr. Trether has a crew that works for him—have you ever seen them—did they ever accompany him when you met with him? A driver, a guard, perhaps?"

"Yes, I have seen a number of his men." The tines of her fork tapping on her plate, Adalia's eyes went to the high point of the stone arch on the wall opposite her as she visualized the faces she had seen. Her gaze dropped to Toren. "Five that I can easily recall. Two more—only marginally. Why?"

"We have a suspicion it wasn't just that one man in Dellington that tried to take Josalyn."

Her fork clattered to the table. "Are the girls still in danger?"

"No." His hand instantly reached over to clasp the top of hers. "Not here. They are safe at Dellon Castle—do not doubt that. But we believe there is another one of Mr. Trether's men in the area—the man has been stopped several times along the far western border of my lands. But there is no way of telling his purpose unless he makes a move to get closer to the castle, or unless we cajole it out of him. If he is Mr. Trether's man, I imagine he is still in the area because he has yet to hear from his boss that the matter has been settled to satisfaction."

"Cajole…" Her right eyebrow lifted. "Cajole with pain?"

Toren's head slanted to the side with a shrug as his hand slipped off of hers.

"But if he is innocent? What if he is just a vagrant passing, looking for work?"

"A possibility—yes," Toren said. "Which is why I would much prefer for you to look at him and tell me if you recognize the man."

"Yes. I can do that. Where is he?"

"In the next village past Dellington. He has been holed up in a coaching inn," Toren said. "It is a half day's ride, if you are willing. And you will need to be mostly concealed; a hood and common clothes would be best so he doesn't recognize you."

Adalia nodded. "Yes." Her bottom lip jutted upward, her eyes pinning him. "Tell me again Josalyn and Mary will be safe here while we are gone."

He grabbed her hand on the table again, squeezing it. "They are safe here, Adalia. Trust me."

*But what about me?*

She hadn't admitted it to anyone but herself, but the incident in Dellington had shaken her to her core. She had grown too relaxed, too comfortable in Toren's world. So much so that her wits seemed to have dulled completely. Dellington was nothing but proof that her guard had slipped so far it had vanished, and she couldn't let that happen again.

For her own sake and for the girls.

She had been such a fool about Mr. Trether. The man was vicious, and she had denied for far too long how dangerous he was. Twice now, he had nearly snatched her niece's from her. So what else was he capable of?

She looked down at the table, focusing on Toren's hand swallowing hers. Strong, his fingers had the capacity for such gentleness on her skin, yet also the brutal ability to crack a man's bones.

She had to concentrate on that—not on worry. If threats upon the girls could be eliminated, she had to help. And Toren knew exactly when to move with delicacy and when to move with brutal strength. She had to trust that.

She would be safe with him.

~ ~ ~

Her head slightly bowed, Adalia surveyed the main dining hall of the coaching inn past the edge of her grey hood.

Her cloak and hood were warm, almost stifling hot in the stagnant afternoon heat pooling under the low, heavily weathered beams spanning the dining room. But Toren had insisted she keep it in place as they slid into a high-backed wooden booth by an outside door at the rear of the dining area.

Toren had found rough, nondescript clothes for himself to wear, and she knew she would look less suspicious without the hood and cloak. But she suffered the heat for

Toren's peace of mind, at least for the time being. She would be able to shed it soon enough if the man Toren wanted her to look at was in here.

The dining hall rather busy for the late afternoon, her gaze travelled amongst the many square wooden tables, benches, and chairs. She spotted three of Toren's guards that had staggered their entrances into the coaching inn. They had settled themselves randomly about to not arouse suspicion.

Two mugs of ale delivered to their table, Toren clutched the handle on his as he leaned forward across the table and looked at her.

"There." He took a sip of the ale, instantly attempting to hide the curdling of his tongue at the taste. He could dress the part of a common man, but his tongue would never be so. He choked down the liquid. "The far square table to the left of the bar. By himself. Blue jacket. Dingy undershirt. Cap pulled down past his ears. Oddly shiny boots. One full and one empty glass in front of him. Half picked through plate of pie."

Adalia blinked at the amount of detail. She had only seen Toren glance in that general area once.

She nodded, scratching the side of her face and casually lifting her hood as she glanced to her left across the dining hall. She spotted the man quickly, just as described. The man chewed slowly, hunched, staring at the table in front of him. Toren had positioned them as far away as possible from the man. Her hood dropped past the side of her face as she looked to Toren. "I can only see his profile from here. And very little of it at that."

"Look again."

She repeated the process, stretching out her peek. Her fingers went to the silver tankard in front of her, fiddling with it. "I think I have seen him before."

He gave one nod, grasping her hand and pulling it away from the tankard. "Good. Then we are leaving."

She yanked her fingers from his grip, her words a rushed whisper. "No, I think—but I am not certain. Not certain it is one of Mr. Trether's men. I am not going to condemn an innocent man, Toren. I have to be positive."

Before he could reach to stop her, Adalia scooted out from the bench of the booth.

"What the hell are you doing, Adalia?" Toren's hissed whisper disappeared into the swish of her skirts.

Moving quickly, she walked across the dining hall close to the front wall where she could approach the man from his rear side and he would not notice her until she was upon him. She fished out one of her kidskin gloves from the pocket in the faded blue cotton dress she had borrowed from Miss Mable, the governess they had hired for the twins.

Just as she stepped past the man's table, she dropped the glove to the floor. Stopping, she stooped, angling herself so she could look at him straight on. The glove in the tips of her fingers, she glanced up, seeing the full of his face.

She gasped.

Half his face had been torn to shreds, partially healing. Ripped apart by teeth—dog teeth. The man that had taken Mary in London.

Hazard had done a beautiful job in marring the man for life. As deserved.

His look raked over her. Jerking upright in his seat, recognition flashed in his cold eyes.

"Well, I be, mousey." His eyes flashed upward above her head for only a moment before his look snapped back to her and he sneered, pouncing. His thick fingers dove under her hood, snagging the thick of her hair at her neck and yanking her upward as he lunged to his feet.

He dragged her two steps. Flailing, all she could see was the beaten wooden boards of the floor flashing in front of her. A scream—his scream, laced with pain. His hand jerked from her head, tearing out hair with it.

Her balance upended, a mess of feet and bodies and arms scuffled about her, and she fell, landing hard into a body. Toren. She could tell by his boots. His clothes he had changed. His boots he had not.

More legs. More boots joined the fray.

An arm clamped around her, pulling her from the scuffle, dragging her to the rear door of the dining room.

Out the door, the sunlight hit her, making her squint as she attempted to get her feet under her. Tucked under Toren's arm, she couldn't right herself completely, and he didn't halt his long strides, moving them down the slight hill toward the stable. It wasn't until they reached the back end of the structure that he stopped, spinning her around the corner—hidden from the inn—and propping her onto the outside wall of the stable.

Breathless, her palms went flat onto the worn wood on either side of her as she caught herself. Toren stomped away from her.

Ten steps, and then his fingers ran through his dark hair as he spun. Stalking back to her, he slammed the butt of his palm on the wood plank by her head, making the whole wall rattle against her back.

"Why in the blasted hell would you do that, Adalia?" His chest almost touching her nose, his palm slammed onto the wood again.

Adalia cringed at the sound, but didn't cower, her chin tilting upward so she could see his face. "Toren—"

"No, Adalia, you don't get to speak. He could have had a damn blade. He could have had a pistol. He could have knocked you down. He could have slammed you into the fireplace, and crushed your head on the stone. He could have bit you. He could have thrown a knee so deep into your belly you could never breathe again. He could have snapped your neck. He could have—"

Her hands lifted, waving in front of his face. "Stop. Stop, Toren. I understand. I was in danger—you don't like that. But I needed to look at him straight on and you were only feet away. Your men were only feet away. I was safe."

"No, you weren't. You don't know what the hell could have happened in those seconds it took for me to reach you." His head shook, his eyes going to the wall above her head as his lip curled in disgust.

"Don't be ridiculous, I—"

"I froze, Adalia." His brutal voice cut her words, his palm slamming into the wall again as his look pierced her. "My damned feet froze."

Confusion creased her brow. "Froze? No—you didn't. You were to me in an instant."

"No, dammit. My blasted feet froze. Dead weight. Watching you—the moment he recognized you—his sneer—I could not move my bloody feet."

"What? You were the first one to me, Toren. A second in time did me no harm."

"It could have."

Her hands went lightly onto his chest, fingers splaying wide. "I am right here in front of you, Toren. Not hurt, not scared. I knew you were there the whole time. I wouldn't have done it otherwise. I knew I didn't have anything to worry about."

"But—"

"No." She reached up to grab his hand on the wall, tugging it down to set his palm flat against the slope of her left breast. "Feel this. Even my heartbeat—it is steady. I am steady. If I had been worried, my heart would still be frantic—out of control—but I am not."

His look went upward, his head shaking again.

"Look at me, Toren—all you have to do is look." She reached up with her other hand, setting her fingers along his cheek and drawing his look down to her. "I am not scared. You have all my trust. You did not fail me in there, Toren."

His brown eyes hard on her, he swallowed, his jaw shifting to the side. "Do not put that upon me, Adalia."

"Put what upon you?"

His voice dropped to a coarse gravel. "Your trust. Your love."

Her hand dropped from his face with a sharp intake of breath. "Why not? You practically demanded a week ago that I give you my unequivocal trust. So you have it. You have it because you demanded it."

*Blast it.* It was bubbling up in her, steam demanding to escape the kettle.

She was going to say it again, and this time it would be no slip of the tongue. This time she would say it because she had to, because Toren was standing in front of her and making her feel it like never before. Because she would say it a thousand times over for the smallest hope that it would someday reach him.

Her hand tightened along the side of his cheek. "You have it because I love you."

He jerked away from her. His hand ripping from her chest as he turned, his face angled to the bright sky.

She stilled for a long second.

*Turn. Turn back to me, dammit. Turn back and tell me you feel something—anything for me. Just turn. Even if it is only in your damn eyes and not your words. Turn.*

The moment passed. Then another. And another.

He didn't turn back to her.

Her knuckles went to her lips, hiding her slight gasp as she pushed herself from the wall of the stable. Dazed, she walked forward, walking to escape him, escape the moment.

Past the pasture. Past the sparse woods. She walked until the ground stopped, her toes at the edge of the brook that ran at the base of the hill behind the coaching inn.

He had told her—been very honest with her about his feelings, or lack thereof. She had sworn to him she could accept it.

She had truly thought she could.

But that was before…before he was the most doting of all uncles to the twins…before he took her, night after night in his bed, his only goal to make her body feel indescribable euphoria…before he had requested his gardener to start work on the rose garden, reviving it to former glory just because it made her happy...before he put the twins and her safety above all other concerns...before he cracked a man in half for her...before he held her when she cried... before he allowed himself to be beaten night after night in whist, and by two eight-year-olds, just because it would make them laugh—make her laugh...

Before all of it. Before he became so very core to the life she lived...before she couldn't imagine her life in any other way but with him.

She stared at the moving water of the brook, wanting nothing more than to lose herself in the swirling bubbles of it.

The man damn well *made* her feel loved. So why? Why could he not bring himself to actually do so—to love her?

And did it matter?

# { CHAPTER 14 }

She didn't turn around to him when his boots crunched onto the pebbles lining the brook.

Toren stared at the back of her head. Her hair in a singular long braid that curled forward over her shoulder, the grey hood of her cloak was now bunched about her shoulders.

She had to be hot. The sun was shining down, soaking into the dark fabric. Yet she hadn't complained once about the extra layer in this unusual heat. Not once. He had asked her to keep it on while they traveled, and especially inside the coaching inn, and she had obliged, not questioning or arguing against it.

Because she trusted him.

Only an arm's length away, he could reach out and touch her. It seemed appropriate in this instance, like something he should consider. Maybe if he could fix this for her. Give her what she needed. Maybe then it would be appropriate.

But he couldn't. So he didn't.

His arms stoically at his sides, his heel shifted, the pebbles clinking together. "Nothing has changed from what I told you at the beginning, Adalia. I am still incapable of love. You know how I grew up."

"Do I?" Her arms curled around her middle. She didn't turn to look at him. "You have mentioned it, but you have never strived to make me understand it."

"That is just it, Adalia." He moved forward, setting himself at her side so he could at least see her profile. If he could watch her, he could figure out what she needed. Her green eyes held so little back. He had learned that about her—if he needed to know what she was thinking at any moment, she held it all in her eyes.

He cleared his throat. "There is nothing to understand. I was raised by a governess that was strict and kept me in line if I veered. Our interactions were, at the most… cordial…at the least, cold."

He paused as Adalia lifted her eyes, but not her chin to him, watching him as an aside. Her arms stayed wrapped around her ribcage. "Her name was Mrs. Marchall. I asked her once about love, because I wanted to understand the concept. I had just read *The Odyssey* and learned of Odysseus and Penelope's great love. I asked her if she loved me. Before I had even finished the question, she told me love was not acceptable. Love was not reality. She told me she was being paid to make sure my needs were met, nothing more."

Adalia's eyes flickered down to the moving water. "How old were you?"

"Seven." He sighed, watching her eyes close as he said the word. "Yes, I know how it sounds. But what you need to understand is that her answer didn't make me sad. I had never known love, I didn't understand it, so when she said that, it made perfect sense. And it troubled me not in the slightest. That was when I knew I was incapable of the emotion. And it has always been so."

"And there was no one else?" The question came softly, barely audible over the bubbling of the brook.

She needed more from him—more explanation. Toren took a deep breath. He had never told another soul about his childhood, other than short, practiced, snippets meant to steer the conversation away from the topic.

But if Adalia needed this—needed this to understand what he could not give her—he would keep talking.

His look centered on her delicate profile. "No. There were no others. Mrs. Marchall was the only one allowed to talk to me. Mr. Octon, our family's solicitor, was my official guardian. I only spoke to him of finances and how to handle the estate, and only when I was old enough to understand. The servants never spoke to me. Nor did they talk to each other—at least not where I could hear them. I knew very little of the world and even how to interact with other people until I went to Eton."

Her green eyes lifted to his look, her full face finally turning toward him. "And that is where you met Theo?"

"Yes. And I was awkward—horrifyingly awkward around other people for the longest time. But Theodore never let that bother him. Where others were distant— reflecting what I was—Theodore was having far too much fun teaching me about the world."

A broken grin crept onto her face. "If you learned about the world from Theo, you got a very skewed representation of the world."

"I imagine I did, but that didn't matter to me. Theodore knew how to talk to people. How to make friends, how to charm. I already knew everything I needed to from the textbooks—but I had never opened my mouth to speak of anything other than numbers or science or geography or the running of the estate until I met

Theodore. He was the one to teach me how to do that."
Toren's hand lifted, rubbing the back of his neck. "In fact, I
had never even questioned how I grew up. I never realized
my life had been so very odd."

Her arms relaxed around her waist, one hand lifting to
tuck away a rogue tendril of hair that had fallen in front of
her left eye. "What was it?"

His eyebrow cocked in question.

"What was that first conversation you had with Theo?"

An instant smile crossed his lips. "He was rambling
philosophical about the mating habits of peacocks. On
whether or not the males were blind—or had severe lack
of sight—since they spent all their time growing ridiculous
displays of plumage and would then end up mating with
females that had nothing at all to recommend them."

His look dipped to the water as he shook his head.
"Theodore thought the males would be depressed if they
could actually see what they were mating with—hence the
blindness he presumed they possessed. He feared that if the
eyesight of the males ever improved, the males would grow
despondent and die, and that would mean the demise of the
species. The only thing he could imagine that would save
the species was if one could encourage true love between the
peacock and the peahen."

Adalia laughed. "That was Theo. He always started
with the absurd and then turned philosophical into fact. I
imagine you began to poke holes in his theories?"

"I did. It was impossible not to."

"Oh, he did love to argue." Her smile went wide. "And
I imagine your explanation of the mating habits of peafowl

was specifically scientific—exactly what the male needs and the female needs to mate?"

"Yes. It was ridiculous how many times we went around that. I wanted him to recognize the reality of facts. He wanted me to recognize the magical possibility of undying love in birds."

Her smile faded. "And that brings us back to the topic in discussion."

He looked away from her, watching the long branches of a willow swing into the water downstream. "Adalia, everyone in my life—all of them—has been there because they are paid to be so. Even with Theodore, I realized I was handy to have around—a duke tends to make people nervous in advantageous ways." His look dropped to her. "And you as well, you came to me looking for something in return."

"To be safe."

He nodded. "So how can I think of this as any different? I pay people to be trusted—to be in my life. This is no different."

Her head snapped back, her green eyes widening. "No different?"

"Well, not exactly—"

"The difference is that I am your wife, Toren." Her left hand went onto her hip. "Your wife. No matter how our marriage began. I am your wife. No one is paying me to be with you. To enter your bedchamber. I do it of my own free will. I am with you because I want to be."

"Yet you are with me for the sake of the girls. For the sake of your own safety."

Her right hand flew up, waving into the air. "You're right—I would do anything in the world for those girls—anything. But I have never been worried about my own safety. I am not in danger, Toren. You think it, but I have not been. Everything has been directed at the twins for some god-awful reason. To make me suffer, I suppose. So if all I wanted was to ensure their safety, I would have married you and then left them safe at the castle weeks ago. I even considered it for days."

He blinked hard at her words. "You considered leaving?"

Her right hand went to her forehead, rubbing it as she looked up at the sky. "Blast it, Toren, how do you not see this?"

"See what?"

A deep sigh shook her whole body, and her look fell to the rocks on the bank of the brook. The toe of her boot flicked a pebble into the water. "Do you know that I did not tell you the full truth about my first marriage?"

Toren's look bored into the top of her head, his words measured. "What do you mean, you didn't tell me the truth, Adalia?"

She looked up at him, her head shaking. "I told you the truth, just not all of it. I blamed Caldwell for choosing Lord Pipworth as my husband—for my marriage being a disaster. I blamed him because I liked to blame him—I liked to pretend I had no hand in the choice, but the truth was, Caldwell was only doing what I wanted him to do—he knew I wanted to marry Lord Pipworth."

"You did?"

"Yes. I idolized the man growing up. He was tall and handsome and brash and my brother's friend. He would come into our house with Caldwell, and he was always so dramatic and funny, and I adored him from afar for years. I was just a little girl, smitten because I didn't know differently. I would have married him whether my brother had arranged it or not. He was the man I thought I wanted and I was that set upon him as my husband."

She heaved a breath. "That is the harsh truth of it. It has always just been easier to blame Caldwell for my marriage. But it was me. Caldwell was just trying to make me happy—he saw how I looked at Lord Pipworth. And Pipworth only married me because he felt obliged to do so after Caldwell's death."

"Why are you telling me this, Adalia?"

Her look fell to the water. "So you understand why I cannot be trusted when it comes to the men that I choose to love. I thought we would be fine as you proposed it at the beginning. A cordial marriage. I would give you an heir. We could live our separate lives. But then…"

"Then what?"

It took a long breath for her green eyes to lift, meeting his gaze, her look piercing him. "Then I damn well fell in love with you, Toren. And I am terrible at choosing a man to love. My choices lead to nothing but pain. So this is too hard. I need to be able to tell you this—need to not have to bottle it away deep inside of me. I love you and if I am damned for doing so, then I am damned. But I cannot keep it to myself any longer merely so you can walk through your days in the comfort of familiarity, with no emotion."

His hands came up, palms to the sky. "What do you want of me, Adalia?"

"Do you really want me to tell you what I want? We both already know what you will allow, so what does it matter?"

His mouth clamped shut, his lower jaw shifting to the side as he shook his head, avoiding her eyes. His voice came out low, rough, unrecognizable to his own ears. "My body needs yours, Adalia. Can that not be enough?"

"I don't know, Toren." She shrugged, her arms wrapping around her belly once more. "I want it to be enough. I do. But I don't know if unrequited love works like that. That it can do anything but distort, morphing into something ugly and angry. I already travelled that path once. And I don't want to repeat that journey. Not with you."

"So don't let it be so. Let it go."

Tears started to brim on her lower lashes. "I am trying, Toren. I am trying."

The words hit him, slicing into him even as he didn't understand why.

She was trying to fall out of love with him.

There was something inherently wrong with that. And he wanted to stop her from even attempting such a thing.

The pebbles crunched as her boots swiveled on the rocks. She took a few steps toward the coaching inn before pausing, looking at him over her shoulder. "This is my failing, Toren. Not yours. Do not blame yourself for the state I find myself in. I own the fact that I could not adhere to our bargain, and I will deal with the consequences."

Tears unshed, she turned and continued her path to the inn.

Toren watched her, his feet rooted to the ground, until she disappeared past the stable.

No. He didn't want her to fall out of love with him. But he couldn't give her what she needed of him. He wasn't capable. He had never been capable.

He took a deep breath, the air lodging in his chest as he stared at the spot where her skirts had disappeared from view. Adalia was the very first thing in his life that he couldn't fix with appropriate attention to need. That was how his world worked. There was a need, and he met it. It had always been simple.

But Adalia. This was far from simple. Because she needed his love.

And he couldn't give her that.

Especially when his lies would destroy her, and in the process, destroy anything she ever felt for him.

She would hate him.

That he was sure of.

# { Chapter 15 }

The letter that had just arrived tapping on her thigh, Adalia walked along the path through the rose garden, the abrupt, heavy scent of newly opening rosebuds filling her head. Her feet slowed as she looked into the flower beds. A slew of rosebuds, with petals of white streaking into tips of pink, had bloomed this morning.

The coloring of the petals was both odd and enchanting. She stopped to stare at them. She hadn't noted this set of roses was near to blooming, as she had with all the others since they started working on the rose garden two months ago.

She hadn't, in fact, noted anything in the last week since her trip to the coaching inn with Toren.

Laughter flitted along the breeze, reaching her ears, and she looked toward the stables. Laughing, Mary leaned forward as she set her pony into a fast trot around the field in front of the stables. Strong, determined, her posture emanated full control over her speckled pony. Adalia's heart swelled. Mary learning how to ride had given her such confidence, it had been magical to see the transformation.

Not to be outdone, Josalyn set her pony onto the worn track, her own laughter ringing into the air. And there at the bottom of the field, clapping with the widest smile, stood Toren.

Pride. Pure pride beaming from his face.

He had shed his tailcoat and waistcoat, and walked about the field in only his buckskin breeches and a white linen shirt open partway down his chest. Easy. He looked easy. Relaxed. Comfortable. Happy.

The swell in her heart grew heavy, weighing down her chest. He was so good with the twins—patient, unfailingly fair with his attention. Each girl thought that she was Toren's favorite—and that alone was an astonishing feat.

The letter she clutched in her hand crumpling, her chest tightened so violently her breath stuck in place. Toren had convinced himself in some long ago world that he wasn't capable of love. That he could not feel it, live it. And she could not convince him otherwise.

Yet there he was, doing that exact thing for the twins.

He did know how to love.

He loved those girls as they were his own. There was no denying it.

He just didn't know how to love her.

The lodged breath in her chest loosened, leaving her body in a long exhale as she watched Toren motion to Mary, having her slow. Mary smiled, breaking into giggles as he exaggerated a whistle at her and waved her down with windmill arms.

Adalia's heart cracked, long and jagged, splitting her chest as she stared at the scene.

She could do this no longer.

She spun, retracing her steps quickly back through the gardens.

She needed to pack.

~ ~ ~

"Adalia, did you need me?" Toren walked into her chambers without knocking, stopping in the middle of the room as he glanced around. "I saw you walking up to the castle from the gardens, but did you need to speak to me?"

Motioning for the maid to excuse herself, Adalia waited until the woman left the room before turning back to her travel writing desk and setting a crisp stack of vellum into the box. "Where are Mary and Josalyn?"

"Digging weeds around the rose bushes with Mr. Fredrick."

She nodded, picking up the inkwell and making sure the stopper was secure.

"Adalia, why are you are packing?"

Holding the inkwell in her fingers, Adalia took a steadying breath and turned to him. "Since I was able to finally write to Lady Vandestile and Lady Desmond about where I was, I just received a return letter from Violet. That was what I came out to talk to you about."

A frown had settled onto his face. "Bad news?"

She nodded, her bottom lip stiffening. "Yes. Her husband died seven weeks ago. Seven weeks and I did not know. She needs me and I need to go to her." She turned back to the travel writing desk to set the inkwell in its compartment. "But I do not feel it is safe for the twins to be away from the castle yet, so I would like to leave them here with you, as I know you will protect them."

"Yet leaving is safe for you?"

"Safe enough. There has never been a direct threat upon me—you know that. And I will take however many men you think necessary. It is just to the Vandestile estate in Derbyshire where Violet currently is. That anyone would even guess I am travelling to her is impossible. Plus, you yourself said that the debt to Mr. Trether was paid in full—that he was forced to accept it. So while I imagine he is irate, I do think the threat from him is passing. Yet I cannot be positive, which is why I would like to leave the twins here for a few weeks, just to make sure."

His mouth tightened into a hard line as his look landed on the open trunk at the foot of her bed. He glanced up at her. "I will accompany you."

"No. It is not necessary."

"When will you be back?"

Her hands needing to be busy, she turned around and picked up the inkwell again, reassuring herself the stopper was tight. She took a deep breath. "I will not."

"Adalia, what are you talking about?" His words were slow, measured, hinting at the firestorm she was about to create.

As much as she didn't want to, she turned back to him, forcing her look upward to meet his brown eyes. "After I can make safe arrangements for the twins, where we will live, I will send for them. I will find a nice cottage to rent near the Vandestile estate. It is close to Glenhaven House, and I may be of assistance to the new Earl of Alton once they determine the heir. I did oversee the estate for two years, mess that it currently is."

"What?"

Her lips drew inward. He heard every word she said perfectly fine, and she was not about to repeat herself.

He strode across the room, ripping the inkwell from her fingertips and setting it into its compartment within the travel writing desk before grabbing her shoulders. "What the hell are you talking about, Adalia? Why would you even contemplate not coming back here?"

Refusing to meet his eyes, she stared at the bare skin of his chest framed by the cut of his white linen shirt. "You know why."

"Dammit, Adalia, I bloody well don't. Whatever it is that you are thinking, you need to tell me."

She chanced a glance up to his face, debating. It would be so much easier if she left, faded into the past without a word. Easier for her. But Toren would never let it be without an explanation. He needed facts, and he would badger her until he got them.

Her look dropped back down to the dip in the center of his collarbone. "I cannot do this again, Toren. I went through this once with my first marriage—constantly questioning myself, my worth—my soul withering until I felt like I was nothing. Just something to be dismissed. I cannot—will not do it again. I cannot live wanting more, every day, every second from you. It is not fair to you—not fair to me."

His fingers dug into her shoulders. "I thought we were past this, Adalia. That this was settled as it needed to be at the coaching inn."

She gave a slight shake of her head. "I had said I would try, Toren. And I have."

"No, you haven't. It has been a week, Adalia. You are rushing into this."

"No, I am rushing away from this. This last week has proven nothing to me except that I need to leave this place. I need to leave before I lose my soul."

"Your soul?" His eyebrows shot up, his hands dropping from her shoulders as he took a step away from her. His fingers ran through his hair as he looked out the window, the bottom pane lifted to let the breeze into the room. His voice went low, barely restrained. "Dammit, Adalia, I have done everything—everything possible—what else can I give you?"

She had to hold in a bitter laugh as she looked up at his profile. "You know exactly what I want, Toren."

He sighed, rubbing his eyes. "Love."

She stared at him, her bottom lip slipping under her teeth to hide her gasp. He said the one word so dismissively it sent a dagger into her chest, stealing further words from her tongue.

His look whipped to her. "You know I am not capable, Adalia."

"Yes, as you have told me." She tried to smile. Tried to make this easier for him, so it would be easier for her. Her lips only managed to pull into a frown. "And that is why I have to leave. You would know. If you could ever love me, then you would already know what love is and you wouldn't question it. Wouldn't deny its existence. And that was what I had been holding onto, the hope of it. But no more."

"So you will just leave this house, leave our marriage?"

Her eyes shifted to the open window. It took her a long moment to nod.

"This is not fair, Adalia." He stepped in front of her, blocking her view. "Have I ever mistreated you? Ever disappointed you? Made you feel like less than a respected wife?"

"No."

"Then what—what—Adalia?"

A chill shivered down her spine, demanding she crumble, demanding she alter course.

No. She had to do this.

Distance from him was the only way. And she wasn't about to let him stop her.

Her look lifted, pinning him. "Respect is cold, Toren. Maybe you will never understand love. But I do. I had love—my brothers loved me, the girls love me. I know what it is. And I cannot continue to give you my heart when what I receive in return is distant respect." Her hand flew up, thumping on her chest. "You cannot imagine how that breaks me every day—every single day—knowing that I am not enough for you to love."

"Adalia—"

"No. I need to leave, Toren. I need to come to terms with…with what is expected of me. To come to terms with being near you and not wanting you to love me. I will still strive to give you an heir. I will. But that time is not now. I cannot have my heart broken every time you roll away from me in bed. Every time you insist you are incapable of love. You aren't incapable of love, Toren. You are incapable of loving me."

"You don't know that."

"I do. You love the girls. I see it."

A growl, and his fingers curled into fists. "I told you I would treat them as my own, and now I am vilified for it?"

"No. Not vilified." Her head trembled as she shook it, a broken smile curving her lips. "It has only made me love you more. It is the only reason I am trusting you to keep them safe."

"No. I do not accept this. Don't go, Adalia."

Her breath caught in her throat. She pushed past it. "Is there a reason for me to stay?"

His chest lifted in a silent sigh, his mouth opening slightly.

In the next instant, his lips clamped shut.

No. No reason at all for her to stay.

"I thought not." She turned and slammed the lid of the travel writing desk closed, the sound of the snap vibrating through her body, a shot to her own soul.

But she could not collapse.

Not now.

In the carriage, yes. But not now. Not until she was out of Toren's sight.

"I will send for the girls as soon as possible." Her hands went flat, smoothing the front skirt of the dark carriage dress she had already changed into. "Now if you will excuse me, I must go tell the girls of my plans."

# { CHAPTER 16 }

Adalia surveyed the busy crush in front of her.

This felt good. For the first time in the last five weeks, she felt like the weight of the thousand stones pressing down on her chest had lifted.

This, she knew how to do. This, she was good at.

The Revelry's Tempest was open again.

Once she and Violet had convinced the current Lord Pipworth to lease the dower house to them, it had only taken three days of preparations to get the first night of gaming underway.

It was none too soon—Violet needed the money—needed it desperately.

After stopping at Glenhaven House to visit Theo's gravesite, Adalia had travelled on to find Violet broken, near a nervous collapse at the Vandestile estate, attempting to hide from the long line of creditors banging at her door. That most of the creditors had travelled from London to do so was highly unusual, and evidence to the fact that the debts were bone crushing.

Reopening the Revelry's Tempest, now with Violet as the proprietress, was the quickest—and easiest solution. Violet had been vital in helping Adalia run the business before, as her prowess with bookkeeping had filled in for the skills Adalia had lacked.

They had opened the Revelry's Tempest two nights before, and what they had planned to be a small event, meant for only the most loyal of patrons, had turned into a crush that had the *ton* on its ear.

Not one to let time cool the strike, Adalia pushed Violet to open again this evening to a much wider list of players.

It worked splendidly. So much so, that the night was two-thirds over before Adalia was able to enjoy her first moment of proper breath as she appraised the scene. Proof of how valuable this evening would be to Violet sparkled in front of her. Table after table was alive with clinking coins, laughter, held breaths, and the general din of money being made. From the first night's profits, Violet had been able to pay down a third of her late husband's debts. Tonight alone would allow her to pay at least the first installments to the rest, if not more.

Best of all, there hadn't been the slightest peep from Mr. Trether.

"You're a mad old bat, woman." The yell came from the drawing room attached to the bustling ballroom, and Adalia quickly scanned the crowd, trying to find the source of the anger.

She found him almost instantly. The comically foppish fellow she had wrinkled her nose at earlier—the first son of Baron Mallsen, Mr. Jawlton—had stood from his card table, the arm in his purple coat flinging out across the table at a lady with white hair and a mess of multi-colored ostrich feathers sticking up from her drooping cap.

Adalia searched the room. Logan and his other guard were in opposite far corners, both searching for the sudden commotion. She was the closest one to the fop. And she could move far faster through this thick crowd than Logan.

"Cheater. I call cheater on you, you decrepit old hag. You yanked that card from your sleeve. I saw it. Saw it with my own eyes." The high pitch of the idiot's voice screeched over the crowd.

Blast it. Moronic fop. Unable to see the face of the woman he was pointing at, Adalia sped across the ballroom, weaving in between the jostling bodies angling for a better look at the sudden fracas.

She was too late.

Already pushing his way to the fop, Captain Trebont was far too quick for a man his age. And he was barreling down on the screeching Mr. Jawlton.

The devil. That meant the old woman was Lady Whilynn. And Captain Trebont was about to defend her honor.

Why Adalia was blessed—or at the moment, cursed— to have Lady Whilynn and her devoted captain attend every one of the Revelry's Tempest events, she would never know. But the woman was elderly. And harmless, for the most part. She had more money than most in the room combined and usually only cheated when she was bored. Or someone annoyed her at the tables. Or she had an itch and a card fell out.

Uncannily spry for his seventy-plus years, the captain had the young fop by his purple lapels in an instant, shoving him away from the table. "You, sir, had better rethink your blasphemous words and apologize to my Buttercup."

"How dare you, sir." Mr. Jawlton flung his hand over the captain's shoulder, still pointing at Lady Whilynn. "The crazy old crone just yanked the queen from her sleeve—she even laughed when she did it. I will no sooner apologize to the hag than eat dung."

Foolish boy. Foolish, foolish boy.

"We will take this outside immediately, you sniveling whelp," the captain barked.

Adalia pushed past the last person in her way just as the captain's hand landed on the hilt of his saber. She grabbed his elbow to still his motion and wedged herself around him, squeezing herself between the two men. The stench of rum emanated from Mr. Jawlton, making her eyes water.

A hand up to each of them, Adalia raised herself onto her toes, looking between the two, buying time until Logan could reach them and handle this. "No. No one is dueling. I will not have it as a result of my tables. Sheathe your sword, Captain."

"You have no control over it, your grace. I am not afraid of this old codger." Mr. Jawlton barreled into Adalia, his arms outstretched for the captain's throat as he shoved her against the table.

Her left hand flailing, it landed under her side as she crashed onto the table, a stemmed glass crunching into her skin. The pain instant, a yelp escaped her just as Mr. Jawlton went flying through the air in front of her—a mass of a man in a black coat rushing past with him.

The captain didn't move like that.

Her toes scrambled back onto the floor to right herself as a primal growl filled her ears. Logan didn't growl. His men didn't growl.

She searched, trying to see the face of the man in front of her.

Toren.

Toren had just ripped Mr. Jawlton off of her, sending him flying into the wall.

And he was not done. Gripping the fop by the scruff of his purple coat, Toren yanked Mr. Jawlton to his feet. "But I have control over it, Jawlton. And if I hear the slightest whisper of your foppish arse attempting to retaliate against Captain Trebont, I will ensure your father cuts you off completely. The title is not yours to squander quite yet, boy."

The crowd parting in front of him, Toren dragged the fop through the drawing room and to the stairs.

Shock stilling her, holding her in place for long seconds, Adalia finally managed to move, rushing after him.

By the time she got to the top of the stairs and could see into the foyer, Toren was shoving Mr. Jawlton out the front door. Her butler ran down the front steps as the fop landed on the sidewalk, rolling in pain next to one of Logan's guards. Her butler and the guard would see Mr. Jawlton properly to his carriage.

A slight twinge of pity for the young fop struck her. Yes, he had been entirely rude. No gentleman of any stature called a lady a cheat. But Lady Whilynn usually did cheat, and Mr. Jawlton had been the only one at her table not knowing that fact.

She shook her head. But to allow his fogged head to take over all proper sense and say the things he did to a woman three times his age—well, he deserved getting tossed from the house.

The door slammed shut, and her eyes landed on the one person left in the foyer.

Toren looked up at her.

"Adalia." His voice slithered up the stairs, chilling her. Never had she heard so much palpable rage vibrating through one word.

*Blast it—no.* Not after suffering the last weeks without him. Not after she had finally been able to breathe again. Sleep again. Imagine a life without him.

Not now.

It wasn't fair.

"Your grace, as always, your evenings are sparkles to my eyes." The lilting voice fluttering happily behind Adalia made her jump, and she turned to see Lady Whilynn and Captain Trebont moving past her down the stairs, their arms entwined.

"Thank you, Lady Whilynn."

Lady Whilynn didn't even look Adalia's way as they moved past—she was too engrossed with her captain at her side. "This one, oh this one." Her words continued, singsong as she patted his arm. "Dueling for me. Like he did when our blooms were fresh. Oh, so very delightful. So strong."

The captain, though, caught Adalia's eye through the feathers sprouting up from Lady Whilynn's cap. He gave Adalia a slight nod, gratitude evident in his crinkled eyes as he tightened a cloak about Lady Whilynn's shoulders.

Lady Whilynn patted his cheek. "Still my hero, Captain."

"Still my twinkling star, Buttercup." He leaned down and kissed her forehead.

Adalia followed them down the stairs, realizing as her hand went to the railing that her palm was bleeding profusely from the smashed glass on the table. She wished she hadn't taken off her gloves earlier. The silk alone would have stopped most of the glass from slicing into her skin.

Just seeing the blood sent pain shooting up Adalia's arm and her head into lightness. Her arm dropped, and she quickly wrapped her hand deep into a fold of her dark skirt.

Lady Whilynn giddy, chattering away to the captain, the couple walked past Toren without a glance as he opened the front door for them.

Adalia hurried down the last few remaining steps and across the marble foyer to catch the couple. Without daring a look at him, she stepped wide past Toren. He reached out to grab her arm, but she flicked out of his reach before he made contact.

Over her shoulder, she braved a glance to him. The anger in his eyes thickened.

"No, I have to talk to them," she whispered as she motioned with her head to the captain and Lady Whilynn. Scanning the street to make sure Mr. Jawlton was, indeed, escorted far from the building, Adalia ran down the front stone steps to the sidewalk, catching the captain just before he joined Lady Whilynn in their waiting carriage.

"Captain, please, a word."

The captain nodded to his footman, and his man closed the carriage door. Taking a few steps to the side away from the coach, his voice went low, almost to a whisper. "Yes, what is it, your grace?"

"You had said it would not happen anymore." In deference to the captain's wish to keep the conversation unheard, Adalia hushed her tone as quietly as the firmness in her voice would allow.

"What is it that I said would not happen?"

Adalia fought back a groan. He knew exactly what she was reminding him of. "Our earlier three conversations we have had in the past year, Captain."

"You will need to remind me, my dear."

"The cheating. You had insisted last time that Lady Whilynn would cease her slips of the cards. I cannot continue to let her sit at the tables here if she insists on cheating every hour."

The captain sighed, his gloved hand going to his sallow, sunken cheek and rubbing it. His ancient eyes closed partially, sad weariness taking over his face. "Please, do not take this from her, my dear."

"Take the cheating away from her?"

He nodded, his hand dropping from his face. "The day my buttercup does not want to attend one of your nights, my dear—the night she does not try to hoodwink her way to victory—that is the night I know she has given up on keeping her mind in this world."

"But—"

"I know she is daft, your grace." The captain's eyes started to tear up, glistening in the low light from the gas lamp behind her. "She knows it as well, at times. But this—she has this." He motioned up toward the light emanating from the drawing room windows above them. "She still has a semblance of normal when she's here, up to her old tricks. There is not a thing she loves more in the world. Here she does not babble. Does not reach for things that are no longer there. Does not talk to people that left this earth long ago. Do not take this away from her. From me."

Adalia's chest tightened. Her lips drawing in, she nodded. "Please, just try and control her—or at least let her only gamble with those you know—she is notorious at it amongst her friends, as you recall?"

"I do, my dear. And I will." He gave her a slight bow, tilting his top hat to her. "You are a princess among pirates, my lady."

A half smile lifted her cheek, and she shook her head at the overt flattery. "Good evening, Captain."

He took a step away from her before Adalia interrupted him. "Oh, and Captain."

He turned back to her.

"She actually loves you more than anything in the world. I have seen it."

A smile broke through the weathered lines on his face. "That she does, your grace. As I do her."

Adalia watched as he got into their carriage, and she stayed in place, waiting until it rounded the far corner. She turned to the front door and jumped. Toren stood on the bottom step, silent, a stone statue staring at her.

Hand on her heart, she tried to still the madcap beating thundering in her chest. If she expired right here on the sidewalk from an exploded heart, it wouldn't matter what caused it—the shock of Toren's appearance in London or the mere fact that his body was suddenly so close to hers—dead was dead.

She looked up at him, her neck craning because of the extra foot of height he had from the bottom step. "You—you didn't have to do that upstairs, Toren."

His jaw shifted to the side, seething. "That fop was about to be handled far too gently by your worthless guards. I merely made sure he was treated with the respect he deserved."

Her eyes narrowed at him. "My guards are not worthless."

"Then why in the hell did I see you between a man with a sword at the ready and a man that rammed into you?"

Her fingers clenched, fists going to her hips. "No, Toren, no, you don't—"

"What is on your hand?" He squinted at her left hand, moving off the bottom step to her.

Blast it. Her hand. She had forgotten. She slowly unclenched her fingers, the movement sending sharp pains vibrating up her arm.

Toren reached down, grabbing her wrist and holding it into the sliver of light casting down from the drawing room above. "Dammit, Adalia, this is blood."

She attempted to pull her hand away. "The glass on the table crushed under my hand. It is fine. Let me go. I need to wash it."

"Glass? Damn, Adalia." He spun, dragging her up the stairs into the townhouse. Inside, his stride didn't slow, and he went up two flights of stairs, skipping the level with the drawing room and ballroom. "What the blasted devil are you thinking?"

At the top of the stairs, she twisted her wrist, still trying to free herself from the manhandling. "I do wish you would stop swearing at me."

"It's better than throttling you." His grip tightened on her wrist as he stalked down the hall, flinging open the doors of the withdrawing rooms she had converted from bedrooms when she first opened the Revelry's Tempest.

It wasn't until the third door that Toren found an empty room.

Her mouth clamped shut. Toren would never hurt her—would he? She couldn't imagine it, but she also never could have imagined him like this—with barely bridled fury raging through his body, so visceral that no mask of indifference could possibly hide it.

The door slamming behind them, Toren spun her onto a chair in front of the fireplace. Releasing her wrist, he stomped over to a dresser. Rummaging through the drawers, he yanked out a sheet, unfurling it before biting into the edge, his teeth tearing the fabric. He repeated the motion, ripping two long shreds free from the rest of the cloth before he picked up the washbowl and pitcher and set it on the floor by the toes of her slippers. He splashed water into the bowl, the liquid sloshing over the side, puddling onto the floor.

Silent except for his seething breath, Toren grabbed her hand and pulled her forward, dunking her hand into the bowl of water, swishing it. Words, harsh and punctuated, hissed from his mouth. "You reopened your gaming house?"

"You left the girls by themselves?" Reaction without thought, her tone matched his.

His look whipped up to her as he lifted her hand from the water. "They are well-ensconced in the castle. No one will touch them—you are aware I know better than most how to create an impenetrable cage for them. Yet you insult me to think I would put them in danger."

She did know.

She knew very well he would never let danger near the twins. "You are right. I apologize."

For an excruciatingly long moment they stared at each other, the water droplets plunking off her hand into the bowl the only sound cutting through the thick air between them.

His breathing heaved in anger. Her breathing heaved because it was too soon.

Far, far too soon. She couldn't see him yet. She wasn't ready.

She wasn't ready a week ago, she wasn't ready fifteen minutes ago, and she was even less ready now.

An exhale hissed from his mouth, and he looked down, dunking her hand into the water again, lifting it out, staring at the haphazard cuts across the butt of her palm. Poking at the cuts, he stretched the skin wide until more blood ran free. Stinging, she yanked her hand away.

He snatched her wrist before she could hide her hand along her body and he held it angled to the fire. With thumb and forefinger, he attempted to pinch a tiny shard of glass from her flesh.

"What are you thinking, Adalia, opening the gaming house?"

Of course. That was what he was doing here. That was why he was so mad. He wasn't here for her. He was here because she had opened the Revelry's Tempest again. "You are upset it reflects poorly on you?"

He held her palm close to his eyes and he yanked, setting a shard free from her skin. He flicked it into the fire. "Damn well I am—but even more so I am beyond irate at the danger you have put yourself in. I never would have allowed you to leave Dellon Castle if I had known you would sneak off to London."

"I did not sneak. I had to change my plans once I saw Violet. Your guards have been with me the whole time."

"But not only did you come to London—you opened this place, putting yourself directly in danger by being in public like this."

He dunked her hand into the water again, the splash sending droplets onto her black skirt. He swished her hand vigorously, pulling it from the water and then holding it close to his eyes to pinch at another piece of glass.

"I did not open this place for me, Toren." She stared at the top of his dark hair. For how angry he was with her, his fingers around her hand were entirely delicate. "I re-opened it for Violet. It is hers now, and I am just helping her. She is in dire straits as her late husband had racked up monstrous debts—he even signed many of them to her name—and the creditors have been harassing her mercilessly."

"There are other ways to handle the debt, Adalia." His focus stayed on her palm.

"You were not there when I found her, Toren. She was near mental collapse with the fear and stress of it all. I merely suggested the gaming house as a path forward, and she latched onto the idea. There has been no swaying her from it."

"So don't help her. That would sway her." He flipped another shard into the fire and set her hand into the bowl of water.

"She is my friend, Toren, and I love her. I would do anything to help her." She couldn't keep her voice at an even level, not that she was bothering to attempt it. "And if she needs this place running in order to stay sane, to pay off debts, to feel in control of her fate instead of getting crushed under it—then I am helping her with that, scandal to your name or not."

He pulled her hand from the water, his voice quiet, measured, when he opened his mouth. "Why did Lord Pipworth allow you to use the dower house?"

"I leased it from him. He needed an influx of funds, as I well guessed for the mess his estate is in. And I needed the dower house for Violet. It is not a loss for him as he wants nothing to do with this house since I already ruined it for all respectability. I did not know a house could own such a trait. But I apparently scandalized the house to ruin for him."

Toren nodded, looking up to her as he released her hand. "Do you feel any more glass in your skin?"

Adalia held her hand up to the light of the fire, squishing her palm back and forth, waiting for more sharp irritations deep in her skin. There were none.

She shook her head.

"Good." He gently took her hand and picked up the clean strip of cloth, his fingers deftly wrapping it around her hand and wrist.

Now that his seething had ceased, the sudden urge to reach out with her right hand and sink her fingers into his hair washed over her, sending a shiver through her body.

How could he be so infuriating and delicate all at once? She wasn't prepared for this, the wanting—aching—to touch him. Aching to feel his skin under her fingertips, his breath on her neck.

She had left Dellon Castle because she didn't want to end up bitter, hating him for not loving her. As much as leaving had been the sane choice, it had done nothing to

quell the burning in her core that exploded when she saw
him again. Did nothing to stifle her need to touch him. She
wanted him more than ever, and denying herself of him the
past five weeks had only made that fire grow hotter.

On its own volition, her right hand lifted slightly from
her lap.

A knock from the hallway, and the door suddenly
cracked open. "There you are."

Her hand falling onto her skirt, Adalia looked to the
door. Violet's head bobbed into the room. "Violet."

"What in heaven's name happened? I was recording
numbers in the office and when I came out the place had
broken into bedlam. Something about Lady Whilynn again?
I have been searching for you everywhere. Who is this?"

Adalia wiggled on her seat, wanting to jump to her feet
and go below, but Toren's grip on her fingers had tightened,
a silent warning that she would be going nowhere. "Do I
need to get to the ballroom?"

"No." Violet waved her hand in the air. "Cass and
Logan and the dealers are handling it. Mostly just gossip
flying about now. I repeat, who is this?"

Adalia attempted to hide a preemptive cringe. "Violet,
I present to you the Duke of Dellon."

His hands still busy and bloody with wrapping her
hand, Toren looked up at Violet, giving her a slight nod. A
very firm mask of indifference was set upon his face, not the
slightest wisp of interest or kindness or curiosity.

Until that very moment, Adalia hadn't realized how
masterful Toren was at hiding anything and everything from
others. She had always assumed he did it mainly to her, and
mostly to annoy her.

Violet barely glanced at him, her eyebrows arching as her lips drew into a tight line. "This is him? This is the bas—"

"Yes." Adalia blurted the word, cutting her friend off. Violet's hold on propriety had slipped in the last weeks, so flummoxed she had been at the dissolution of her entire life. Slapping a smile on her lips when greeting someone she had an inherent dislike of was not one of the things Violet could yet manage. "This is my *husband*. I cut my hand earlier and he is helping me. You should go below. I will tell you all about the skirmish later, but I imagine at the moment Cass needs your help in keeping the evening on keel."

Frown settling onto Violet's face, her arms crossed over her chest. She had a few more things to say, and Adalia knew they were not good. But to her friend's credit, Violet nodded and moved toward the door. "I will talk with you later, Adalia." Violet made sure the last thing she did before leaving the room was to pierce Toren with a glare of death.

"Thank you, Violet," Adalia called out across the chamber, breaking Violet's stare.

Violet left the room, closing the door behind her.

With a sigh, Adalia glanced down to her hand.

"Your friend does not like me." His fingers busy tying off the white strip of cloth, Toren did not look up at her.

"She is loyal to me and she does not understand…" Her voice trailed off.

"Understand what?"

She stared at the top of his head. "How you cannot love me."

His eyes jerked up to meet hers. "You told her of that?

"Of course I did. She is one of my dearest friends."

His head tilted to the side, genuinely curious. "Why would she care?"

Adalia strangled back a growl. She wasn't ready for this—wasn't ready to have to validate every feeling she had to him. Especially not when a waterfall of opposing feelings was currently drowning her. "She cares because she loves me, Toren. She's loyal. She thinks you're blind. She does not understand how you cannot see what a *wonderful* person I am."

"She gets to lay judgement upon that?"

"She loves me, so yes. Yes, she gets to judge that. I do not live in a world where there is only one person and that one person is me, Toren."

Still on his knees, he leaned back, landing on his heels. "That is what you think?"

"That you live in a world that consists only of you?"

"Yes."

"Yes—no—maybe." She sighed, her right hand lifting to her forehead, rubbing it. "I don't know what I think at the moment, Toren. You appear out of nowhere, angry as a demon out of hell in one second and wounded that my friend doesn't like you in another. I don't know what to think. And I definitely don't know what to feel."

He looked around the room, his hands slapping on his thighs. "This place, there are too many people here. It is not private."

"Private for what?" Her eyes narrowed, wary. "No. Absolutely not, Toren. It will be the death of me if you think you can burst in and out of my life, take me to bed when the mood strikes you and then leave. I cannot handle that—not yet."

"I was not the one that left, Adalia. That was you."

That was true. Brutally true.

He stood, holding his open hand down to her. "Please? Somewhere else?"

"Fine." She glared up at him, taking his hand. "But my home, not yours."

"Then I bow to your needs."

# { CHAPTER 17 }

His hands clasped behind his back, Toren moved about the perimeter of the room. The study in the Alton townhouse was well-appointed. Classic furnishings with staid, thick chairs that wouldn't break under a man's weight, a wall of well-used tomes, a walnut coffered ceiling that matched the straight lines of the mantel, and centering the room was a wide mahogany desk with ledgers piled high on opposite ends.

After a painfully silent carriage ride to the townhouse, Adalia had quickly moved to the back side of the desk once in the room, sitting in the wide chair. Her back was ramrod straight, her elbows propped on the desk with her hands clasped, fingers entwined.

Toren hid the slight cock of his eyebrow at her movements by turning away from her to study the paintings on the wall. If Adalia needed to have twenty stone of well-oiled mahogany furniture between the two of them, then he would give her that. Her actions also told him exactly what he would be dealing with as far as his wife was concerned.

What had he hoped for? That she would see him and immediately fall into his arms? Declare her love over and over? Beg to come home? Apologize profusely for being so idiotic as to come to London and reopen her damn gaming house?

Fanciful notions, all of them.

But the lack of any and all of that hadn't stopped his own body from flying into a licentious rage. The second he saw her in the crowd at the Revelry's Tempest, he had wanted her pressed up against him, naked, her body writhing—no, not wanted—he *needed* her body on his. And then in the next instant, she'd been slammed onto that table, glass cutting into her delicate skin, and he had lost all rational thought, a guttural, ancient fury taking a hold of his body.

He had thought he had been prepared for anything with her.

But not that.

Not blood. Not Adalia's blood. Not his wife's blood.

Facing the wall, he closed his eyes, drawing a deep breath in effort to battle the fury exploding in his veins. She was fine. Cuts, nothing more. And she currently needed space. Space from him. He could give her that courtesy.

At least for a few minutes.

He opened his eyes.

An oil painting framed in gilded, delicately carved rosewood hung before him, a man and woman dressed in the most exquisite finery from two decades ago. He exhaled his breath slowly, concentrating on the thin strokes of cobalt blue along the woman's gown.

"These are your parents?" he asked, not turning around to Adalia.

"Yes."

He studied Adalia's mother. She bore a striking resemblance to Adalia. Beautiful, the artist had captured an elegance—an innocent refinement about her. He wondered if that had been the artist's interpretation of the woman before him, or if Adalia's mother had actually possessed the same sharp cunning as Adalia.

Not that Adalia wasn't refined—she was, but she also possessed a fearless independence that skirted her to and fro along the line of propriety. Being raised by three brothers had prodded that peculiar trait to the top. A trait Toren had found, begrudgingly, that he enjoyed—until she had left him.

That was when his amusement of her independence had waned. When, night after night, his body had screamed out for her, unsatisfied—with nothing to calm the craving that had not dissipated in the slightest since she had left the castle.

He had grumbled through the first two weeks without his need for her sated. It wasn't until the moment in the middle of the third week when he had snapped at Josalyn at the breakfast table that he realized something had to change. He had never once snapped, never even considered speaking sharply to the girls. But in that moment, his voice still echoing against the stone walls of the breakfast room, he had watched Josalyn's tiny face crumble in front of him. Innocence turning into tears she stubbornly refused to shed, even as Mary took her hand and pulled her away from the table.

Stubborn. Josalyn was stubborn. And it only pointed out the fact that he was damn well more stubborn. He missed Adalia, and he hadn't allowed himself to admit it.

Hell, he more than missed her. It felt like his life had unraveled in a thousand disparate shreds, everything fraying a little bit more and more each day, until he had snapped and yelled at Josalyn.

Josalyn's reaction had been something he never wanted to witness again—never wanted to cause again. Especially when she hadn't deserved it—she had merely been chatting about the roses with an enthusiasm that reminded him of Adalia, and he had barked at her. He had apologized, of course, fearing he had irrevocably wounded her spirit. But she had forgiven him once he explained he wasn't mad at her, and that it wasn't her fault, she had merely stumbled in front of his misplaced anger. She even giggled at his words, all forgotten.

Also like Adalia. She forgave easily, dismissing anger with nary a look back over her shoulder.

He hoped to high heaven Adalia had not lost that trait.

The devil, he had to get this right. Say the right words to Adalia. He had no clue what they were, but he had to get them right.

He studied the slight smile on his mother-in-law's face. Adalia would have that same serene smile if she wasn't so canny. But no, not his wife. Her likeness would someday be painted with the grin that was so quick to her face. The grin that just waited for life to amuse her, and if life wasn't doing so, she would create the mayhem herself.

He had realized in the time she was away how the very air around Adalia spun with excitement. It always had. So much so, that the air had crackled around her on the silent carriage ride to the Alton townhouse.

His eyes flickered to Adalia's father. He looked like a slightly older version of Theodore.

"Your parents appear young here."

"They were, though not as young as one would think," she said, her voice soft. "It was the last portrait done of them. They had commissioned an artist to do one of our entire family after I was born, with all four of us and them.

But their ship sank along the coast before it was started.
Caldwell had told me he remembered my parents sitting
for this painting, and it had been utterly boring for him.
He remembered watching it being done with Theodore and
Alfred, and that they kept stealing the artist's brushes and
creating general mayhem. There are some smaller portraits
of them in the house, but I always liked this one the most
for the obvious pride on their faces. I imagine it was pride
of their three boys."

Toren nodded, leaning closer to the oil painting to
study it. "Your mother was with child at the time?"

"She what?" Adalia's hands slapped onto the desk.

Toren glanced back to her and then stepped to the side,
pointing at the painting. "These lines here, they look to be
a swollen belly, yet your mother is slight in the rest of her
frame. Her hand is splayed on her belly. It looks protective.
I believe it is a common sign."

Adalia jumped to her feet, rushing around the desk and
across the room to study the painting. For a long moment,
she said nothing. "Yes. You may be right. I had never
noticed that—I tend to look at their faces. Caldwell never
said exactly when it was done."

"Maybe it was pride at the fourth babe on the way."

She looked up at him. "No…" Her eyes went to the
portrait, studying her mother's face. "Do you think?" Her
voice dipped small, vulnerable, an obvious lump in her
throat.

Toren watched her profile, recognizing the hope in her
green eyes. He set his hand gently on her shoulder. "I think
it is very possible."

She awkwardly dipped away, dropping from his touch and skittering several steps from him. After a quick glance back to the safety of the desk, she looked at him, her feet holding her ground. "What are you doing here in London, Toren. Truly?"

"I came for you."

"Because I opened the Revelry's Tempest?"

"Yes. Because it is not safe for you here. It is not safe for you to be exposed to people in that situation—there is no control."

"I am perfectly safe there—your guards have more than made it so."

His look drifted down to her left hand, wrapped thick with the strip of white linen. "Yet that happened."

She glanced at her wrapped hand and then set it slightly behind her skirt out of view. "A mere skirmish that was being handled, Toren. I was safe." Her green eyes pinned him. "Do you mean to shut down the Revelry's Tempest?"

"I do not know yet what I mean to do."

"Why not?"

He took a step toward her. "I thought I was here for one purpose, but I did not know everything I needed to. Not until tonight. When the guards I sent with you reported back to me that you had travelled to London and were preparing the gaming house for opening, I set off as soon as I knew the twins were secure." His right fingers curled into a fist that he had to forcibly relax. "You were quicker than I, though, and opened it before I could stop you."

Her right hand went onto her hip as her eyebrow arched. "You think you could have stopped us?"

He shrugged. "I could have sufficed whatever needs you were attempting to satisfy. That alone should have done it."

"You don't understand the Revelry's Tempest in the slightest, do you, Toren?"

His head slanted to the side at her sharp words. Challenging. Always challenging. "What is there to understand?"

"That the house is about control over one's own future, Toren. You wouldn't have stopped us from opening it, because I wouldn't have allowed it. The Revelry's Tempest is the one thing that Violet needs right now. Control over her own future. Her life was decimated—everything around her had been a farce—and she hadn't known it. Merely paying off the debts would have solved one problem, yes, but I needed to tether Violet to a future she could want."

"Tether her to the future?"

Head shaking, Adalia's hand slipped from her hip, flattening on the front of her black silk gown, her thumb and forefinger pressing in against her ribcage. "How I found her, Toren..." Her voice faltered for a moment before she took a quick breath and rushed on. "Violet needed something, anything, as a reason to wake up the next day. That is what the Revelry's Tempest is right now for Violet. A future she will wake up for. Do not take it away from us. I need my friend."

Her green eyes pleaded with him, and not for her own benefit, as he had thought this whole debacle to be. She was doing this for her friend, and Toren doubted he could ever sway her off that course.

Not that he would try. It was quite possible that he was actually, to his own amazement, beginning to understand his wife. "Your friend, Violet, do you consider her your family?"

"Yes. Of course I do."

His jaw shifted to the side. "I had always only believed family was by blood. That was the very direct meaning of the word that I understood."

"And now?"

Now? Now what? How could he answer that? He cleared his throat. "I am reconsidering."

She took a small step toward him. He could stretch out his arm, touch her now if he so chose. But he kept his hands firmly clasped behind his back.

"Why did you come to London, Toren? You could have easily sent word to your men to close down the Revelry's Tempest."

"I…" He sighed. "I lied to you, Adalia."

Her eyes went wide, her chin bowing as she looked up at him with a mixture of bewilderment and trepidation. "What did you lie about?"

"When we first married you asked me why Theodore trusted me."

The suspicion thickened in her eyes. "Yes." The one word left her lips, slow, drawn out.

"I lied when I said I did not know. I do."

"Why?" Her shoulders relaxed slightly, but her green eyes still harbored heavy suspicion.

"Theodore and I were once drunk—near to oblivion—in a tavern a day's travel from London—don't ask why or how we ended up there."

"A Theo plan of mayhem?"

"Yes, and if I recall correctly it had to do with an actress and a certain bauble she wanted him to recover for her." Toren waved his hand, dismissing the absurdity of the situation. "Regardless, it was not the most artfully designed adventure, and we quickly found ourselves in trouble that would not end well—at least for us. But then your eldest brother, Caldwell, appeared and he got us out of the tavern we were about to die in. All of it—the entire thing—was nothing but a grand time for Theo. And your brother was furious with him."

"As it always was." Adalia's face had softened as he talked, a small smile warming her lips.

"Yes, and I saw it. I saw your brother's anger at Theodore, and I wanted it." He stopped, his eyes closing as he envisioned the scene from years ago. "Wanted it to be directed at me. Wanted it to my core. It was the first thing I ever truly wanted in my life. Stupid really, to want someone to be furious with me. But I wanted it because all of that ferocity came from blood…from family."

"From love."

He opened his eyes to her. "I was drunk and I told Theodore as much as we were drifting off to sleep. That I wanted that. I wanted his family."

"You said those words?"

"Yes. And I didn't even think he heard me. But he did. And he knew. He knew if I ever had that—a family—there wasn't anything I would not do for them." He met her wide green eyes fully, his voice rough. "I don't think Theodore could say the same about anyone else he knew. Which was why he extracted the vow from me to marry you, should the need arise. Why he sent you to me. He knew what you needed."

"And he knew what you needed." She took another step toward him, her look not wavering from his as she reached up and set her fingers gently along his cheek.

Toren nodded. "Better than I could ever recognize it myself. Your brother was smarter than I ever gave him credit for." He paused, glancing to the coffered ceiling for a moment, bracing himself.

How he just wanted this to be enough. He wanted to reach out and grab her, haul her up to his lips, kiss her, strip her down and let everything in his body say the things he could not.

But that would not be enough for her, and he knew it. She would still demand more. And he would fail her. The lies he had told guaranteed it.

Her hand dropped from his face, and his breath stopped in his chest. This was the moment she would walk away again.

He concentrated on the dark wood of the ceiling, manifesting indifference.

Let her go. This was not fair to her.

Her sudden hand on his chest, fingers slipping inward past the lapel of his dark tailcoat, startled him, and his look fell to her face.

She stared up at him, a wicked smile on her face. Wanton. Purely wanton.

"Well, I can be the one furious with you, Toren, if that is what you need of me." The twitch of her grin showed pure delight at the prospect. Her fingers maneuvering, she unbuttoned his waistcoat in short order.

He exhaled, relief shuddering through him.

She hadn't disappeared. Hadn't turned from him. He hadn't given her enough—he knew that—yet she had accepted what little he had to offer. And this—this he could give her. His body had always known exactly what to do with hers.

His head dipped to her neck, inhaling the sweet smell of honey from her hair as his lips brushed her skin with his words. "You have already proven your capacity for anger at me, Adalia. Far too often for my liking, I daresay." He started unlacing the ribbons along her spine that held her dark gown in place.

She moaned, soft and lusty as she angled her head to improve his access to her. "Too often, or not enough? Just remember it is because I am your wife and we are family."

He chuckled into her neck, her skin already hot to the touch beneath his lips. It had been far too long since he'd tasted her, felt her body under his fingertips.

Pushing off his coat, Adalia suddenly jerked away from his hands, holding his coat up. "What is that?"

In between them she draped the dark tailcoat over her left forearm and plucked an obnoxious pink and turquoise striped handkerchief from the inside lapel pocket. She snapped the fabric, sending it free from its square folds.

He chuckled, tugging the silk handkerchief from her fingertips. "The twins are working on their embroidery." He pointed to the two "D" initials on the opposite ends of the fabric. "Somewhat warped, but one can possibly make out the letter."

"You managed to convince Josalyn and Mary to embroider? That is a feat in itself."

He shrugged. "They discovered my mother's sewing box and were fascinated by the many tiny hidden compartments and shelves that swing open. The box was an engineering wonder. I said they could have it only if they knew what to do with it, so Miss Mable started giving them lessons. They gave this to me for my birthday."

She stared at the fabric in his fingers, a frown tipping the edges of her full lips.

"I apologize, Adalia, should I not have had Miss Mable teach them?"

She shook her head, her eyes lifting to him. "No. It is not that—that part is commendable. It is just…it was your birthday? While I was away?"

"Yes. Mary found the date of my birth recorded in the Bible in the library. They surprised me with the handkerchief."

"When was it?"

"A fortnight ago."

She fingered an edge of the silk, the tip of her forefinger brushing against his thumb. "And you are still wearing it?"

The tips of his ears tinged with heat. He shrugged. "Yes. I told them I would wear it unfailingly. So I do."

"It was thoughtful of them." Her fingers slipped from the edge of the fabric.

"Yes." He folded the handkerchief neatly, slipping it back into the inside pocket of his tailcoat that Adalia still held over her arm. "It was the first present I ever received."

"What?" Her mouth widened in a disbelieving smile. "No. Surely you have had presents before."

His shoulders lifted again, the heat in his ears spreading down his neck. "No." He took the coat from Adalia's arm and turned, moving to the simple wooden chair by the desk to drape it over the back rails.

A footstep behind him, her hand landed on his shoulder. "I am sorry I was not there. I am sorry I missed it."

"It is no matter, Adalia."

Her hand stayed on his shoulder and she stepped around him, planting herself in front of him, her sparkling green eyes intent on his face. "It does matter, Toren. It may not matter to you, but it does to me. It matters to me that you have lived your whole life without the joy of receiving something well-crafted from someone that loves you. Proof, however small, that you matter, that you are the world to someone else. Mary and Josalyn—they adore you."

"I am fortunate."

"You say that with bewilderment, as though you are surprised they could do so."

He shrugged.

Her head shook, a frown settling on her face. "I should have told you. Before I left I didn't tell you that you… matter…that you are worth loving. That was my failing. When I left Dellon Castle it was about me, about my love for you and how I needed to reconcile that. But I should have told you—about you—about who you are as a person and how I see you for the man you are. That you are a man that can be loved. How would you know that unless I spoke the words?"

She slipped both of her hands upward, wrapping them around his neck, even as traces of the frown lined her lips. "And as much as I wish it were not so for the pain I fear is ahead for me, I have reconciled nothing about my love for you. I thought…I thought I had. But then you appeared tonight and everything—everything I had been lying to myself about collapsed."

Toren stilled. This was what he had dreaded. This was the moment she decided what he could offer was not enough.

For a long breath she stared up at him until her frown slowly stretched, turning into a grin. "I adore you still, and I think I need to give you a delayed birthday present."

He gave a slight exhale. "There is no need, Adalia."

Her fingers went onto his lips. "Shhh. You will accept this gift. You will close your mouth and not deny it. No matter how you may want to scream out against it."

"Scream out against it?"

The smile widened on her face, the return of wantonness. She nodded, her fingers leaving his neck to remove his waistcoat and work his shirt upward on his torso, stripping him free of the cloth.

She started on the dip at the base of his neck, her tongue flickering, tasting his skin. Trailing down the center of him, her lips teased, tongue swirling along the swells of his muscles. Muscles that grew taut under her touch, fire building. With every caress he flinched, his body needing to grab her, needing to strip her free of every last piece of cloth on her body.

Lower and lower her mouth travelled.

Dropping to her knees, her fingers ahead of her mouth, she worked the buttons free on his trousers.

Just as she freed him to the air, her mouth pulled away from his abdomen and looked up at him. "Lift your foot."

Toren did as commanded with his right foot, and she pulled off his boot, followed by his left. Within seconds, she had stripped him, naked to the air. He drew a deep breath, his control frayed almost to the edge. He knew he was not long for just standing naked before Adalia on her knees, his cock hard and straining for her.

His fingers twitched.

She slapped his left hand, looking up at him, wicked. "No screaming. No ordering me about. You will suffer this."

Her hands went flat onto his stomach, splaying wide, rolling along the ridges of muscles. Watching her stare at his body, planning, he almost lost his balance as he fought to not yank her up and drive himself into her.

"Not yet. I can see you flinching." She didn't look up, just said the words to his stomach, soft, as though she needed to seduce his skin to remain under her control.

Her hands slipped lower. Her right hand wrapped around the base of his shaft, holding him.

Warm. Strong. Commanding.

Her lips clamped around him, her tongue swirling along his cock as she took him deep into her mouth.

The devil take him. He almost dropped to his knees.

She sucked, hard, then withdrew, softly teasing. Diving forth, pulling his shaft deep into her throat.

Her lips had been on him before. But this—this was far different, for he had always directed her. She was in full control, and from the way his body shuddered with every movement she made, the growls erupting from his throat, she was enjoying every second of her mastery.

His hands dove into her hair, clutching at her, pins falling as strands fell freely down her back. She drew him deep into her mouth, again and again. A height he had never known. And hell. He could not stand it any longer.

He yanked himself from the torture of her mouth.

She would not get through this unscathed.

Looking up at him, eyes wide, she yelped as he dropped to his knees in front of her, grabbing her about the waist and flipping her onto her back. He hovered above her for a long second, taking in the swollen red of her lips, the lust flushing her cheeks. Reveling in the pure, wanton joy on her face.

He needed to be in her. But not yet.

His hand went down, yanking her skirts upward. "And I imagine I have missed your birthday. Or I am early for it."

Her hands lifted, attempting to stop him, take back control, but he would have none of it. Dipping down before she could alter his course, he pushed her skirts fully up, his thumbs running up her thighs.

"Dammit, Toren."

Not giving her a moment to fight it, he dove without preamble, his tongue finding her nubbin, already swollen and ready for his touch. Flicking, teasing. She jerked under him, throaty moans escaping her as her back arched, holding herself to his mouth. Resistance evaporated as she yielded every bit of control to him, letting him build, pull, take her to the edge before yanking her away.

He lifted himself up, ignoring her gasps, her grasping at completion.

"Toren." The word was breathless, begging, demanding. She reached for his arms, fingernails clawing into his biceps.

"No, Adalia. I have waited weeks for this, and I am inside you, nowhere else."

"Yes."

The demand of a devil angel.

He slammed into her. Her body instantly started to ripple, gaining strength as he filled her.

"Toren."

She shook, her body arching, screaming, and he lifted her, steadying her body against his strokes pushing her through to completion.

"I have you, Adalia. Heaven to hell I have you."

He drove into her again. Fast. Withdrawing slowly. Her body contracted in brutal waves demanding he return. Again and again until he could take no more. Into her depths, his body lost control, the earth and skies and heaven and hell blending into one explosion.

The roar in his own ears deafened him, his eyes blinded to nothing except the green of Adalia's eyes. Wave after wave pulsated from him, emptying into her body, and he collapsed, gripping her body tight to his.

Even as the sensation infiltrating every shattered fragment of his body was foreign, he understood it instinctively on a raw, innate level.

He hadn't been wrong. His body needed hers—a vice that refused to release him.

But even more so—he needed *her*.

# { CHAPTER 18 }

Sitting in the drawing room at the Revelry's Tempest, Adalia scanned the ballroom beyond the open double French doors that connected the rooms. Not a thing was out of place, the entire level cleaned top to bottom. One would never know a night filled with voracious gaming had happened only a few short hours ago on these floorboards.

Violet truly was remarkable at managing these events. Adalia's friend had always offered invaluable help, but now that it meant her own livelihood, Violet had poured every modicum of her energy into making these evenings successful.

Adalia sipped her tea, eyeing her friend over the rim of the cup. They had just finished going over the books from the previous night. All was perfectly in order. And after the excitement of Lady Whilynn and Captain Trebont, the betting of the evening had reached a new high. Violet was now in position to pay off the rest of the debts within a month, if all went well.

Violet would be fine. She wasn't going to like what Adalia had to tell her next, but Adalia knew her friend would be fine.

Violet set the teapot down on the delicate inlaid rosewood table between them. "So you have obviously reconciled with him in some fashion—I can tell by the flush in your cheeks." Violet picked up her tea cup and took a sip from it. "Where is your duke now? And why have your guards below multiplied? Were there not only four of them before? You are not in dire danger, are you?"

Adalia said silent thanks that Violet held her tongue where Toren was concerned—her friend had listened to all of Adalia's tirades about her husband, and she knew Violet possessed, at most, an unkind view of him.

"Toren insisted with the guards." Adalia set her cup down. "My presence here in London makes him nervous, especially when we cannot completely control the crowd that comes to the gaming nights. So he wanted to add two more guards and I have not fought him on it. He believes the issues with Mr. Trether have been resolved, but he is still uncomfortable with how exposed I am."

"And good riddance to that charlatan."

"Yes. And I will be able to breathe in my own space again once we are back in the countryside."

Violet's cup clattered to the table. "You are leaving?" Instant worry sent Violet's blue eyes wide in panic.

"Yes. At least for the time being. Toren has insisted." Adalia's fingers tapped on the table. "But it is odd that he is still worried as to Mr. Trether's motives. I did not miss something, did I? Mr. Trether has not shown up at either of the two nights, has he?"

"No. And Logan knows to alert me if he sees Mr. Trether."

Adalia nodded. "Good. You need to be wary of the man as well. But beyond that blackguard, and more important, I miss the twins desperately and want to be with them." Adalia reached across the table, grasping Violet's hand. "And you need not worry. You are splendid at this,

Violet. You manage this place better than I ever have. Plus, Cass is here to help with the gaming nights."

Violet opened her mouth to speak, but Adalia squeezed her hand, interrupting what she knew would be protest. "And I have other news about this place you will be happy to hear."

Violet's head tilted, wary. "What?"

"That is where Toren is. He is buying this house as we speak."

"He is what?"

"He told me this morning. He wants me—us—to own it with no connection to the Pipworth estate. So he is arranging it right now."

Violet's look narrowed, her voice pitching desperate. "No—you cannot let him—he's doing this only so he can close down the Revelry's Tempest."

Adalia's head snapped back slightly. Violet had been deeply wounded by her late husband's betrayals—and there were multiple—but Adalia hadn't realized how deep her mistrust of men had cut. "Violet, no. Toren would not do that. He has never once been dishonest with me—even when it would benefit him."

"Such as?"

"Well, he could have lied long ago, told me he loved me, and kept me in his bed, a willing and dutiful wife. But he couldn't. His honesty is irreproachable. He is even putting the house into a trust owned solely by me. Mine to do with as I see fit."

Violet looked down at her fine bone china, fingering the delicate handle of the cup. "You are positive of his intentions? You know I trust you, Adalia. You and Cass, and that is it."

"And I trust Toren. So yes, yes, I am positive."

Violet gave a slight shake of her chestnut hair. "Well then, I can only applaud you, Adalia. What did you do to make this happen—to make him want to buy this house?"

"Nothing." Lifting her cup to her lips, Adalia smirked. "Well…it is quite possible there was some tongue exploration involved."

Her friend laughed. "No, seriously." Her eyebrows arched, the elegant lines of her face turning grave. "Tell me you are not accepting less than you are worth, Adalia. Does he love you? Is that what he came to London to tell you?"

Adalia took a slow sip of her tea. "Not exactly. But before you admonish me for surrendering, I believe there is hope. I left Dellon Castle because I believed Toren could not love me—but last night—last night I saw a flicker of it in him. More than a flicker. Even if he didn't understand himself what it was he was feeling. I truly have hope that he can love me—that he can figure out what love is and embrace it. Even if he never admits to it."

"You are going to give him that chance?" Violet leaned in. "I know you, Adalia. I have since we were thirteen years old, giggling at old Mrs. Swanson and her swatting ruler. I had to watch your marriage to Lord Pipworth, how it crushed your heart. So I ask this with caution. Will ambiguity—especially where love is concerned—be enough for you?"

Violet's stare pierced into her, and Adalia resisted the urge to squirm. The problem with having such incredibly close friends was that they knew her far too well. But she wanted this—wanted Toren—and after what she had seen the previous night, she had to try.

And that didn't even take into account how quickly her defenses had fallen around him—she hadn't been able to resist touching him for more than ten minutes.

"I am not going to send Toren to his knees, begging, if that is what you think I need to do, Violet. I left him because I had no hope. But I believe, to my soul, that I saw it in him last night—enough to give me hope. And he cannot discover that he truly loves me if we are living separately." Adalia set down her cup. "I think he loves me, Violet. It is why he came to London. He wanted to shut this place down, yes, but he came here for me."

The skepticism heavy in Violet's blue eyes, she gave a half smile. "You are so adept at recognizing what others miss in people, Adalia. And you unfailingly want to see the best in everyone. I just pray your unique view is not clouded by misplaced hope in this instance."

Adalia sighed. It was a real possibility, whether she liked to admit it or not. "As do I."

"Well, if you are wrong about your duke—and I pray you are not—you must remember you will always have me and Cass and the twins." Violet's fingers flipped in a circle above her head. "And this place. This place will always keep you more than busy."

"It is more than enough." Adalia offered up the right words, even as she wasn't sure she meant them.

The door on the far end of the ballroom opened, and Mr. Walt stepped in, looking around. Spying Adalia and Violet, the butler walked across the deep expanse of the ballroom, his heels clicking evenly on the polished oak floors.

Adalia had hired Mr. Walt when she opened the Revelry's Tempest, as he was a man that adhered to the utmost in propriety. If she couldn't bring full respectability to the place, at least she could hire people with the veneer of it.

Mr. Walt stopped before them, one hand bent behind his back as he bowed to her with the silver salver balanced on his fingertips. "This just arrived for you, your grace, with an air of urgency."

One red-wax-sealed note sat in the middle of the gleaming silver.

She gave Mr. Walt a smile which he did not return. The man was stone—even more so than Toren. She plucked it from the salver. "Thank you, Mr. Walt."

Mr. Walt left them and Adalia pulled off her short gloves, careful not to rub the scabs forming on her left palm, and set them on the table. Her name on the front of the note, she flipped it, using her fingernail to crack the red seal she didn't recognize. She tapped the excess broken wax from the folded paper before opening it to beautifully shaped letters.

The note was short. Not signed.

*Question what you believe of your brother. Come to corner of Berwick and Broad Street for truth.*

Her brow furrowed.
*Brother?*

She ran over the cryptic line several times before flipping it to the back side to make sure it was addressed to her. It was.

She read the words again, noting the two odd absences of the word "the."

"What is it, Adalia? You are growing pale." Violet's eyes dipped to the paper and back to her face. "Your duke? Not good news?"

"I am not…" Her voice trailed off. *What you believe of your brother.* A chill snaked down her spine. Her brothers were dead. Buried. All of them. Who would even dare to besmirch their memory—to care about them in the slightest?

Adalia shook her head slowly, starting to rise. "I am not sure."

Violet gained her feet, grabbing Adalia's arm. "Wait, you do not look good at all, Adalia. Do I need to speak to your duke? Set him into the right? It is beyond the pale, but I will do it for you."

Adalia's eyes shot to Violet. "No. This is not about him." Toren. She needed to show this to him. "It—I am fine. But I do need to talk to my husband. You will excuse me?"

Without waiting for Violet to reply, Adalia rushed to the door of the drawing room and ran down the stairs. She skidded to a stop in the foyer at the sight of her guards in the parlor adjacent to the foyer, realizing she had no carriage handy. Toren had dropped her off much earlier, promising to be back with haste.

Where the hell was he? She needed to get to Berwick and Broad Street.

Just as she spun to go back up the stairs to tell Violet she was commandeering her carriage, Adalia caught sight through a window of Toren's carriage going past the townhouse. It didn't stop to let him out, so Adalia opened the front door to watch where it went.

The shiny black coach turned at the end of the block. The mews. Toren must need to speak to the stable master. Adalia slammed the front door closed and raced through the house to get to the back alleyway.

She had made it halfway through the rear gardens when Toren came through the back gate from the mews.

He jumped at seeing her running full force at him. A smile flashed, and then vanished as he realized what was on her face.

Panic. Pure, terrifying panic had taken a hold of her.

"Adalia—what—what has happened?"

She stumbled at the last second, falling into him and catching herself on his chest. His hands were instantly on her upper arms, bracing her from falling further.

She waved the note in his face. "This. This came, Toren."

His worried eyes didn't leave her face. "Adalia, you are near hysterics."

She shoved the piece of paper in front of his eyes. "Look at the note, Toren. Just look at it."

He stilled, reading the note. The paper between their faces, she couldn't see his reaction, but his fingers tightened, digging into her arm muscles before he abruptly released her and took a step backward.

Her hand dropped, the crinkled paper no longer between them.

Toren's face had gone impossibly indifferent. Cold.

She waved the note. "What could this be? Who would do this? About Caldwell? Alfred? Theo? Why?"

He didn't answer her—no reaction.

She stared at him, at the stiffness his body exuded, at the mask—void of any emotion—that had taken over his face. *Dammit.* No. Not now. Not when she needed him.

And then a possibility crept ever so slowly into her consciousness. "Wait—you understand—you know what this note is about, don't you?"

His brown eyes left her, his look going to the top of the tall evergreen hedge that lined the perimeter of the garden. "I had thought…there is no way out of it." Belying the mask of indifference he had erected, the words slipped, muttered, from his lips.

But Adalia heard. She heard perfectly clear.

"What? No way out of what? What are you not telling me, Toren?"

"I thought I could, but I can hide the truth no longer, Adalia. Not with your safety at stake."

His look dropped to her, his facade of detachment splintering, cracking in his brown eyes. That alone chilled her, her blood turning to ice, heavy in her veins.

"Truth?" Her whisper escaped, so soft she wasn't sure he heard her, and then he flinched.

"Theodore is alive."

"What?" The question came abrupt, loud from her lips, what she thought she heard so ridiculous she knew she had misunderstood.

"Your brother is alive, Adalia."

Her hands flew up, her palms blocking him. She couldn't have heard him correctly. She couldn't have.

Toren stepped toward her, his chest almost to her hands. His voice was low, a growl, forcing upon her what she didn't want to hear. Didn't want to believe. "Theodore is alive. He has been all along."

Her hands started to shake. "No. Stop. What you are saying—impossible—stop it, Toren."

He grabbed her wrists, the shaking in them so violent his own steady hands could not calm them. "He is alive, Adalia. We thought he was dead, but he is not. He was taken months ago and they are attempting to extract information from him."

"Alive?" She jerked her wrists from his grasp, jumping backward, her voice shrill. "They? Who is 'they'? No. No. No. You are mistaken. Theo died. And extract information? What does that mean? What information? What could he possibly have to talk about?"

"We are in the midst of war, Adalia." He took a cautious step toward her with his palms raised, attempting to calm the panic in her. "Theodore was not lost in Caribbean waters for the past two years. He was on the continent, an agent working for the crown. He has been all this time. The intelligence he has gathered is admirable. He manages a number of active spies infiltrating Napoleon's army. And he is extremely valuable. But once your eldest brother died, and the title was his, we have been attempting to bring him home. Yet he insisted…he insisted…month after month he refused to board a ship—there was always one more mission he had to complete. He—"

"What…what are you telling me? What…" Savage spikes of disbelief ravaged her body, sending her quivering, staggering backward.

Theo was alive.

And Toren knew.

He kept advancing, and she kept retreating through the lanes in the garden, her legs quickly failing her. Toren had known for months—months that Theo was alive.

Lied. Toren had lied for months.

And then it welled. A storm swirling in her gut, taking her breath. Tingles spiking up and down her arms. Sweat breaking along her brow.

She bumped into the corner of the evergreens, the needles pricking her bare neck.

"Adalia…"

She spun, curling over as she vomited, losing all control of her body. Trembling uncontrollably, she bent, unable to stop the heaves, stop the horror of what Toren was trying to tell her.

His hand on her back, stroking her spine didn't surprise her. Not that she could stand his touch at the moment, but she was incapable of removing herself from him.

Minutes passed where she gasped for breath, bent over, her fingers gripping her thighs as she fought to not collapse to the ground. She stared at the black hem of her muslin dress.

Theo was alive.

He was alive and she was in black mourning because he was dead. Toren had lied to her. She blinked hard, the black muslin blurring before her eyes. What sort of hell had just happened?

A silver flask in Toren's hand appeared in front of her, the stopper already removed. Where he had produced it from, she didn't know, but she took, taking a quick swallow and swishing it around her mouth. Brandy. It stung, yet she held it in her mouth for seconds, the sharp pain grounding her to the moment at hand.

She spit the liquid out, now so far past the devastating embarrassment of upending her stomach in the corner of the garden that spitting seemed like the least of her worries.

Without looking up or uncurling, she held the flask out for Toren to take it. He did so, and her hand dropped to brace against her knee once more.

Breathe. She had to get a full breath into her lungs. She sucked air. It got no further than the base of her throat.

His hand settled onto her back again. "I am sorry, Adalia. I know it is a shock that Theodore is alive."

"Don't touch me." His words spurred her body into sudden action, sending a solidifying burst of energy into her legs. She stumbled to the side, out of his reach, pulling herself upright. Or at least partially upright. She still needed to curl her belly around her forearms. But she managed to look up at him, her eyes piercing him. "Who are you? How do you even know this?"

His hands lifted, presumably to steady her. She stepped backward, running into the evergreen hedge. She didn't need to be steadied. She needed answers.

He froze, his hands poised in midair. "I know because Theodore works for me. At least while we are at war. I head one of the many bands of crown agents. My title does not allow me to participate past English soil, but I can strategize, wield the power of the ducal title and reserves as needed. And I am effective at the work because I hold no emotion. I merely do what is necessary."

His voice low—they were standing in the middle of the garden and not in the privacy of the townhouse—his words came fast. He took the slightest step forward, his hands still in the air. "This note—it is proof. I am positive now Theodore was the reason there were attempts to steal the girls—to use them to get Theodore to talk. I suspected as much when you first came to me, but then the threat of Mr. Trether made me question everything. But this note—it is them. There is no doubt."

"But the man at Dellington—he gave you Mr. Trether's name."

"They know all about you, Adalia, all of your dealings, and they merely used Mr. Trether to deflect suspicion. Theodore has war secrets—he knows at least half of our spies currently in their country. They are trying to break him—and they will not stop at stealing a little girl—or you—to get him to talk. They were the ones that tried to take both Mary and Josalyn—not Mr. Trether. That is what the note is about, Adalia. They are attempting to lure you to a place where they can take you."

"Where is he?"

A pained look flashed across Toren's face. "We don't know where they are. Somewhere outside of London, within a day's ride, but we have not located them yet. We were close once, but they had a half-day's start on us. We are doing everything we can to find him, Adalia. Everything."

Her eyes closed as his words washed over her, numb in her ears.

Theo was alive—and a spy—and a prisoner.

And her husband knew. Knew the whole time. A stranger. She was listening to a stranger. A stranger that had lied to her.

Her eyes cracked open to him. "You lied to me? This whole time? The whole time we were married—before we were married." Her hand went to her forehead, attempting to hold in the thousands of thoughts flying like rabid bees in her head, swelling into a swarm. "What else did you lie to me about, Toren? Oh, hell, you came here for me—you made me think you cared for me—and you don't. This is all part of your plot to keep your secrets safe."

"Don't you dare say that, Adalia. I came here for—"

"For what? This whole time for what?" Her fingers moved up from her forehead, digging into her hair.

His jaw twitched to the side, his ire starting to rise against her own.

He took a full step toward her, bearing over her, his voice a hiss. "There is no plot, Adalia. The only plot I have is to keep you and the girls safe. And if you are too obstinate to see that—"

"How could you lie to me—about his body—about his *death*, Toren?"

That made him pause. He leaned back slightly. "When I first did, I did not think on it—honestly. You didn't need to know. And you were so distraught about the twins I knew it was better if you believed him to be dead."

"Better for who?"

"For you. For Theodore. For all of us."

"You told me he was dead—*beaten to death. Not whole.* You told me you had him buried. What did I visit at

Glenhaven? Whose gravestone did I cry against? Whose dirt did my fingers rip from the ground?"

His face went steely. "No one. No one is buried at his gravesite. Not yet…"

"What?" Her voice shot into a shriek. Damn to hell anyone who was listening.

She had lost all ability to be discreet. Her dead brother was alive. The man she had fallen in love with had lied to her about that very thing—and who knows what else. And now he was talking about burying Theo again.

The churning in her stomach started again. She bit back bile.

"I apologize." Toren's head shook. "I should not have said that. I still have hopes that we can locate him."

"Locate him?" Wetness hit her cheeks, tears she didn't even know she cried streaming. "Wait—we can still find him, can we not? I—I can help."

Toren stilled, suspicion thick in his look. "No, you cannot, Adalia. You cannot and you will not."

"I can—you said they were after the twins to try and make him talk—so they would take me just as easily as one of the girls." She wiped her face and then grabbed his arm, tugging it. "That was what the note was about—you said so yourself. If they took me then that would lead you to them."

His hands curled into instant fists, the muscles in his arm going impossibly hard under her fingers. His voice dropped to a dangerous growl, each word ground out between gritted teeth. "Dammit, Adalia, you are not bait— do not even suggest such a blasphemous idea."

"No? Why not? This is my brother, Toren. If there is a chance that Theo is alive I will do anything within my power to help him."

"Do you even know what they would do to you, Adalia?" His mouth had pulled back into a furious line. "How they would use you to make him talk?"

She blanched with a quick breath. "Torture?" Her hands fell from his arm, wrapping across her stomach.

"You cannot even imagine what these men are capable of, Adalia."

Her head shook slowly as she tried to imagine just what they could do to her. The picture in her mind was not pretty. And if they would do that to her…

Her look jumped to Toren. "So what are they doing to Theo right now, Toren? You said yourself they were trying to make him talk—just how are they doing that?"

His lips drew inward, refusing to answer her.

"Exactly. Torture. I cannot stand by in a safe cocoon while they are doing that to Theo." Her eyes narrowed at him. "But you wouldn't understand—you have no idea of what I'm feeling—what I would do to save him. Because you were right—you have no concept of love."

He winced. Her blow piercing its target.

The line of his jaw pulsating, it took a long second for him to answer. "You think I can't imagine what I would do for someone I loved?"

"No." Her lip snarled, her chest expanding, wanting to expel all of the hurt, all of the pain that had just consumed her. "You will never understand love, Toren. Never. If you did, you never would have lied to me. And I would be on that street corner, inviting an abduction at this very moment in order to get to Theo—whatever it takes."

"You are not going to be used as bait, Adalia."

"You cannot stop me." She spun from him, moving toward the back gate of the garden.

Three steps, and he grabbed her arm, twisting her back to him, his anger palatable. "I damn well can, and we both know it, Adalia. Do not make me have to do it in a way that we both will regret—because, make no mistake, I refuse to let you put yourself in the way of harm. So you can stop the idiocy running through your mind this instant. I don't give a damn about what you think you must do, because you aren't going to do it."

She heaved a breath, stewing, her eyes whipping daggers at him. She should have been faster. Should have run. Damn him. "Were you ever going to tell me about Theo?"

"Yes. No."

"Blast it, Toren, that is not an answer."

His hand on her upper arm refused to loosen. "Yes, I was going to tell you after we found him alive."

"And the 'no'?"

"No, I never would have told you if we were too late in finding him and he had been killed. There would have been no purpose to tell you. I would have quietly had his body interred into the gravesite at Glenhaven."

"And I would have been none the wiser to the fact." Her heart contracted, so much so, she knew a piece of it was dying. Her fingers lifted to her mouth, pressing on her lips, her words eerily quiet. "You were just going to let me think, for the rest of my life, that Theo died in the rookeries."

"Correct."

She looked down to his hand gripping her arm, her voice calm. "I need you to leave, Toren."

"You can go inside and I will wait for you in the study. That is all I will allow. We are leaving for Dellon Castle this afternoon, Adalia."

"No." The yell echoed up against the brick of the surrounding townhouses as she twisted violently, yanking her arm. He didn't let her escape. "I need you to leave. Leave my life. Leave me alone. Leave me. I don't want to see you. Don't want to hear your voice. Don't want your hands anywhere near me, Toren."

"I am not leaving you here in London, Adalia. We are going back to the castle."

With all her weight she shoved off from him, ripping her arm from his grasp. "I am not going anywhere with you, you bloody liar."

He stood, hands twitching to grab her, heaving a sigh as he shook his head. "I don't want to do this as I am about to, Adalia, but I cannot trust you and I need you safe."

"What?" Her hands flew up, palms to the sky. "What the devil could you possibly do to me now?" She spun before he answered, stomping toward the rear door of the townhouse.

Her feet left the ground in a whoosh, her body twisting in the air until his shoulder jammed into her stomach. It stole her breath for a moment, and Toren was through the back gate to the mews before she comprehended that he had actually thrown her over his shoulder.

She beat at his back with the one fist she managed to free. "Of all the blasted, high-handed, moronic,

Neanderthal things to do—every insult I ever hurled at you was true, you pious ogre. You infuriating, tyrannical—"

Her words cut off as he tossed her into his carriage still waiting by the mews. He was in, slamming the door of the coach before she could right herself on the bench.

The carriage lurched forward. She slipped off what little balance she had gained. Two sharp turns that stretched the capacity of the coach's springs, and they were a full block away from the townhouse before she managed to sit upright.

Centering her look on Toren, the well of insults had only just begun. She opened her mouth.

"Do not test me, Adalia."

Her mouth clamped shut.

He was right. She needed to be quiet. Needed to conserve her energy. Needed to strategize.

For she couldn't figure out how to escape Toren and find Theo if she was too busy yelling at her husband.

The fiend probably planned that as well.

She sat, arms crossed over her chest, refusing to look at Toren for two hours. Through the London streets, past the outskirts of tiny cottages and into the countryside. She couldn't bear to acknowledge his presence.

Nor did he attempt to make her.

Still stuck deep in stewing, Adalia at first didn't realize that the carriage had begun to tip. Gradually, heavy in the fall, the center of gravity shifted beneath her so slowly that by the time she knew what was happening, she was helpless to do anything about it.

Toren had no such problem.

He launched himself across the carriage, grabbing her, wrapping her into his chest just before her body flew off the bench, weightless in the air for a moment.

The embankment was steep—she had seen that out the window as they had turned onto this road. And the last thought she had before Toren shielded her head, blocking all sight of everything but his black coat, was that this was going to be painful.

The weightlessness lasted only a moment, and their bodies hit the side of the carriage, tossed from wall to floor to roof to wall as the coach rolled over and over. His grip not faltering, Toren blocked her from the blows the entire way down.

The last crash, deafening.

And then nothing. Silence. Splintering wood creaking. Silence.

Toren's arm around the back of her head went slack, and she shifted. Instant, bruising pain invaded every muscle.

If she was in that much pain—Toren had to be pulverized from head to toe. And he was still. So very still.

*No. Heaven no. Please.*

Fear gripping her, she forced herself to move. Wedged against one of the carriage benches, she lifted her head awkwardly to find his face, only to see blood creasing his brow, his eyes closed.

Before she could even poke him, reach her hand up to his face, wood creaked above her.

The coach door. She could hear it being yanked open above her head. Their driver. He could help.

She tried to twist, looking up.

A figure blocked the daylight from above. A man she didn't recognize.

"Aye, she be movin'. Hold me leg."

The man rustled above her. Adalia squinted, trying to see who it was, trying to untangle herself from Toren's limbs enough to turn fully upward.

"We be watchin' ye, lil mouse." A burly hand came down at her.

She realized just before his thick fingers wrapped around her head what he intended.

Her head slammed into the wood of the bench.

The world went blank.

# { CHAPTER 19 }

He could still feel her body on top of him. As long as Adalia's body was on his—safe—he could stay in the darkness. Just a minute more.

His arm moved.

The sensation odd, as he hadn't moved it. Had he?

His arm flopped wildly.

Shaking. Someone was shaking his arm.

Adalia?

He focused on his chest. It was cold. The space in front of him where she had been—cold. She wasn't on top of him.

His arm shook again.

Against the weight of blackness that fought to stay in his mind, Toren cracked his eyes open. It took a long moment to focus on the person above him. A person straddling him. Awkward.

What was around him? The coach. He was still in the coach, flattened against the inside of the crushed vehicle.

"Adalia?"

"Sir?"

"Adalia? Where?"

"Sir. Ye are awake? Yer driver be sittin' near."

Toren reached up, grabbing at the sleeve he could see swinging above his head. He forced himself to focus on the man above him. "My wife?"

The man, thin, wore farmer's clothes and looked down at him, bewildered. "There be no lady here, sir."

Toren pushed off the side of the carriage to sit upright. Pain sliced down his back and around his side. A rib, probably two out of place.

Light as a feather, the man hauled himself upward out of the carriage door opening above Toren.

Brutal pangs lancing through him with the slightest movement, Toren bore down, shoving all pain to the deep recess of his mind. He didn't have time for pain. Not when he didn't know where Adalia was.

He crawled up the broken interior of the coach, following the farmer up and out with not nearly as much grace. Dropping heavily onto the ground next to the overturned carriage, Toren looked up the embankment. Steep. The coach must have rolled at least four times on the way down.

The farmer bent, balancing on his haunches next to where Toren sat. "Ye ain't lookin' well, sir."

Some semblance of coherent thought finally firing through his brain, Toren grabbed the farmer by the back of the neck. "Where the hell is my wife?" He looked around, screaming into the oncoming darkness. "Adalia."

"It is just ye here, sir. Ye and yer driver."

"Adalia." His voice thundered over the cacophony of birds at dusk.

Mr. Benson staggered around the end of the coach. His driver looked worse than Toren felt, blood covering half his face. "I only just awoke, your grace. And she is not here. We were run off the road, your grace." Leaning against the upturned step of the coach, Mr. Benson glanced at the farmer and then looked back to Toren. "There are tracks."

"What kind of tracks?"

"Two men. Two horses. Down here by the carriage. And this, your grace, stuck on a shard of the carriage." Mr. Benson tossed a balled up cloth at Toren.

Toren caught it with one hand and unfurled it. A sleeve. The black sleeve of Adalia's dress. Torn. A waft of blood hit his nose. He dropped the cloth to the ground, nodding to Mr. Benson as his entire body pulled itself into steely efficiency. "You know what to do."

"Yes, your grace."

Toren hauled himself to his feet as his look swung to the farmer.

"Do you have a lantern, man? A torch?"

"I have a lantern on my wagon."

"I am taking it. Get it now."

The man turned and started to run up the side of the grassy hill next to the road. Within a minute, he was back to Toren, the lit lantern swinging as he handed it over.

"Horses. We need horses," Toren said to the farmer.

"Yes, sir." A bob of his head and the farmer scampered to the hill.

Toren stalked over to his driver, holding the lantern by his head. Mr. Benson shuffled along the ground on his hands and knees, his fingers over the upturned dirt.

"Do you have it, Benson?"

Mr. Benson looked up at Toren. "Yes, your grace. I believe I do."

"We move."

~~~

Breaking through the crust that had formed along her lashes, Adalia opened her eyes.

The bright light of flames across the floor assaulted her pupils. It took a long minute for her eyes to adjust to the glow.

A dirt floor. No. A stone floor covered in dirt. A fire.

The smell, dank and putrid of death, seeped into her brain from the floor her cheek was pressed against.

Haltingly, her senses came back to her, filling her mind, identifying just where and how she had landed.

The last thing she remembered was the carriage rolling down the bank of the road, her body wrapped in Toren's arms and legs as they were tossed about the interior of the coach.

And then they had landed. Landed and what…

The man. The man that knocked her head into the bench.

And Toren—he was still. Not moving.

Panic seized her chest. No. He was fine. He had to be fine. He would not leave her. Would not die. He had sworn as much to her. Said he would always protect her.

He couldn't have died. No.

He had to take care of the twins.

She gasped a breath, trying to calm her panic.

Where in the bloody hell was she?

Lying on her side, on the floor, she tried to move. Pain shot down her arms, all her movement denied. Blast it. Her arms were stretched high above her head, her wrists tied together around a wooden leg. She craned her head up between her arms. The leg was attached to a table. A beastly

thick table above her. And the sleeve of her left arm was
missing.

Every muscle aching, her head now pounding, she tried
to pull her legs upward. No. They were not moving either.
She looked down her body to find her ankles tied to the far
wooden leg of the table.

Stretched out like a pig to be roasted.

Aside from the missing sleeve, her clothes were still
intact. Thank the heavens for that.

"Look. The mousey moves."

Her head tilted, her eyes following the sound of the
rough voice.

Twisting her neck along her arm, she searched
the room, and her eyes finally adjusted well enough to
see. Vaulted ceilings, the stone of them crumbling and
pockmarked with time. She was deep in the undercroft of
an ancient castle or abbey.

She saw the boots first, worn, moving across the floor
toward her. And just behind them, someone else.

Theo.

Her sharp intake of breath cut through the dank air.

Theo sat across from her next to the fireplace, tied
to a chair, bare from his waist up, not conscious. Blood
splattered his body. Cuts, lines of flesh boiling—singed. His
dark blond hair hung past his face in long locks—clumps
of muck meshing the strands together. His jaw looked
wrong—crushed in on the left side. She stared at his chest,
willing it to move. They wouldn't have brought her here to
him if he was dead, would they?

No. Impossible.

She stared longer, her eyes drying out. Breathe, dammit. Breathe.

A flicker of a movement. The tiniest of breaths.

The boots stopped in front of her face, interrupting her view of her brother. Adalia wiggled, trying to crane her neck so she could see past the boots.

The man attached to the boots dropped to his haunches, fully blocking Theo from her sight. The bastard poked at her cheek. "Your brother is sleeping again." His gravelly voice sliced into her ears, making the pounding in her head intensify. "Never knew one to fall to blackness as much because of the pain. A mite weak, that one."

Instant indignation flared through her, the need to defend her brother's character instinctive and seemingly ignorant of the fact that she was also tied up and at the mercy of the man in front of her.

Her eyes dropped to the floor between them, concentrating on the ridge of dirt made by his boots. This wasn't the man that had gone after her in the wagon. This one was more refined, his accent odd, English not his native language.

"Watch him carefully, mouse." The man's thumb pointed back over his shoulder to Theo. "You will be needing to speak to him when his senses come back about him."

Talk to him? Talk to him about what? About how he was alive? Not dead? She still had not wrapped her mind around the thought—even if Theo was currently sitting across from her. Beaten to grotesqueness, but still there. Still alive. Still breathing.

The man stood, his boots spinning in the dirt before her eyes. He walked back across the room, stopping by the hearth to pick up an iron poker and then nudge the tip of it into the fire.

Her look drifted to Theo. The horror that he had lived through the past months was evident all over his body. But still alive—a miracle. Or hell on earth. They were keeping him alive for a reason, and she didn't imagine that bastard by the fire wanted her to have a pleasant chat with Theo about the weather.

The fat leg of the table wedged between her forearms, she twisted her wrists with as little movement as possible, testing the knot of the rope binding her hands together.

Tight. And every shift of her hands made the ropes dig into her skin. She turned her attention to her legs. Her boots were gone, the rope looped around her ankles, holding her legs together. She bent her left knee, trying to wiggle her foot free. The rope didn't budge.

A scream—tortured and curdling—echoed in the stone chamber.

Her look whipped to Theo. Wide awake, he was frantic, pain rolling across his face.

Then she saw it. Skin still sizzling on his chest. Flesh bubbling. The poker the man had been tending the fire with was raised in front of Theo, still glowing red.

The putrid smell of burning flesh hit her nose, making her gag.

Theo's eyes landed on her. He stared at her for a long moment. Too long. And then recognition hit him. Hit him with a blast that sent his head shaking, sudden tears streaming down his face.

"No, Theo. No." Words failed her as she yanked on her limbs, desperate to free herself, to go to him and hold him, take away his pain.

His breathing going rapid, Theo's arms strained against the ropes holding him captive to the chair and he looked up at the man that had turned back to the fire, shoving the tip of the iron poker into the blue of the flames.

"No…" The one word came from Theo's lips, strangled as though he hadn't spoken in weeks.

The man at the fire looked to Theo. "We had hoped for one of your wee nieces, but your sister will do nicely."

Adalia's mouth went instantly dry, brutal terror coiling down her spine and invading her body. The world slowing, disbelief seized her, his words flooding her mind—she would do nicely.

The man took a step backward, pulling the poker from the fire. He looked at it with a nod, its black tip glowing a molten orange-red.

No. He couldn't mean.

Holding the poker tip in front of him, he brushed it in front of Theo's eyes—close—but not close enough to burn. A taunt. And then he continued across the room to her.

*No.*

His boots edged closer.

*No.*

Her eyes could go nowhere but at the waning glow at the tip of the poker.

"You know exactly how this feels, dung heap. Now your sister will feel the brunt of your pain."

"No." The choked word came from Theo.

Adalia's look flicked desperately to her brother. He could barely keep his head up. Yet he fought it. Fought the pain. He had suffered beyond what anyone should have to suffer for whatever he had refused to tell this man during the past months. And now she would be the end of it.

Theo would do anything to save her, and she knew it.

Her eyes flew around the room, desperate for anything to help her escape. The table atop of her. Maybe if she could yank a leg out, the table would fall. It would crush her, yes, but Theo would not be forced to make an impossible decision.

"You say no, yet I don't hear you talking, dung heap." The bastard's gravelly voice stayed even, almost bored with the idea of sizzling away Adalia's flesh.

She yanked as hard as she could on her arms, pulling the leg. Nothing. Not the slightest creak of the wood. She jerked up on her legs. The same result.

The bastard took his last steps to Adalia, stopping in front of her. He turned himself slightly to the side, giving Theo a full view of the red-hot poker hovering above his sister.

"No."

"No, what, dung heap?"

The bastard lowered the poker in front of her face and then close to her neck. Heat radiated from the tip, near to burning her bare skin by mere proximity.

Her neck open and vulnerable, she twisted, a trapped animal frantic to escape, a whimper stuck in her throat. Frantic and helpless.

"Are you going to tell me before I burn her perfect skin? Or after you have heard her tortured screams?"

The poker dipped closer. The tiny hairs along her neck crisped, burning, the smell making her retch.

"No. Don't." The garbled words came out of Theo in a cough.

The bastard looked down at her, a vicious smile snarling his lip.

He was going to enjoy this.

Adalia gasped a breath, bracing herself, her eyes closing against the horror of the iron near to searing into her flesh.

A whoosh of air. Metal clanking.

Embers sparked down onto her neck as the poker went flying through the air. Her eyes flew open with her scream at the sharp pain, even as the embers quickly fizzled on her skin.

The poker sailed through the air, clattering down to the stone in front of her. Shouts, screams—a scuffle that had two men struggling fiercely for control, until the bastard trying to burn her was flipped onto his back.

A fury of fist after fist came down upon the man, blood splattering, until his head fell to the side, his body motionless.

The man on top of the bastard stilled, looking over at her.

Toren.

His brown eyes savage, the ferocity of his face, his body, made her heart stop. A second that seemed like a lifetime. It wasn't until he moved that her body jolted into motion again.

He was to her in an instant, a knife pulled and cutting through the ropes at her feet and wrists within seconds.

He paused as she drew her limbs inward, curling against the pain coursing through her muscles after the unnatural stretch they had been in. She could feel him watching her. But she was fine. Fine. Or she would be in a moment.

"Toren—Theo, get him." She managed to grit out through the pain.

"Can you walk? We have to get out of here—Benson has two upstairs he is holding off."

"Get Theo."

Her words barked and Toren finally jumped from her side. "Yes."

He ran to Theo and started sawing through the ropes holding her brother to the chair.

Adalia rolled onto her back, staring at the rough underside of the table, bearing down against the pain of blood rushing into her limbs.

A clank sounded next to her, cutting through the heaving breaths she was taking. The poker lifted from the ground.

The bastard had woken up and grabbed the iron. The tip raised high to swing, he was headed straight for Toren's back.

For one instant, Adalia's world stopped.

*Not Toren.* She could not lose him. And even if she screamed out, the bastard was too close and Toren would only turn into the swing of the poker at his face.

She had nothing. No knife. No gun.

Nothing but her body. She could stop him for only a moment, but it would have to be enough.

Scrambling to her feet, pain ravaging her every movement, she lunged, diving low, ramming herself into the back of the bastard's legs.

He grunted as they both toppled forward, the poker flying out of his hand.

She hit the stone floor, rolling, just as Toren turned from Theo, knife high in his hand.

By the time she stopped rolling, knocking into Theo's bare feet, Toren was standing over the bastard, knife bloody.

The man wasn't moving. Dead, she hoped.

Her look lifted to Toren, and he was staring at her with a strange mixture of wonderment and rage in his eyes. And then he grinned. Pure, unadulterated pride beaming in his look. "Well done, Adalia."

She nodded, unable to speak, her body still moving purely on instinct.

His eyes darkened. "But do not ever dare to do something so foolish again." He nodded to Theo. "Let us remove ourselves."

Slitting the last rope free from Theo's ankle, Toren slid his arm around her brother's back, lifting him from the chair. At standing, her brother instantly swayed, and she could see Toren take almost all of Theo's weight as his own.

Not that there was much left of Theo. Her brother was tall, but the skin she could see through the blood and wounds hung loosely from his bones.

Within a minute, they were up a tiny circular stone staircase and moving out into the daylight.

Her hand lifted to cover her eyes from the bright early morning light. She shook her head, slightly confused at how time had moved to morning. She had to have been unconscious for some time.

Mr. Benson rushed toward them, quickly wrapping his arm around Theo to support the other side of him.

"The others?" Toren demanded over the top of Theo's slack head.

"Taken care of. But I do not recommend we stay in the area," Mr. Benson said.

Both men supporting her brother, they started moving along an overgrown lane leading from the side of the castle toward a line of trees. "Adalia, your feet—can you walk out here?"

She looked down. Bare feet. She had forgotten she lost her boots and stockings. The dewy grass cold against her toes, she nevertheless nodded. "Yes. Nothing has hurt them yet."

"Grab the reins of the horses." Toren flicked his head to the two horses tied a few steps into the forest by the trail they were walking toward. "The road is only a quarter mile ahead. It will be easier if we don't have to balance Theodore on a horse."

Adalia ran ahead, untying the leather straps from the low-slung branches. Waking them, she tugged the horses to follow Toren, Theo, and Mr. Benson.

Rogue sticks poking into the soles of her feet, Adalia bit back a blasphemy at each prick shooting up her leg. She would never complain about pain again. Not after that. Not after seeing what Theo had been through.

Unimaginable pain.

In front of her, she watched the limp rolling of her brother's head as Mr. Benson and Toren carried him forward. He was awake, grasping at threads of consciousness, but her brother could not even hold his head up.

Unimaginable pain. But he was alive. Alive.

She just prayed his soul had somehow survived the last three months as well.

The trees thinned as they approached the road and within minutes of walking, a man and a wagon crested the hill before them.

Toren waved him down. "You. We need your wagon."

Hay piled low in the back of his wagon, the farmer slowed, his grey donkey coming to a lazy stop.

Adalia stepped up beside her husband, poking him in the ribs. "You cannot just take someone's wagon, Toren."

Toren glanced down at her, his eyebrows arched as though the thought was novel. He gave a slight shrug, glancing to his driver. "Benson?"

Shifting Theo's weight onto his one arm, Mr. Benson awkwardly fished out a heavy sack of coins from the inside of his black coat. He tossed it up to the farmer.

Squeezing the pouch, the farmer heard the coins clinking and a toothless smile broke onto his face. "It be yers, sir." He jumped off the driver's bench and with a tilt of his worn cap, he turned and walked away in the direction he had come from.

"Let us get Theodore in the back on the hay," Toren said, and he and Mr. Benson walked Theo to the rear of the wagon, lifting him up onto the flat boards. Stripping off his coat, Mr. Benson jumped up onto the bed of the wagon, laying the coat down and then dragging Theo forward until his entire body was splayed on the coat and hay.

Toren turned to Adalia to take the leather reins of the horses.

Through the fog she was still in, she felt his knuckles brush the back of her hand and it sent a shock up her arm. Her eyes lifted slowly, almost afraid to meet his eyes in case she was dreaming and he was about to dissipate to the wind.

His chin. Dark stubble along it. His lips. A cut along the bottom left.

She held her breath.

His eyes. The warmest brown, tender in the midst of the rage that still pulsated under his skin.

Real. He was real.

"You…you didn't die. I feared…" She could only now utter the words that had been stuck in her chest since he had appeared in the bowels of that castle.

His free hand lifted, settling against her neck, his fingertips pressing into the muscles along the base of her hair. "No. I didn't die. You do not curse those around you, Adalia."

She blinked hard, still afraid to believe he was alive and in front of her. Maybe he was right. Maybe she didn't curse those around her. "And you found me."

His eyes closed to her. He visibly swallowed, his head shaking. It was a long breath before he opened his eyes and met her look fully. "I did. I will always find you. Always protect you, Adalia. I swore that. For that alone I will live through anything."

She nodded, her chest swelling. In spite of all his idiocy—his lies—she loved this man. Loved him fully, unconditionally, and she knew she would until the day she died.

A slight grin lifted the side of his mouth. "Though I must give due credit, Adalia. I did not technically find you. Mr. Benson did."

"Mr. Benson?" She leaned to the side, looking at Mr. Benson still getting Theo's limbs comfortable on the bed of hay. It appeared as though her brother had lost consciousness again.

"Benson is one of the crown's preeminent trackers. I borrowed him when I learned you were in London. He shadowed you until I arrived. He was going to accompany us back to Dellon Castle."

"Yes." She nodded, Mr. Benson's face registering. "I recognize you from the Revelry's Tempest."

Lifting one of Theo's legs, the ragged shreds of her brother's trousers tangling in his fingers, Mr. Benson glanced up at her, tilting his head. "That you do, your grace. Pleased to be of service."

She looked up at Toren. "I wondered why Mr. Beal was not driving the carriage last night."

"I left him at the castle. He is teaching the girls about how he trains the horses."

"Why on earth?"

"Mary wants to learn how to drive a carriage."

Adalia chuckled. "She is about ten years and a quarter of the weight she needs to do that properly."

"Yes. But she can learn. And whatever those two want to learn, I am going to move heaven and earth to teach them."

Adalia smiled, her thumping heart expanding hard in her chest.

Toren motioned to the wagon. "Where do you want to ride, Adalia? On the bench or the back?"

She glanced at her brother and then looked up at him. "I want you—no—I need you, Toren. You. I need you holding me."

"Then I bow to your needs." He nodded, a glow sparking in his brown eyes. "We will ride in back together with Theo."

"I think that best."

His hand dropped from her neck and he moved to tie the horses onto the wagon, but she stopped him before he escaped her, her hand going up to his cheek, turning his face toward her. "Before I forget to argue over your latest edict, you should know that I will foolishly tackle a thousand men for you, Toren, whether you wish it or not. Do you understand there is nothing I would not do for you?"

He stared down at her, his brown eyes piercing her. The twitch of his cheek under her hand said volumes. But then he sighed. "I know it, Adalia. I know it full well."

"Good." Her hand dropped from his face and she motioned to the wagon. "Then let us make our way home."

# { CHAPTER 20 }

Pleasantries with the Earl of Bayton satisfied for the evening, Toren sipped from a thick cut glass, watching the fire in the guest quarters.

The brandy slid down his throat slowly, fighting past the clenched muscles along his neck. That his hands were not shaking at this point was a miracle.

He had almost lost her.

He leaned forward, his hand gripping the heavy oak mantel above the hearth to steady himself.

Even now, even though his wife was physically safe, he quite possibly *had* lost her for his actions the day before. For the months of lies.

But she had needed him above everything else after being strung up in the undercroft of that abandoned castle.

*She needed him.*

He clung to that wisp of hope. Adalia had been overwhelmed, he knew that. The entire wagon ride, she had needed him to hold her because of it. Her fingers clutching her brother's hand, she watched Theodore like a hawk, ignoring how her own body shook, the reality of what had happened to her manifesting in her uncontrolled tremors.

And he had held her. Happily. Gratefully. For there had been moments in the last twenty-four hours when he had thought he would never get the chance to again.

Those moments had nearly destroyed his soul.

Mr. Benson had driven the wagon to the nearest haven Toren could think of, Lord Bayton's Berkshire estate.

Theodore needed a surgeon, and he needed it sooner rather than later. In residence, Lord Bayton was happy to welcome them under the circumstances.

Toren knew Adalia would have been more comfortable getting as quickly as possible to Dellon Castle, and they would travel onward to there once they could properly move Theodore.

He guessed he would have a fight on his hands with Theodore to get him to remain at Dellon Castle for the immediate future, but Toren wasn't about to chance someone else coming after him or Adalia or the twins. So there they would remain until this bloody war was over.

The door opened, and his wife walked into the questionably appointed room. Decorated in cherubs and soft pastels, it was the furthest thing from his taste—but he wasn't about to complain. Lord Bayton was one of the few men in parliament that actually had the ability to practice discretion, and Toren didn't want a soul to know of their whereabouts. Not to mention the man knew his horseflesh.

"How is your brother?" He set the glass of brandy onto the mantel and walked across the room to her. Her left hand had been rewrapped after the scabs from the glass had reopened, and she had changed into a simple, yellow muslin dress a maid had procured. Touches of pink had also returned to her ashen face since he had left her with Theodore a half hour before.

Progress.

"Sleeping, mercifully." She sighed, exhaustion lacing her breath. "I thought he would lose consciousness when they set all those bones. I needed him to, but he didn't. I don't know how he suffered it."

"Theodore has always been strong."

She nodded, rubbing the back of her neck, rolling her head to stretch her muscles. He had seen how stretched out she had been tied up, and imagined the aches in her own muscles and limbs were screaming. He stepped around her, brushing her hair to the side and slipping the pads of his thumbs up and down the muscles of her neck and shoulders.

Her eyes closed and her body leaned into him, near purring within seconds.

More progress.

Her face dipped downward to stretch the lines of her neck as his fingers kneaded through the tightness. "Will the girls be safe, Toren? I am worried."

"Josalyn and Mary are no longer valuable as a device to make your brother talk, so yes, they are even safer than they were a day ago. And the war will end eventually, sooner if all goes well with Wellington's plans. After that, hiding them away will not be necessary. But you know I will take every precaution until that time."

"I do." She took a deep breath. "I want to be back with them."

"We will leave tomorrow if we can find a suitable, well-sprung enclosed wagon to carry your brother laid out. Even at that, I feel we should not move him until he heals more, but that could take weeks, and I prefer the safety of Dellon Castle."

"As do I." She nodded. "So we are safe?"

"Yes."

She stepped away, turning to face him. "Good. Then I can currently be irate with you."

"Irate?" Toren blinked hard. His wife was purring a moment ago, and now she was irate? He deviously grinned—purely manipulative. He would use whatever means necessary to veer her off whatever irate course she was determined to follow. "I do not think irate is allowed. Not now."

"Yes, now." Her hands went onto her hips. "Your lies. Potatoes."

"Pota—what?"

"Potatoes. You tossed me over your shoulder like a sack of potatoes, Toren." She thwapped his shoulder. "Your blasted shoulder. Like I was nothing. Like I was a…a… thing. A sack of potatoes you bought at the market."

"Ah…"

Her head shook, her lips pursing as her green eyes skewered him. "Overbearing tyrant."

"At least you dropped the 'fiend.'" His head cocked to the side with a wry smile.

She was not amused. "Fiend" would be added back to the insult if he did not step carefully around his next words.

He sighed, his hand rubbing against his forehead. "I have no defense, Adalia. I did toss you about like a sack of potatoes. In that moment in the garden, all I could think of was keeping you safe—safe from yourself. I had no idea where you were going—what you were about to do. The need exploded so brutally in me that I was blinded to everything except getting you out of there—getting you out of London before you did something stupid."

He shrugged. "So, yes, I was tyrannical. I apologize for that. But at the same time I cannot profess that I would have done anything differently. Anything to keep you

safe means *anything,* Adalia. Even throwing you over my
shoulder if that is what is necessary. Even if it means I have
to face down the look you are currently giving me."

Her hands slipped from her hips, her arms crossing
over her ribcage. "And the lies? The lies were not a sudden
uncontrollable urge, Toren. They were premeditated. You
lied to me for months—months—about Theo." Her voice
had gone soft, near to cracking.

Toss her about, and she was mad—but this, this had
caused real hurt. A wound that she attempted to cover with
a veil of anger, but it was there, plain as day.

The lies were trickier, for he had no defense. He had
hauled her away from London to protect her from her own
idiocy. But the lies. The lies about Theodore's death were all
of his own making.

Mercy. The only thing he had left was to ask for mercy.
Beg if necessary. "I cannot defend the lie, for when I did so,
it was entirely for my own benefit, and I thought nothing of
it. But you are well aware of that, aren't you, Adalia?"

She nodded, her lips drawing back into a tight line.

"There were moments after…after we married, when I
wanted to tell you. But I could not do so, Adalia. Some lies
just need to remain lies—for the hurt they would cause if
revealed. Hurt for no reason. Hurt I could not inflict upon
you."

"Hurt is not a reason to hide truth, Toren."

"No. Yet I still could not do it. Could not watch you
crumble as you did. It was selfish of me and I can only beg
your forgiveness on the matter."

Her mouth opened, ready to retort, ready to unleash a
maelstrom of condemnation upon him.

He deserved all of it.

But then her lips suddenly clamped shut, her head shaking, her green eyes pinning him.

Toren pounced on the slight hedge. "I only have one question for you, Adalia."

"What is it?" Her words seeped out through gritted teeth.

"Do you trust me?"

She stared at him. Wavering. Wavering enough that Toren could not discern to which side she would end—forgiveness or damnation.

"I always have." She exhaled, defeated, her eyes not leaving his face, her voice weary. "I cannot deny that truth, as much as I want to in this moment."

His held breath seeped from his lungs, an inordinate amount of pride filling his chest. "I know how much that just cost you."

"You do? How?"

"You said the words, yet you are still staring at me like that."

Her eyebrows cocked in question.

"Like you would like to see me roasting on a spit over a fire. It would curdle my toes if I didn't know you possessed the exact opposite of that look, and on occasion, you grace me with it."

Curiosity sparked in the center of the raging storm brewing in her green eyes. "What look is that, exactly?"

"Like you want me naked in the middle of the bed, suffering your fingers slipping into nooks to torture me. Like lust. Like wanton devilry. Like I am the only man you will ever want. Like wonderment." He took a step toward her. Any means necessary.

She fought it, but the slightest crack slipped into her ire, her lips softening.

He set his hands upon her shoulders, gentle, pressing just slight enough to draw goose bumps up along her neck. "I am never going to let harm come upon you, Adalia. I swore it when we married. And I swear it every day, every minute, every second. Everything I have done was to keep you safe—from both man and harm to your soul."

Raw vehemence shook his words and slowly—far too achingly slow—he watched the last of her ire dissolve, her green eyes turning to resigned adoration. She lifted her right hand to his face, her palm flattening along the line of his jaw.

That one touch from her was the moment—the one moment in his life that would stay with him until the end of days—the moment his life truly began. And he knew it, recognized it fully, and accepted it with every fiber of his being.

His mouth opened, his words near to cracking. "Will you listen to one other thing I need to tell you?"

She drew a deep breath, her chest rising, brushing against his. "If you are about to tell me I was an idiot for how I acted, I do not think I will remain soothed, Toren."

"I wanted to tell you what I saw two nights ago, Adalia."

Her brow creased. "At the Revelry's Tempest?"

"Yes. I did not comprehend it at first—it had to sit in my mind for a while." Searching her face, he found and concentrated on the darkest shards of emerald green in her eyes, letting it bolster him. "Something I never understood until now. Something that made more sense to me than anything else ever has."

Curiosity sparked into her eyes. "What?"

"Lady Whilynn and Captain Trebont. I want them."

"What?" She chuckled. "You want the captain and Lady Whilynn? I do not think they are available to keep as pets, if that is what you are dreaming."

Her hand started to drop from his face, and he caught the back of it, holding it in place along his cheek, refusing to give up the one part of her that was touching him.

"No. I want what I saw. I want—no I need—to be the man that will unfailingly fight for your honor, Adalia. I need to be that man no matter what life brings us—when we are old and you are deep into madness and I am still mad beyond measure for you."

Her jaw dropped, her intake of breath shaking her entire body. "Toren, you…you love me."

His fingers on the back of her hand tightened to near crushing. "If this is it, that I need to be your champion. That I need you by my side. That I need you in my bed. That I need you to be happy, because without your happiness, I cannot recognize my own. That I stand taller when you are near me. That I want you to be the first thing I see when I awake. That I want my face buried in your hair, the last scent I smell before sleep. That this last month without you left me with a gaping hole in my chest, a torture that would not yield, every breath a struggle. That I suffered unimaginable pain when you were stolen from me—that I did not know how I would move onward if I could not find you." He stopped, a last breath fortifying his

lungs. "Then yes, if all of that is love, then I do, Adalia. I
not only need you, I love you."

Her green eyes glistening, she smiled so wide, so
heartfelt, it split his chest in two. Her bandaged hand came
up, clasping his face. "I thought so."

He laughed. "And just like the captain and Lady
Whilynn, I need this love to last forever, for I cannot
imagine my life without it. Those two love each other. No
matter what has happened to them. They love each other
above everything else. As ugly as life can become, as much
as reality has slipped for them, they still love each other—
through anything. Seeing that…" His head shook. "Love
like that makes unequivocal sense to me, Adalia. We make
sense."

She jumped to her toes, her lips meeting his hard with
passion—love—that had been bridled for far too long.

He broke then.

His arms wrapped around her and he dragged her body
into his. He had said what he needed to. What he should
have told her weeks ago if he hadn't been too stubborn to
stay away.

And his glorious, smart, beautiful, kind, forgiving wife
had accepted him as she had left him. With love in her eyes.

Only this time her love had a place. A home in him.
Treasured beyond compare.

Her lips moved against his, her smile stealing her from
the kiss. "Give me a few years and I do believe I can go mad
for you, Toren."

"And I do believe I will always defend your honor,
Adalia." He drew his head back slightly, searching for her
eyes. "It took me a lifetime to understand this thing—

love—Adalia. Do not think I have come upon this lightly. Do not dare to think it will ever leave my heart. Ever leave my soul."

"You come upon nothing in life lightly, my love." Her right hand ran up along his face, moving back through his hair until she had him captured by the neck. "So do not dare to think I would ever doubt you."

He buried himself into her.

Heaven. Love.

This was it.

Who knew they were the same thing?

# { EPILOGUE }

Adalia stared at the gnarled tree. The willow along the border of the pond to the east of the castle had grown with multiple thick limbs—each thinking they were the main trunk. One of the fat limbs had long since broken off from the center—the perfect spot to sit and hide, completely still, in a game of hide and seek.

The willow branches shuffled in the breeze, giving her a view to the trunk. Flat, curled into a ball, still as a rock, sat Josalyn. Adalia smiled. For how much her niece liked to talk, no one was better than Josalyn at silently hiding. And she could do so for an inordinate amount of time.

Hazard's nose lifted into the air, his head cocking about as he whimpered. Adalia set her hand on the nape of his neck, trying to calm him—or at least keep him in place. Hide and seek meant hiding without a nervous wolfhound divulging all the best hiding spots. Something Hazard had a very hard time respecting.

Adalia wouldn't have allowed this nine months ago. Never. The twins out of her sight—out of anyone's sight—but this, this she could now give them. Their childhood while they were still children. They were safe, and she knew that fact in her heart.

The war had settled. Napoleon banished to a far-off island. She had underestimated how free she would feel with that fact. For as much as she had always felt safe at Dellon Castle, now the world was open to her again. Open to the twins.

The heavy scent of rose wafted to her and Adalia twisted in the chair she had set under the shade of an ancient oak to look over her shoulder. Toren walked down the sloping hillside toward her, bringing the smell of the flowers with him.

"You have been in the roses?"

"I have." He smiled. "However did you know that?"

"I could smell it. It is all over you. My nose has been oddly strong as of late."

He stopped behind her, leaning down to kiss her neck as his hand slid downward to flatten atop the rounded mound of her belly. "The first blooms of your hybrid with the pink tips have opened."

"I did not know you were observing them so closely."

"I like to watch your experiments." He nipped at the tip of her ear and then moved to stand next to her, his look taking in the pond and trees as his fingers settled along the back of her neck, tracing circles down the line of her spine.

"Speaking of experiments, Violet wrote to report your idea of turning several of the withdrawing rooms into private card rooms at the Revelry's Tempest has been quite the success."

"Good. Yet she still does not care for me, does she?"

"The credit did come begrudgingly." Adalia's head tilted to the side, her hand reaching out to rub the back of his leg. "She will, eventually. I am sure of it. If it is any consolation, of all the men in the world, you are by far, the one she trusts the most."

"I do not know if that is good for the men of the world or not."

Adalia pinched the back of his leg and he chuckled.

"Look." His head gave a slight shake, a wry smile lining his lips as his gaze landed by the pond's edge. "Mary is really bad at hiding."

Adalia laughed, her look swinging to where Mary sat bunched behind a fat rock by the water. Her blue skirts ruffled out in all directions. "Yes. But so bad at it, I suspect she just likes to get found first."

"Does she realize your brother is sneaking up on her from behind?"

"I doubt it." Adalia clasped her hands, resting them on the top of her swollen belly as she watched Theo limp his way toward Mary. A sudden squeal, and Mary jumped up, starting to run just as Theo caught her around the waist, tickling.

Instant strain on Theo's face, his eyes cringed as he lifted Mary, pretending to throw her into the water. It pained him. Greatly. But Theo kept the smile wide on his face, laughing for the sake of his niece.

What Theo had suffered—the ravages from those days. His limp. His jaw that was still slightly askew. Scars that had healed to rough white threads along his skin. The war was over, but this—the wounds of empire against empire— had lost their nobleness. No man should have to suffer as her brother had.

Toren's look grew serious and he nodded toward Theodore. "How did you manage to get him out here?"

She looked up at her husband, mischievous glimmer in her eye. "I told him I would make you delay his move back to Glenhaven if he didn't come out into the sun and play with the girls."

He shook his head. "Remind me never to bet against you."

She laughed. A laugh that was reflected fully in Toren's brown eyes. Brown eyes that were once so distant from her, now were her every breath.

It swirled around, settling upon her in that moment—a sudden happiness so thick it almost suffocated, stealing her breath away.

All of it, all of the pain, the heartache, the worry of the past years—worth it.

Worth it for this one moment, when uncompromised happiness was truly hers again.

Full, all-encompassing happiness.

Happiness born of love.

# ~ ABOUT THE AUTHOR ~

K.J. Jackson is the author of the *Hold Your Breath,*
*Lords of Fate, Lords of Action, Revelry's Tempest,*
and *Flame Moon* series.

She specializes in historical and paranormal romance,
loves to travel (road trips are the best!), and is a sucker for a
good story in any genre. She lives in Minnesota with
her husband, two children, and a dog who
has taken the sport of bed-hogging
to new heights.

Visit her at www.kjjackson.com

# ~ Author's Note ~

Thank you for allowing my stories into your life and time—it is an honor!

My next story in the *Revelry's Tempest* series will debut in fall 2017.

If you missed the *Hold Your Breath, Lords of Fate,* or *Lords of Action* series, be sure to check out these historical romances (each is a stand-alone story): **Stone Devil Duke, Unmasking the Marquess, My Captain, My Earl, Worth of a Duke, Earl of Destiny, Marquess of Fortune, Vow, Promise, and Oath**.

## Never miss a new release or sale!
Be sure to sign up for my VIP Email List at
**www.KJJackson.com**
(email addresses are precious, so out of respect, you'll only hear from me when I actually have real news).

## Interested in Paranormal Romance?
In the meantime, if you want to switch genres and check out my Flame Moon paranormal romance series, **Flame Moon #1**, the first book in the series, is currently free (ebook) at all stores. **Flame Moon** is a stand-alone story, so no worries on getting sucked into a cliffhanger. But number two in the series, **Triple Infinity**, ends with a fun cliff, so be forewarned. Number three in the series, **Flux Flame**, ties up that portion of the series.

## Connect with me!
www.KJJackson.com
https://www.facebook.com/kjjacksonauthor

68085493R00176

Made in the USA
Lexington, KY
01 October 2017